MICHAEL L. CLARK

Raven's Lady of Blood

Raven's Lady of Blood
Library of Congress Control Number: 2025914508

Historic Traces Publishing
Pensacola, Florida

Hardcover ISBN: 978-1-965756-12-6
Paperback ISBN: 978-1-965756-13-3
Ebook ISBN: 978-1-965756-14-0

Dedication

I would never be able to do what I do without the help of so many people who have found their way into my life. The most important being my wife, Cindy. She has put up with my dreams and schemes for forty-four years, and I don't know what I would do without her being by my side to encourage me along the way.

My daughters, Casey and Savannah, have also played a crucial role in my success as an author.

Finally, the people listed below have played a significant role in the finished product you will read within this cover. My Beta Team is:

Christie Schneider
Darlene Seaman
Jeff Neely
Julie Leffert
Marcia Wright
Melanie Hendrix
Sarah Gatian
Steve Lindsey
Summer Brewer-Bryan

PROLOGUE

April 12, 1709

The recently married young captain stood at the rail, watching through her spyglass as the dory rowed closer and closer. She moved the spyglass from one person to another. She had the strangest feeling she had seen these men before, but where?

Raven had sent a few of her crew out to investigate a small, unrecognizable craft floating in the middle of the Atlantic. The small boat was like no other she had ever seen. From her vantage point, it looked flimsy and unreliable, especially this far out to sea.

Slowly, the dory returned to the ship. Seremala threw a line up to the crew aboard *Destiny* to secure the dory from floating away. Each man climbed a rope ladder to the ship's main deck with Seremala in the lead. He led the three strangers to Raven and introduced them to her.

The strangers saw the beautiful young woman standing before them, her bright red, curly locks flowing freely down her back. She was dressed in leather trousers and a leather waistcoat, with a wide leather belt wrapped around her midsection. Hanging from her belt was a sword, and two antique-looking pistols hung from two braces that were crisscrossed over her chest. Suddenly, the men were speechless.

"Captain, these men were in the little boat we saw floating in the sea."

Raven looked at them suspiciously and said, "My name is Raven Ashworth, but everyone calls me the Red Raven. Who are you?"

Jeffrey felt his stomach flip as Raven introduced herself as Raven Ashworth. They hadn't discussed her name change. *Was it just a slight faux pas on her part, or did she have no intention of changing her name?*

Taylor replied, "I am Lieutenant Charles Taylor, and these are my men, George Devlin and Walter Parpart."

"Did you say, Charles Taylor?"

"Well, yes. I did."

Raven felt faint, "Oh no!"

CHAPTER 1

A tall, muscular African man stood on the deck of his ship, watching and waiting. His ship, *The Sea Witch*, was near *Raven's Destiny*, but not near enough to hear what was happening on the neighboring ship.

Captain Pharaoh was co-captain of the Spanish galleon that now belonged to Raven after being captured nearly a year ago. His co-captain, Alexander, and he would share duties on *The Sea Witch* until another suitable ship could be captured by Raven and her band of mixed-race pirates. About eighty percent of Raven's crew were Africans she had rescued from slave ships over recent years. There were also English, Spanish, and a couple of Irishmen as well. Raven was more commodore than captain, but she refused the title. She simply wanted to be known as Raven or the Red Raven, a name Pharaoh had dubbed her with because of her red hair.

Pharaoh was the first to be rescued by her. That was nearly nine years ago, and they had been together ever since. Raven, disguised as a twelve-year-old boy, served as a ship's boy on the original ship, *Destiny*. Richard, as she was known then, met Pharaoh, then known as Batimkoo, who had been captured by slavers in Africa and sold to Captain Billings of *Destiny*. Richard developed a friendship with the big African. Although they spoke different languages, Richard and Batimkoo found a way to communicate with each other. Richard learned Swahili, and Batimkoo learned English. By the time they reached their destination, Charles Town in the Carolinas, Richard had convinced Captain Billings to allow him to purchase Batimkoo's freedom in exchange for Richard's wages. Billings reluctantly agreed and then hired Batimkoo to serve onboard *Destiny* as a regular seaman.

On each of their voyages over the next two years, Richard freed four more slaves with his wages after proving himself worthy to his captain and receiving promotions along the way. These slaves eventually became known as the five kings, with Richard changing each man's name. Batimkoo became Pharaoh, Shujaa Shujaa became Alexander, Mtu Waoga became Attila, Mwama wa Mfalme became Nero, and Muuaji Simba became Caesar.

It wasn't until after *Destiny* sank in a hurricane that the five kings discovered Richard was not a boy, but a girl named Raven. Raven managed to save all five of them, along with most of the slaves being held captive below decks during the storm when the ship broke up and sank.

Pharaoh stood at the rail and remembered his early life in Africa.

1692 eSwatini in East Africa

One hundred fifty miles west of the African coast and the Indian Ocean, a tiny village stood in the center of a clearing surrounded by acacia trees. In the village stood twenty grass huts, erected in a circle with a community fire at the center. The clearing was only about five acres in size and was entirely surrounded by the dangers that the jungle held. The village was known as Nyumbani, meaning "home."

The village was situated in the southeast corner of eSwatini, a part of the continent that would eventually be called Swaziland. The people who lived there were outcasts from a much larger village near the center of eSwatini, called Mji wa Mlimani. The village of Mji wa Mlimani rested on a mountain top and was fortified with a pole wall standing twenty feet tall on the north side. The mountain's escarpment naturally protected the other three sides.

The people of Nyumbani were driven off the mountain because the king of the mountain village banished their patriarch over a disagreement regarding how the village should be governed. Tobasi, Nyumbani's leader, felt that King Urogu was taking too much from the people in the way of taxes to supply his own greed. Tobasi challenged Urogu on the matter but was defeated and exiled from the mountain. Tobasi left, taking with him his five wives and their relatives to build a new village elsewhere. They wandered for two years searching for a suitable place to build their village. They lost loved ones to disease and animal attacks along the way, but they also increased their numbers through natural propagation. When they finally settled on a place to call home, they built a village they could be proud of and feel safe in.

Batimkoo was the seventh son of Tobasi, but the first son of his mother, Wygugi. Wygugi was only sixteen when her son was born. She was the fifth wife of Tobasi and, therefore, was at the bottom of the family's lineage. Although she was at the bottom in the eyes of the other wives, Tobasi favored her over the other four wives because of her youth and beauty.

Batimkoo learned very early in life to take up for his mother to protect her from the other wives. At the age of ten, Batimkoo threw rocks or elephant dung at the other women whenever they bullied his mother. It wasn't long before all the other wives learned to avoid Wygugi, especially whenever Batimkoo was nearby.

Batimkoo was very tall and strong for his age. His half-brother, Muwaji wa Joka, was two years older but shorter and much thinner than Batimkoo. Joka and Batimkoo were very close. The brothers did everything together, and although Batimkoo was younger, he was always leading the way in whatever they did. The two boys played together daily along the stream that ran past their village. They would fish early in the morning and late in the evening to help provide food for the families.

Although Batimkoo and Joka were close as half-brothers, their other two half-brothers were not so accommodating. They were at least three years older than Joka, and much bigger. They constantly berated the two younger brothers whenever they could. As Batimkoo got older, he began to fight back, but the older boys were too much for him to handle. But one day, Batimkoo had an idea.

The sun hung low over the Lubombo foothills, casting long shadows across the acacia thornveld. Dry grass crackled underfoot, and the scent of cattle dung fires drifted through the village like a lazy spirit. Joka sat beside a worn stone near the cattle kraal, pretending to patch a broken clay bowl. His fingers trembled, not from fear, but from trying to hold in laughter.

"Do you think they took the bait?" he whispered in siSwati.

Batimkoo, crouched beside him, eyes scanning the bush path, gave a slow nod. His chest was broad and his face calm, but Joka knew him well enough to spot the fire beneath.

"They're greedy," Batimkoo said. "And greedy boys don't think."

That morning, Batimkoo had wandered past the edge of the village, through the knobthorn trees and past the shallow stream, to a rocky kopje where bees had made their hive inside a split in a marula trunk. He had taken a small piece of honeycomb, just enough to bait a trap, and left the rest. He'd also stirred the hive, gently, just enough to make them restless and alert.

The boys had buried a small earthenware pot near the path to the river where the older brothers, Wabene and Tagora, often passed on their way to set snares or to swim. Inside the pot was a smear of honey and some crushed wild mint for scent. Around the tree, Batimkoo had smeared honey drops, forming a trail from the hive to the bait.

Then came the whisper, spoken "accidentally" near the cattle troughs: "The trader from Ngwenya said he'd return for his honey before the full moon. If someone found it…" Just loud enough for Wabene to hear.

Now, hiding in the tall grass near the footpath, Joka and Batimkoo watched.

The two older boys emerged, arguing softly.

"I told you I heard them say something," Wabene muttered.

"Then dig faster," Tagora hissed. "Before someone else finds it."

Wabene knelt at the base of the tree, uncovering the pot. "There's not much here," he grumbled.

Batimkoo whispered, "Wait."

A faint hum tickled the air, at first like flies. Then louder. Angry.

From the trees came a black cloud. The bees had followed the trail.

Wabene jerked his head up. "What—?"

Then he screamed.

Tagora swatted at his ears. "*Tinyosi!*" he shouted. "Bees!"

The two bolted from the path, flailing wildly. Wabene's reed sandals flew off as he dove into the scrub. Tagora dropped his knobkerrie, shouting something about witchcraft.

Batimkoo doubled over with laughter. Joka snorted with laughter, trying to stay silent.

"Did you see Wabene's face?" Joka gasped.

"Like he sat on a puff adder," Batimkoo said.

When the laughter calmed, Batimkoo pulled a small twist of dried bark from his goatskin pouch. He unwrapped it and handed Joka a piece of fresh honeycomb, golden and sticky.

"From the real hive," he said. "The bees won't miss this much."

Joka took it reverently. "You're not just strong, Batimkoo. You're dangerously smart."

Batimkoo shrugged, chewing slowly. "They forget that we are *bomfana* now. Boys grow. One day, we'll be men."

They sat together in the tall grass, the honey sweet and wild on their tongues. Behind them, the cattle lowed as the herders brought them home. Smoke curled from the cooking huts. Somewhere, a drum sounded faintly—perhaps a girls' initiation song. But here, hidden from the world, two boys laughed like kings.

Pharaoh stood at the stern of *The Sea Witch*, remembering that day. The corners of his lips curled upward as he remembered his brother, Joka. He wondered where Joka might be now if he were still alive.

Alexander interrupted his trance, "Where are you, my brother?"

"Many years away from here."

"The past, or the future?"

"I was thinking about my childhood back in eSwatini."

"Good memories, I hope."

"Aye. I was with my brothers. Some good memories, others, not so good. I was just wondering what my brother Joka might be doing, if he were still alive."

"Joka was older than you?"

"Aye. All my brothers were older, but Joka was smaller than I was. Two years older, two years smaller. He should have been my protector from our older brothers, but I was his."

"Have you ever thought about trying to find your other brothers?"

"Yes, many times. Alas, I wouldn't know where to begin. I am not sure I could even find our old home. I was so young when I was taken, and that was so long ago."

Alexander let the subject drop for now. Pharaoh looked around to find that *Raven's Destiny* was sailing off their starboard bow about a quarter mile out. Both ships were sailing northwesterly through the Atlantic heading toward Barbados. Raven had decided the timing might be suitable to find Spanish ships sailing from South America toward Spain full of gold and other treasure. The Spanish galleons were likely heavily loaded with treasure but well-armed. Their best strategy would be to find a ship sailing alone near the back of the fleet and attacking it from the rear. Raven and her band of pirates might be lucky enough to pick up another ship or two along the way to add to her fleet.

Just as Pharaoh was about to walk away from the stern, a call came from the crow's nest.

"Ship off the port bow!"

Pharaoh took his spyglass from his leather satchel that was draped over his head and shoulder and pointed it in the direction that had been announced. He scanned the horizon looking for a ship.

Alexander asked, "Do you see anything?"

"Not yet."

"How about Raven? Do you think she has seen it?"

Pharaoh swung his spyglass to the right in *Destiny's* direction to see if there was any indication that Raven was aware of the approaching ship. He had Raven in his sights, but she seemed unaware of the ship coming into their path.

Pharaoh called his signaler over and said, "Send a call out to *Destiny*. We have a ship approaching from the west."

"Aye, Captain."

The young man took a large conch shell from his leather satchel and blew the signal in *Destiny's* direction to let her know of the approaching ship. Pharaoh watched through his spyglass as Raven heard the signal. She looked toward *The Sea Witch*, then out over the water to find the ship in question. Raven took out her spyglass and scanned the western horizon, and there, coming toward them, still half a mile out, was a ship. The ship was still too far away to identify it, but Raven had good reason to believe it would be a Spanish vessel.

Pharaoh continued to watch Raven as she scrambled her crew. She then turned to Pharaoh and signaled for him to bring his ship alongside hers.

"Helmsman, 30º starboard. Make way to *Destiny*."

"Aye, Captain!"

"Boatswain, full sheets! We need to come alongside *Destiny*! Master Gunner! Prepare all guns for battle!"

"*Aye, Captain!*" both men replied.

Pharaoh's crew scrambled across the decks. Some climbed the masts to unfurl more sails. Others began preparing the cannons in case they needed to fire upon the approaching ship. Pharaoh called up to the crow's nest to the lookout, "Let me know as soon as you have identified that ship!"

"Aye, Captain!"

CHAPTER 2

The call came from the crow's nest. "Pharaoh! She is a Spanish Galleon! There are more ships beyond her! I can't tell how many yet!"

Pharaoh turned to the helmsman and said, "Keep steady toward *Destiny*."

"Aye, Captain."

Pharaoh looked once more through his spyglass and saw Raven standing on her quarterdeck at the port side, anxiously staring at him. Pharaoh put his spyglass back in his pouch and sent Raven hand signals to indicate there were more than just the one ship heading their way.

Moments later, *The Sea Witch* came alongside *Destiny*, and they tied together so the captains could converse about the situation.

"Raven, there are more than one ship coming toward us."

"How many?"

A call came from *The Sea Witch's* crow's nest, "Pharaoh, I now count six ships. They sail about a quarter mile apart in a single line."

Pharaoh turned back to Raven and waited for her orders.

"Alright, Captain Pharaoh. How would you like to handle this?"

"Me?"

"Yes. How would you go about taking at least one of these ships?"

Pharaoh paused, "Well, if the galleons are loaded, they will be slower and deeper in the water than our ships. We should be able to catch them from behind. I still have the Spanish flag from when we captured *The Sea Witch*. I will fly the flag to fool them into thinking I am another Spanish galleon. I'll come up from their port flank while you travel on the starboard side. We will come up alongside them and force them to stop. If all goes well, we can capture the ship without damaging it."

"That sounds like an excellent plan, Captain. Let's give it a try."

Raven turned to Jeremy Finch and said, "Get our new passengers to a safe place until this is over."

"Aye, Raven!"

Jeremy collected Lieutenant Taylor and his two men to the officer's quarters under the forecastle.

"Stay here until this is done."

Charles Taylor asked, "What's goin on?"

"We're about to attack a Spanish galleon and take her captive if possible. She should be loaded with treasure this time of year."

Jeremy disappeared, leaving them to mull over their situation.

George Devlin asked, "What have we gotten ourselves into, Lieutenant?"

"It seems we stumbled into the past. These people must be pirates. Although I've never heard of a woman pirate captain."

Walter Parpart asked, "Lieutenant, how are we going to get home?"

"Steady, Walter. I'm not sure. I don't even know how we got here in the first place."

Destiny and *The Sea Witch* parted ways, Raven moving toward the galleon's starboard flank and Pharaoh to the port. They were at least half a mile from the fleet heading their way. Pharaoh ordered his men, "Strike our colors and hoist the Spanish flag!"

Pharaoh knew the captain of the ship would be looking at any vessel that might be following in the open sea, but *The Sea Witch* had the advantage that most of her crew were Spaniards. Ricardo de la Cruz was the first mate of Pharaoh's vessel. He beckoned the first mate to him on the quarterdeck. Pharaoh then called Zachery Thacker to join him to translate.

"Mr. Thacker, please tell Señor de la Cruz I need him to dress in his best uniform and pretend he is the captain of this vessel while we pursue the galleon at the rear of that column."

"Aye, Captain."

Zachery did as he had been instructed and noticed the curious look on Ricardo's face.

Ricardo asked in Spanish, "What does he plan to do?"

Zachery asked Pharaoh, "What is the plan, Captain?"

"Tell him we are going to capture at least one of those ships sailing to our south. If they see a Spanish vessel sailing towards them with a Spanish captain on the quarterdeck, they won't be alarmed when we approach them. We will have a better chance of taking their ship and its cargo without damaging any of it."

After Zachery translated again, Ricardo replied, "What will he do with the ship and its cargo?"

Without consulting Pharaoh, Zachery answered, "The ship will be conscripted into our fleet, and the cargo will be split among the crew. All of you could be very rich if all goes well."

Pharaoh noticed Ricardo's brows raised with whatever Zachery had told him. Ricardo bowed to Pharaoh, then left to return to his quarters to change his clothing.

"What did you say to him?"

"He wanted to know what we intended to do with the ship and its cargo. I told him the ship would be added to the fleet and the cargo would be split among the crew. He seemed to like that idea."

Pharaoh smiled.

"Let us get to it, then. Call the men together and inform them of our plan. Let them know of the stakes for each of them, and they should act accordingly. We want to take this ship without damaging it, if possible, and possibly the next ship in line as well."

"Aye, Pharaoh."

The waters southwest of Barbados glistened like spilled coin under the dying sun. Six Spanish galleons, heavy with gold and dreams of empire, cut through the sea with the slow majesty of a funeral procession. Their gunports were closed. Their captains were unworried. No clouds on the horizon. No sails that did not bear the flag of Castile.

Except one.

Far astern, a lone galleon flew a Spanish ensign—a red and gold banner fluttering obediently in the Caribbean breeze. Her hull was dark, sleek, and her sails well-trimmed. She bore the appearance of a loyal escort catching up after being delayed in port. But the flag was a lie, and although her crew were Spaniards, they weren't what they appeared to be.

They were pirates.

Aboard *The Sea Witch*, Captain Pharaoh stood on the quarterdeck, next to the helm, the red silk of his sash snapping in the wind, his dark eyes locked on the trailing galleon less than a league ahead. His posture was calm, but the crew could see the tension in his jaw, the controlled power of a lion before his pounce.

"Steady," Pharaoh murmured to his helmsman. "Let them think we are a lost sheep returning to the fold."

High above, his lookout called down, "No signal from their sterncastle. They haven't spotted us for what we are."

Pharaoh smiled. "Good. Ready the boarding teams. Quiet as shadows."

Off his starboard beam, just within the curve of the sea, a second ship ghosted along—*Raven's Destiny*, cutting through the water like a blade. On her quarterdeck, Raven watched Pharaoh's approach through her spyglass. Her crimson hair fluttered like a banner of blood.

She lowered the glass and nodded to her helmsman. "Hold position. Pharaoh's the bait. We strike when they're blind."

The plan was elegant: *The Sea Witch* would fall in behind the rearmost galleon, appearing as just another Spanish vessel. Once close enough, her Spanish crew would swarm aboard and seize the ship quietly, without cannon fire. Then they would mimic her signal lights, deceive the next ship in line, and do it all again.

The Sea Witch signaled a distress to the last ship to allow them to come alongside for aid. It worked. *La Real Victoria* trimmed her sails to slow down for the approaching vessel. The captain of the ship was an elderly gentleman who looked much too old to be out on the open seas leading an expedition such as this. Captain Miguel Juan Carlo was leading his final voyage as captain of this treasure vessel. He was set to retire at the end of this voyage.

His weak eyes squinted at the new ship as it pulled along the port side of his ship. He smoothed his snowy white moustache away from his parched lips as he watched Spanish sailors tossing their grapples over the side of his ship's rail.

Captain Carlo stepped to the port rail to welcome the captain of *The Sea Witch*, a ship he knew by reputation. What he did not expect was to meet a young man posing as the captain of *The Witch*. Captain Fernando Arguello was well known by seamen throughout Spain, including Carlo. However, the man who now stood across the rails from him was not he.

"Where is your captain?" the man asked in Spanish.

"I am the captain. I am Ricardo de la Cruz. Who are you?"

"I am Captain Miguel Juan Carlo. Where is Captain Arguello?"

"Oh, I am afraid he died several months ago. He became ill and did not survive his sickness."

"How may I help you, Captain de la Cruz?"

"Oh, thank you for asking. Please have all of your men assemble on the main deck. I have an announcement to make before we proceed."

The old captain obliged and called all his crew together, as he nervously watched with anticipation.

"Is this everyone?"

"All except my man in the crow's nest."

"Call him down, too, please. This will also concern him."

Carlo signaled for his man to climb down and join the others. When the young man reached the deck, he approached the captain and softly spoke to him, "Capitån, another ship is approaching."

Carlo looked around and saw *Raven's Destiny* approaching on his starboard stern. He looked at de la Cruz with concern as he asked, "What is this? Who are you really?"

"We are the crew of the Red Raven, and you and your ship must consider yourselves our prisoners."

The old captain was agast. He couldn't believe he had fallen for such trickery. What would happen to him and his crew? Would he ever see his family again, waiting for him in Spain?

Carlo looked at the young de la Cruz with contempt and asked, "What would you have us do?"

Lay down all your weapons, Half of your men will transfer to *The Sea Witch*, the other half will move to *Raven's Destiny*. It will be decided later what will happen to you.

The old captain instructed his men to move to the other ships while a crew from *The Sea Witch* moved over to *The Royal Victory*.

Alexander moved to *The Royal Victory* and took control of the makeshift crew.

One ship taken. No shot fired.

She turned to her papa, who was standing next to her on the quarter-deck. "Now for the next. Bring us in close to her starboard stern. No flags this time. Let them wonder."

But as Alexander moved his newly captured galleon closer to the fifth in line, something went wrong.

Aboard the Spanish fifth ship, sharp eyes spotted irregular movement on the deck of their sister vessel. A lantern swinging too high. Too many armed men. No Spanish captain would be so careless.

The alarm was raised.

Suddenly, the fifth galleon's gunports yawned open like mouths ready to spit fire.

"Cannons!" cried Alexander's lookout.

The Sea Witch, still disguised, was sailing between the two galleons—too close to fire or flee. But *Raven's Destiny* was already moving in.

"Battle sails!" Raven shouted. "Run out the guns—aim for the waterline!"

Black smoke curled from her broadside as her cannons thundered. Iron balls punched into the fifth galleon just above the sea, bursting planks and shattering gun crews.

The Spanish ship returned fire, its first volley raking the captured galleon's rigging. Men screamed. Sails tore. Flames licked up a mast.

"Don't let them scuttle her!" Alexander roared. "Snuff those fires!"

On *Raven's Destiny*, Raven paced the deck like a storm-witch. "Ready another volley. Sink her if we must, but keep the others scared, not angry. They must still think we're many ships."

The second galleon shuddered under the second barrage, then listed, smoke pouring from her gun decks. Her crew tried to abandon ship, some leaping into the sea, others clinging to broken spars.

When the masts cracked and the ship rolled, Raven gave a grim nod. "One ship sunk... but now the rest know we're not the Spanish navy."

The remaining four galleons scattered, turning hard north or east, their captains choosing flight over engagement. The pirates had lost the element of surprise—but not the prize. One galleon was held in their hands. Another was slipping beneath the waves. And there were four more out there, heavy with gold and terror.

Raven turned to the wind, eyes fierce. "Not bad. It could be worse."

Pharaoh turned to Raven and waved to her from the deck of *The Sea Witch*.

CHAPTER 3

The morning sea shimmered like polished brass as three ships drew together in a quiet cove tucked along the windward side of an unnamed islet south of Barbados. The breeze was steady and warm, and the skies overhead were a cloudless blue, a rare day of calm in a world where warships and storms were never far apart.

The Sea Witch arrived first, her hull intact and her decks bustling with crew excited by the recent battle. The captured Spanish galleon, *The Royal Victory*, loomed behind her—majestic and slow, her white sails heavy with humidity, her lower decks bristling with riches. And lastly, *Raven's Destiny* glided into the cove like a dark-winged bird, her crimson sails catching the wind, her sleek hull slicing through the surf.

On the quarterdeck of *Raven's Destiny*, Raven stood at the rail, watching the approach of *The Royal Victory* with a sharp eye. She wore her usual brown leather coat, cinched at the waist with a scarlet sash. Her boots gleamed, and the polished hilt of her cutlass caught the sun like fire.

"Drop anchor," she ordered. "Signal the others to prepare for boarding."

From the deck, Attila blew the conch shell to signal the other ships to be ready to receive her boarding. A trumpeted sound echoed across the cove, and the new crew of *The Royal Victory* scrambled to attention.

Moments later, Raven climbed down into the dory, accompanied by her quartermaster, Jeffrey Hamilton, and four of her best blades. The rowers dipped their oars in rhythm, ferrying her across the calm waters to *The Royal Victory*, now under the command of Alexander.

Alexander, tall and broad-shouldered, stood waiting at the top of the boarding ladder. His coat, once that of a naval officer, had been trimmed and tailored in crimson and brown, matching Raven's own. His hair, thick and bound in braids, was pulled back beneath a bandana. Gold rings glinted in his ears, and a quiet pride burned in his eyes.

"Captain," he greeted, offering his hand.

Raven took it and climbed aboard. "*The Royal Victory* is yours, Alexander. She sails under your banner with all my blessings."

"She carries enough gold to buy Neptune's favor a hundred times over."

Raven smiled, then turned to Jeffrey, "See to the treasure. Make a full inventory before it's divided."

"Aye, Raven," her husband replied, already unrolling a leather-bound ledger.

They walked the length of the upper deck, passing stunned former Spanish sailors still under guard. Below, in the belly of the ship, lanterns were lit as Jeffrey and two others descended into the treasure hold.

The chamber was suffocating with wealth.

Crates of gold ingots, chests of minted coins bearing the face of the Spanish king, velvet-lined boxes overflowing with emeralds and rubies, and polished artifacts looted from temples deep in the forests of New Granada—jewels set in obsidian, figurines of jade and bone.

Jeffrey whistled low. "It's more than we guessed."

Raven crouched beside an open chest. "The priests in Cartagena will be lighting candles for these baubles. And the crown in Madrid will wonder what sea swallowed their treasure."

"And the men?" Alexander asked. "Their shares?"

Raven stood. "We'll divide it by the Articles. One share each to the crew, one and one-quarter shares to the doctors, junior officers, gunners, and boat swains, one and one-half to senior officers, and two shares to captains. You'll command *The Royal Victory* going forward, unless you'd rather return to *The Sea Witch*."

Alexander shook his head. "She's a fine ship. I'll see her fly our colors."

"Good."

Above deck again, Raven turned toward *The Sea Witch*. "Now to the prisoners."

The brig aboard *The Sea Witch* was little more than an iron cage below deck, dark and damp with the scent of sweat and defeat. Three dozen Spanish sailors were held there—some sullen, some fearful, others defiant. Among them was Captain Miguel Juan Carlo, once commander of *The Royal Victory*.

He rose when Raven entered, his face lined with both rage and pride. "You'll not find loyal men among us, pirate. We serve Spain."

Raven tilted her head, "Spain is far away. The sea is now your master, and she is less forgiving."

"You can kill me," he said. "But I will never serve under a thief's flag."

"I don't need every man," Raven replied, stepping closer. "I offer a choice. Swear loyalty to me, live free, and earn your share. Or... take your chances in the water."

A murmur spread through the prisoners. One young sailor, no older than twenty, stood shakily. "I'll serve. Spain never gave me enough coin to buy a loaf."

Raven nodded to a nearby guard. "Bring him topside. Feed him, give him water, then see he earns his keep."

She turned to the others. "You have until sundown."

Miguel spat at her boots. "You'll hang one day. You and your black devils and your red rags."

Raven looked to Pharaoh, who stood beside her, silent and watching.

She turned back to the guards. "He and anyone who won't swear allegiance. Drop them into the drink at dawn. Let the sea judge them."

When Raven returned to *Destiny*, she had the Spanish prisoners brought up on the top deck to receive their choice to swear allegiance to her or suffer their fate in the deep. Twenty-eight men stumbled up the ladder leading from the lowest deck to the main deck. Raven offered them the same choice as those captive on *The Sea Witch*.

Charles Taylor, George Devlin, and Walter Parpart watched from the port rail. None of them had realized until the battle that they were aboard a pirate ship being led by a woman.

"I offer you men a choice. Swear loyalty to me, live free, and earn your share. Or... take your chances in the water."

The men grumbled among themselves as the captain's words were translated to them. Many of them were underfed, wearing ragged clothing barely covering their golden brown hides. One man spoke out in broken English, "I serve you."

After a silent pause, man after man repeated his words, *"I serve you."*

Raven joined the crews gathered on the beach of the islet to witness the division of the treasure. The sun was high, and the surf broke gently against the sand. Chests were opened, the gold gleaming as Jeffrey called out the counts.

Raven stood beside him, watching her crew with pride. These were not mere cutthroats—they were survivors, freedmen, outcasts who had carved their own nation from the sea.

Jeffrey's voice rang out: "By the Articles and by the authority of the Red Raven, shares are tallied as follows. One share to each able crew. One and a quarter shares to your junior officers. One and a half shares to first and second mates. Two shares to your captains. Three shares go for Commodore Raven. The rest goes to the fleet, to pay for powder, sail, and repairs."

Cheers rose as the first chests were opened for distribution. Men laughed, slapped backs, and poured coins through their fingers. The new Spanish men who had recently joined the ranks were overjoyed to hear that they too would receive their share.

Raven stepped away, walking the shoreline as the sun set fire to the western sky. Pharaoh joined her.

"We've drawn Spain's blood," he said. "They'll send hunters now."

"They always do."

"Then what's next?"

Raven watched the waves. "We find another prize. Another galleon weighted with gold and pride. Until one of them sinks us, or we drown in riches."

Pharaoh smiled. "I'd prefer the riches."

"So would I."

The wind picked up. Gulls cried overhead. And in the glow of dusk, three pirate ships lay anchored like kings in exile, their flags snapping against the sky, their holds heavy with treasure—and vengeance yet to come.

Later that night, as Pharaoh lay in his bed, his mind drifted back to his boyhood.

The rainy season had just begun when Batimkoo turned thirteen. The skies over the hills of what would one day be called eSwatini swelled with thunder and split with lightning, and the dry ground drank deep of the long-awaited rains. For the village boys, it was a time of daring—racing the streams that formed in the gullies, climbing trees slick with rain, and chasing goats too stubborn to return to their kraals.

Joka, Batimkoo's half-brother, was fifteen at the time. Though they shared the same father, they came from different huts—Joka's mother was a quiet woman of noble clan blood, while Batimkoo's mother had been a much younger woman, a fierce healer from the hills. The boys were as different in body as they were at birth—Batimkoo was broad and robust, Joka was lean and quick, and had the clever eyes of a jackal. But their bond was stronger than bone.

That week, their father had tasked them with repairing the upper water traps—stone channels built to catch and divert mountain runoff into the dry fields. They hiked up the ridgeline with calabash gourds of water and bundles of cut grass, laughing and pretending to be warriors guarding a fortress.

But the sky turned quickly. As they worked on the cracked stone troughs, clouds gathered, black and roiling, and a wind swept through the trees with a shriek.

"We should go," Joka had said, already shouldering his bundle.

But Batimkoo, proud and stubborn, insisted on finishing the work. "One more stone. Then we run."

Lightning forked above them as they scrambled down the wet slope. The trail, once clear, had become a river of mud and broken roots. Halfway down, they heard it: a roar like a beast waking.

A landslide.

The hillside above gave way in a cascade of stone, mud, and trees. Joka shoved Batimkoo forward with all his strength. "Run!"

Batimkoo tumbled into a ravine and was buried waist-deep in muck, coughing and choking. The hillside was silent when he clawed his way free and looked back. Joka was gone.

It took the villagers two days to dig through the rubble. They found Joka near the edge, his body broken but his arms still wrapped around a branch that had held back the worst of the fall from crushing the path entirely—buying Batimkoo the seconds he needed to live.

At his funeral, Batimkoo's father said Joka's spirit would walk forever with the rain, whispering warnings to those who wandered too high in the storm.

Batimkoo never returned to the hills. But he wore Joka's bone-carved armband from that day forward, and when the older brothers mocked him for his size or questioned his bloodline, Batimkoo would only stare, silent and unflinching, as if he were waiting to be tested by the mountain again.

Years later, when Joka's name was mentioned, Batimkoo would say simply:
"He went first so I could go farther."

Pharaoh thought about that phrase concerning his former friends, Nero and Caesar. They had both served on another of Raven's ships sunk by the French Navy at the bay of Port St. Felix a few years back. Caesar was captain of the *Tryton*. Nero was his first mate and second-in-command. They, along with Alexander and Attila, had been Raven's five kings that she had saved while living under the disguise of Richard Ashworth.

"They went first so I could go farther."

CHAPTER 4

As morning broke, the skies were filled with hovering black clouds as dark as if the sky had swallowed the sun. Raven gathered her crew on the main deck to hear Captain Carlo's decision about his fate. He and his officers had all abstained from joining Raven's crew the previous day.

"Well, Captain? What have you decided?"

Captain Miguel Juan Carlo lifted his chin, eyes steady on Raven as if she were merely a squall to be endured. Behind him, his officers stood like carved stone, unbent by fear or fortune. Though unarmed and bruised from the fight, they carried themselves with the pride of men who had sworn an oath not just to a flag, but to each other. Their silence spoke louder than any threat—they would not bend, not even for gold.

Captain Carlo stood stiff and proud before the congregation joined together on *Destiny's* deck. "My officers and I have discussed your offer at length. We will remain loyal to the Spanish Crown, regardless of the consequences."

Raven seemed indifferent to his answer. She had expected it.

"Fine, Captain. As I pronounced yesterday, you and your officers will be dropped into the sea."

Raven ordered one of the dories to be lowered into the water to carry the captives to their final resting place. Captain Carlo and his officers were placed in the dory while Attila and four of the crew joined to row the craft away from the shore.

Once again, Charles Taylor and his men nervously watched from the rail.

The sky had turned the color of old iron, and the waves were rising fast as *Raven's Destiny's* dory pulled away from the shore of the islet. The sea hissed beneath the wind, rough and restless, as if eager to receive what was coming.

Captain Miguel Juan Carlo sat rigid, hands bound before him, his once-pristine coat now salt-stained and torn. Beside him, his five officers sat silently, their pride intact but their futures dissolving like mist. None had spoken since Raven's final offer had been refused. None had begged. None had bowed.

Raven sat at the boat's bow, her coat snapping in the wind. Behind her, Attila held the tiller, guiding the vessel toward the deep water where the reef fell away into darkness.

"You made your choice," Raven said over the wind. "The sea has a long memory. Perhaps she'll forgive you sooner than I would."

Carlo remained unspoken.

At her signal, the crew hauled the men up one by one and cast them into the sea, with their hands still bound. The men didn't scream. They hit the water with splashes swallowed quickly by the rising chop.

By the time the last officer vanished behind a wave, the dory was already turning back to shore. Overhead, thunder grumbled in the distance, and the wind carried the scent of rain. Raven didn't look back.

The storm would arrive before noon.

Back on the beach, the crew of *Raven's Destiny* watched the boat return in silence. No cheers, no jests—only the low hiss of wind through palm fronds and the distant rumble of thunder rolling across the horizon. Even pirates knew the weight of judgment when it fell.

Attila leapt out first, securing the boat as Raven stepped ashore. Jeffrey approached her, eyes searching her face.

"It's done?" he asked.

She gave a single nod.

Jeffrey had seen it before on other occasions, "A hard sentence," he murmured.

"Not hard," she said quietly. "Only final."

The men who had gathered began to drift back to their duties—sharpening blades, tying down sail, securing hatches in preparation for the storm. They had seen such endings before, and would again. Still, a few of the Spaniards stole glances at the sea, where six specks bobbed faintly on the swells before being swallowed by the coming squall.

Raven walked to the edge of the beach, boots sinking slightly in the wet sand. She looked out across the grey-green water. The wind tugged at her coat, sending her red scarf trailing like a banner. She thought of men's choices—some for glory, some for loyalty, and some simply because they couldn't bear to yield.

She felt no triumph, only the quiet ache of command. This sentence was unlike the others. On other occasions, those who had been dropped to the sea had been guilty of selling slaves. This time it was for riches. There was no morality to lean upon that. She knew if she had not sent the officers to the sea, they would be trouble in the end. But maybe she should have simply left them on the tiny islet as punishment. It was too late to think of that now. She would put it away from her mind.

Behind her, the crew moved with purpose. The sails would be reefed. The treasure secured. The night would come fast and wet. And they would sail again in the morning—fewer in number, but heavier in gold.

Taylor and his men approached Raven.

"Captain, may we have a word?"

"Certainly, Leftenant. What can I do for you?"

"Captain, we've been watching you and your crew. Please don't be offended if I ask...but are you and your men...pirates?"

Raven's lips curled with amusement at his question.

"Whatever gave you that idea?"

Raven's smile grew.

Taylor realized her sarcasm. "How long have you been a pirate?"

"About four years. We weren't always pirates. It was born out of necessity actually. When I was sixteen, I served as a junior officer onboard the original *Destiny,* a merchant ship out of Bristol. My three captains and I, along with two other Africans sailed on that ship until it was destroyed by a hurricane and sunk. We worked together to free the slaves that were being held below decks before the ship was taken under. Those of us who survived eventually drifted to an island where we were stranded for about a month. We built long boats and when a merchant ship sailed nearby the island, we rowed out and overtook the ship. We offered the crew a place among us to remain on the ship or be marooned on our island. Some of the crew remained with us. My husband was one of them who remained."

Taylor surmised, "And so, you go about robbing ships of gold now?"

"Not just gold, mind you. Our primary purpose was to free any slaves we could. Many of them have joined our crew, others have found new lives back in Africa."

Raven examined their faces.

"Would you like to join us?"

Taylor looked at his companions and saw them shrug to him.

"Well, as we don't have anything else to do, we might as well join your crew."

"Fine. I'll have Mr. Hamilton read the Articles of Code to you and have you sign them. Then, we'll put you to work."

As Taylor and his men followed Jeffrey to the captain's quarter, Raven finally turned back to the sea, her face set against the wind.

There would always be storms.

And she would always sail through them.

Days later, the three vessels sailed through the Caribbean, prowling for Spanish galleons that might be sailing eastward back to their native home. Alexander was getting familiar with his new crew on *The Royal Victory*.

Alexander was an excellent captain when it came to sailing. He had done so on *The Nightingale*, a merchant vessel captured by Raven and her crew nearly three years ago. *The Nightingale*, *The Lady Falcon*, and *The Matilda* were lost in a battle with the French Navy while Pharaoh, Attila, and Alexander were aboard *Raven's Destiny* in conference with Raven.

Alexander discovered that one of the Spaniards spoke English. Hector Fernandez was a young man of about twenty whose mother had worked as a maid for an English family who ran a merchant business while living on the Spanish coast, near Barcelona. Alexander made Hector his special aide to translate his orders to those who spoke no English.

Now, despite their strength and numbers, the sea remained silent.

Week by week, they scoured the lanes of the Windward Passage and shadowed the coast of Hispaniola, their sails dark against the bright horizon. Lookouts strained their eyes from the topsails, and the crews grew restless. The few merchantmen they'd encountered were Dutch or English, not worth the powder to chase or fight. Especially since they no doubt would be without the one cargo Raven could not let them keep.

Slaves. Slaves were always carried toward the Americas, not away.

Once thick as gulls in the sky, Spanish ships had grown scarce. It was as if word of Raven's vengeance had sailed ahead of them.

The men passed the long hours sharpening blades that wouldn't bite, mending sails that hadn't been torn. Dice games grew sharper, tempers shorter. Even Pharaoh, usually the most measured among them, had snapped at a crewman for a tangled line on *The Sea Witch*.

Jeffrey enforced the articles, ensuring no infighting escalated into violence, but even he admitted the tension was rising like a kettle left too long over a flame. He allowed men to settle their differences by hand-to-hand battles on the main deck. It was both entertainment for the men and a way to work out their frustrations. Raven was alright with it as long as no one was seriously injured.

One night, as the three ships anchored near a crescent island unmarked on any chart, Raven sat with her captains beneath a lean-to of canvas and spars, the surf whispering behind them.

"They're hiding," Alexander said, brooding over a half-emptied mug of rum. "The Spanish know we're out here. They're either hugging the coast or holding back their treasure until they can move in force."

"Or they've rerouted through the north," Pharaoh offered. "Toward the Bahamas or even the open Atlantic."

Raven nodded, her eyes fixed on the fire. "They can run. But sooner or later, they'll have to move their gold. The Crown needs its tithe. And when they do…"

"We'll be waiting," Attila finished.

But even as she agreed, Raven felt the itch behind her ribs—the unease of a predator too long denied the hunt. She could see it in her crew as well:

the hunger, the restlessness. They were not meant for long silences. They were men and women of the blade, forged in the storm, and storms needed wind.

"We move east come morning," she said at last. "Out beyond the reefs. If they've slipped past us, we'll ride the open current and cut across their path."

And with that, the meeting broke. The captains returned to their ships, and the campfire hissed into coals. Above them, the stars blinked cold and watchful.

The sea had gone quiet—but not forever.

Two nights later, with the moon hidden behind a curtain of clouds, *Raven's Destiny* sliced through the black water east of Guadeloupe, her lanterns dimmed to slits of flickering gold. The wind had gone strange—erratic, and whispering, like a voice just beyond hearing. The crew felt it in their bones.

Just after midnight, the lookout's cry broke the silence.

"Ship! Dead ahead, bearing nor'east!"

Raven was on the quarterdeck in moments, spyglass in hand. She trained it toward the dark horizon, and there it was: a vessel, barely visible, its sails blood-red, yet glowing in the moonlight that filtered through the clouds. No lanterns. No flag.

The ship didn't rise and fall with the sea—it glided, smooth and silent, as though the waves parted for it.

Jeffrey stepped beside her. "She's not on the wind."

"She's not making a wake," Raven added, lowering the glass. "That's no galleon."

The crew gathered at the rails, speaking in hushed tones. Some of the Spaniards crossed themselves, while the African sailors simply stared. Even seasoned hands, who had braved hurricanes and French broadsides, looked unsettled.

Pharaoh joined them moments later alongside from *The Sea Witch*, his own crew murmuring similar unease.

"Looks like a Spanish caravel," Jeffrey commented to them both. "Old build. Fifteenth century, maybe."

"She shouldn't be sailing," Raven said. "Not unless the dead learned the ropes."

Lightning forked faintly in the distance, and in the flash, they saw her again—closer this time. The hull was scorched black in places, as if it had been burned in battle. Her sails hung in tatters, yet she moved as if at full wind—no figures on the deck. No crew. Just silence.

Then, with no sound at all, the ship veered slowly southward and faded into the mist that clung to the sea like breath on a window.

Raven turned to Jeffrey. "Did we get a name off her?"

He shook his head. "No colors, no markings. Could've been a mirage."

"No," Pharaoh said. "That was real. I've heard stories from my Spaniards of lost Spanish ships... treasure fleets sunk in storms, their crews cursed to wander the sea."

"Ghost stories," Jeffrey scoffed. But even he didn't sound sure.

"Whatever she was," Raven said, "she passed us by. And that means something."

"What do we do?" Jeffrey asked.

"We keep sailing. But keep watch, close and tight. If the sea's stirring up spirits, then the Spanish can't be far behind."

The order was given, and the ships resumed their silent course. Yet the crew spoke little through the night. Eyes drifted often to the horizon, half expecting to see those red sails again.

And deep below deck, where the gold from *The Royal Victory* lay stacked in the hold, some swore they heard the faint clinking of chains—like footsteps dragging across wet wood.

CHAPTER 5

A week later, Raven's fleet found themselves back near the island of Barbados. They needed supplies, and the men needed to relax a bit, so Raven directed the ships to pull into Bridgetown for a time of rest.

Raven asked Jeffrey to ensure that supplies were purchased and distributed to all three ships. Jeffrey brought Jeremy along to both help and to learn. Jeremy was a bright young man who would no doubt command a ship, whether it be in Raven's fleet or a ship of his own.

They walked through the streets of Bridgetown together like brothers. Although Jeffrey wasn't a captain of any ship, as quartermaster and once a second mate, he was well versed in seamanship. At one time, Jeffrey had hoped to command a ship of his own until Raven came along. Jeffrey quickly fell in love with her, and all he wanted from then on was to be near her.

Most men would want to be the head of the household, but Jeffrey had no such ambitions. As Raven's husband, he shared her bed, and that more than fulfilled all of his wants and desires. He melted with love whenever in her presence, when most men shrank in fear.

As the two young men walked through the streets, Jeremy asked, "What do you think about the ship we saw last week?"

"You mean the phantom ship?"

"Aye."

"I don't know. It could be a mirage, but I think it's strange that so many of us saw the same thing."

Jeremy then asked, "You said it looked like a caravel?"

"Right."

"Have you ever seen a caravel, Jeffrey?"

"Not with my own eyes, only in books or drawings. I don't think one has existed for at least a hundred years."

"Jeffrey, have you ever seen a ghost?"

"No. Have you?"

"Well..." Jeremy hesitated to answer.

"Go on."

"My mama died when I was ten. Soon after, I thought I saw her standing in the garden beside my grandfather's home. She was standing near the roses, watching the goldfinches that were lighting on the rosebushes. I called to her. She finally looked back at me, and when I approached, she faded away to nothing."

Jeffrey asked, "Did you mention this to your papa?"

"Aye, but he said it was probably just a lingering memory."

"Could be...but then...you never know."

Raven and John went into Bridgetown to look around while Jeffrey and Jeremy took care of supplying the ships. Her three captains were left to tend to the ships and ensure they were in good condition for their upcoming journeys.

As they walked down the cobblestone streets of the town, Raven spotted a tavern up ahead with a sign above the door that read, "The Pelican's Roost".

Raven asked, "Are you hungry?"

"I could eat. Especially if Louis Hardy has nothing to do with cooking it."

Raven smiled, "Mr. Hardy isn't a bad cook, he just doesn't have much to work with."

"Well, let's see what the Pelican has to offer."

They stepped inside and found a dimly lit room. Its walls were white-washed but faded so that they failed to reflect the light coming in from the single six-paned window at the front of the establishment. They looked around and found an unoccupied table in the corner of the room. Raven nodded to the man standing behind a bar at the back wall of the room.

The place wasn't entirely filled with patrons. However, it wasn't empty either. Raven and John sat at a table to the right of the front door, where only one other table was occupied by one single patron.

A young woman walked over to Raven and John's table and asked, "What'll it be?"

The woman appeared to be a little younger than Raven, less attractive, and significantly heavier. Her hair appeared not to have been washed or brushed in at least a week. Raven was already having second thoughts about dining here.

Raven said, "We'd like some food. What do you have?"

"All's we got is some roasted mutton, turnips, and carrots. I can bring you some fresh-baked bread and goat cheese, too."

"That will be fine."

"What do yuh want to drink? Ale or rum?"

Raven replied, "I'll have ale."

John acknowledged, "Same here."

"Name's Faye. If ya need anything, give a yell."

Raven said, "Thank you, Faye."

Raven looked around the room to see who or what might catch her eye. She noticed the man at the next table staring at her. It wasn't unusual for men to stare at her. She was pretty used to it. This man, however, caught

Raven's eye. He was dressed like a seafaring man. The saltwater and the sun had bleached his clothing. His face was rugged and wrinkled by years of being baked in the sun. His eyes were bloodshot from too much rum. Raven thought at first the man might be drunk, but when he spoke, his speech was clear and his words were unslurred.

"Good afternoon, young lass. And, to you, sir." He nodded to them both.

Raven replied, "Good afternoon."

He spoke with an Irish brogue not much different from Sean O'Toole's, but this man seemed well-educated from his manner of speech.

"Might you both be from one of the ships that entered the bay this morn?"

"Aye. I'm Raven Ashworth, and this is my father, John Ashworth."

"The name is Geoffrey Neely. What kind of vessels might you be sailing? Merchants?"

"Aye, we sail merchant ships. I have three."

"YOU have three? You mean you own these three ships?"

"Aye. I am the owner."

"It's very unusual for a young lass like yourself to be the owner of three such ships and to be sailing on them as well."

"Well, I'm a hands-on kind of gal." She smiled.

"Are you a seaman?"

"Once was. Not anymore. I've seen too much of the sea, and too much in the sea."

Faye brought out two platters of roasted mutton surrounded by sliced turnips and carrots. She then placed a warm loaf of bread in front of them, along with a hunk of pale yellow cheese. She walked back to the bar, collected two tankards of ale, and delivered them to Raven and John.

Raven returned her attention to the old sailor as she began to eat. "What do you mean, you've seen too much of the sea and in the sea?"

Geoffrey Neely looked around before whispering his answer. "Ghosts!"

Raven paused mid-bite of her mutton, then chewed again. After she swallowed, she leaned toward him and asked, "Ghosts?"

"Aye, young lassie. A ghost ship travels through these waters. Many a man has seen her."

"What kind of ship?"

"A Spanish caravel."

"Really? What can you tell me about this caravel?"

Geoffrey read Raven's face and realized something. "You've seen it, haven't you?

"We've seen something we couldn't identify. One of my crew said it could have been an old caravel. What can you tell me of this, ghost ship?"

"They say she first appeared two lifetimes ago—when Admiral Gaspar de Mendoza, a man of noble blood and black ambition, sailed from Cartagena with a fleet heavy with gold stolen not just from the jungles of New Granada, but from the temples of the old gods.

Mendoza, drunk on greed, defied the Spanish crown and set a new course—one that would carry the treasure not to Madrid, but to a hidden island said to be rich in dark powers—with him sailed a witch, a Castilian noblewoman condemned by the Inquisition. He spared her life on the promise she'd keep his ships safe, come storm or cannon fire.

But, you know, power has a price. As his fleet crossed the Bermuda passage, a storm unlike any seen before struck. Ships were swallowed in the black waves. Cries were lost in the thunder. And as Mendoza's flagship, *La Dama de Sangre*, disappeared into the maelstrom, the witch was said to have stood atop the deck, her arms raised to the sky, calling the winds by name. Whenever Spanish treasure is stolen, she follows those ships carrying the scent of stolen gold."

Raven flashed back to her supposed dream, which she had had several months back, in which a similar maelstrom had trapped *Destiny*. She shivered at the thought.

"Only one ship limped home, and its crew—half-mad with terror—spoke of red sails glowing in the night, of whispers on the wind, and of the dead walking the decks of a ship that should have sunk."

"*Red sails*? She thought to herself. "*I thought Destiny was the only ship with red sails.*"

"Now, *La Dama de Sangre* is said to prowl the Caribbean, shrouded in storm mist, her sails torn but still full, her deck forever lit with lanterns that burn without flame. Wherever great treasure is taken from the Spanish, she follows, drawn to the scent of stolen gold and betrayal.

They say if you hear a woman weeping in the wind just before a squall, it's the witch searching for what was lost—and warning that the sea has a long memory."

Raven was still thinking about the red sails when Geoffrey finished his story.

"*Did the ship they had seen fly red sails?*" She couldn't remember. It was too far away, maybe, to have been able to distinguish the sail's colors. Raven slowly and silently ate her food.

Geoffrey, without another word, stood and walked away.

Raven and John continued to eat their meal and drink their ale without much conversation. Both were deep in thought about what they had heard.

Raven had heard many ghost stories over the years from old timers who had sailed the seas. Some of the men she sailed with on the original *Destiny* told such stories. When Raven was barely thirteen, working the sails of *Destiny*, a merchant ship that made frequent and profitable runs to Madagascar, the older sailors used to speak in hushed voices of a ship called *The Hollow Star*.

She was once a whaler, they said, out of Whitby. Her captain, Elias Thorne, was a stern and righteous man, a widower who sailed with his only son, a bright-eyed boy named Micah. One bitter January, Thorne took *The Hollow Star* north of the Hebrides, a large group of islands off the west coast of Scotland, deep into hunting grounds cursed by the locals, where the whales moved like shadows and the sun never rose more than a hand's height above the sea.

The crew grew restless. One sailor vanished. They claimed he'd been lured overboard by a pale woman with black eyes, singing from beneath the ice. Then another disappeared. Then the boy, Micah. Captain Thorne, broken and maddened, refused to turn back. "The sea took my soul," he whispered. "Now I take hers."

The Hollow Star was last seen drifting off Flamborough Head, her sails in tatters but upright and billowed full, moving against the wind. No crew was aboard. Only a single lantern burned in the crow's nest—a widow's lantern, the old men said, meant to guide lost souls homeward.

Since then, on fog-heavy nights along the Yorkshire coast, sailors swear they've seen her—a ship, no sound but creaking wood, no sail but gliding fast over the waves, and always the lantern above, swaying slow like a hangman's noose.

They say if you follow her light, you'll never return—drawn to the same fate as those who went before, swallowed not by storm or beast, but by a grief that refuses to die.

Faye came back once more to check on her new patrons to see if they needed anything else.

"Will there be anything else I can get you?"

Raven replied, "No, thank you. How much do I owe you?"

"Five shillings will do."

Raven reached into her leather pouch and pulled out a £1 silver coin, handing it to Faye.

"I'll be right back with your change."

"No need. Keep the rest for yourself."

"Blimy! Thank you, miss! No one has ever been so generous to me. Is there anything else I can do for you?"

"What can you tell me about the man who was sitting at the next table just a moment ago? Where might I find him?"

Faye looked at Raven, confused. "What man do you mean?"

"I believe he said his name was Geoffrey Neely."

Faye's mouth dropped open in shock. "Blimy, miss! You say Geoffrey Neely was here?"

"Well, yes. He was right here at this table, talking to us while you served us. Didn't you notice him?"

"Miss, Geoffrey Neely died twenty years before I was born."

CHAPTER 6

Raven grabbed her papa's arm to steady herself after hearing what Faye had just told her. John took Raven by both arms and held onto her until she was strong enough to walk. John was feeling a little unsettled himself. He hadn't spoken to the man, only listened as he and Raven conversed. But he had seen Geoffrey Neely as clearly as the cloudless sky.

John spoke to the young woman who had delivered the news of their apparent spectral encounter. "Thank you, Faye. We'll be leaving now."

He took Raven to the door and delivered her into the bright light of the afternoon, hoping it would clear their minds. Raven had lost all ambition to explore the port city any longer. She was ready for her bunk.

John led her back up the cobblestone street to the dock where *Destiny* and the other ships were moored. He led her up the gangplank, where Attila met them.

"What is wrong with Raven?"

"I'm afraid she's had a bit of a fright. I'll tell you about it later. I need to get her to her cabin."

"Allow me."

The rather large African swept her up into his arms and carried her to her cabin with John leading the way. John opened the door and allowed Attila to carry Raven to her bed, where Captain Billings was anxiously waiting. The monkey squealed when he saw his owner passed out, lying on her bed.

The captain jumped to her shoulder and began rummaging through her hair with his tiny primate fingers.

John scolded the monkey, "Now, you let her sleep. No nonsense, mind you."

As John and Attila exited her cabin, they were met by Pharaoh and Alexander.

Pharaoh asked, "What is wrong with Raven?"

John motioned for the three of them to follow him to the quarterdeck for a bit of privacy. Once on the quarterdeck, John began to explain, "I'm afraid we've both had a bit of a shock. We were having a meal at a tavern called The Pelican's Roost. There was an old seaman sitting at the table next to us who struck up a conversation with Raven. He was telling her a tale about a ghost ship—a caravel that sails through these waters from time to time. A ship called *La Dama de Sangre*. She was captained by an Admiral Mendoza who had spared the life of a witch who had been tortured during the Spanish Inquisition. He told her she would remain under his protection as long as she protected his ships. A storm came upon them one night and destroyed all the ships but one. That lone ship limped home with a half-mad crew onboard, screaming about a ship with red sails glowing in the night. Its crew was all dead, but their bodies walked the decks during the night."

Alexander asked, "And this story frightened Raven?"

John shook his head, "Not the story. The man who told us the story. He wasn't there. The young woman who waited on us told us that the man who told us the story had been dead for many years. He wasn't really there."

Pharaoh asked, "You believed this young woman? Could it not have been a prank?"

"No. I thought back and remembered. The man never spoke while the young woman was present. He only spoke to us while she was away. He must have been only visible to us. When Raven asked her about the man who called himself Geoffrey Neely, she said Neely died twenty years before she was born."

Pharaoh then asked, "Did you say the ship's name was *La Dama de Sangre?*"

"Yes, that's right."

"I have been trying to learn Spanish from Zachery Thacker. If I am not mistaken, that means, *The Lady of Blood.*"

Jeffrey and Jeremy soon returned from their supply run. As they walked up *Destiny's* gangplank, they were met by John and Attila.

John said, "Jeffrey, I'm afraid Raven has had a bit of a fright."

"Where is she?"

"She's in her cabin, resting."

"What happened to her?"

"I'll tell you all about it later. Let's say, for now, she may have seen a ghost and it has startled her."

Jeffrey was confused by John's suggestion as he trotted to Raven's cabin and quietly opened the door to check on her. Captain Billings greeted him with a squeak as he sat on Raven's bed. Jeffrey carefully walked over to her, trying to be silent. He then sat on the edge of the bed and softly touched her face with the back of his hand. Raven stirred from her light sleep and looked up to find her loving husband gazing at her with concern.

"Are you alright?" he asked.

"Yes, I'm fine. How did I get here?"

"John and Attila brought you in. John said you've had a bit of a fright. Some kind of encounter with a ghost?"

Raven suddenly remembered, "Yes! We were at a tavern, eating. A man spoke to us from the table next to ours. He spoke of a ghost ship called *La Dama de Sangre.* Then the man just vanished. I asked the young woman serving us about him. What was his name? Oh, Geoffrey Neely! She said that Geoffrey Neely died twenty years before she was born."

Jeffrey raised his eyebrows, "Oh, dear. Well, what did this...ghost...this Geoffrey Neely have to say about *La Dama de Sangre?*"

"It is a ship with red ripped sails that glides through the sea under an unknown power, whether winds are present or not. A witch of some sort stands on her deck, screeching at those who sail in their path. Whenever Spanish treasure is stolen, she follows those ships carrying the scent of stolen gold."

"Are you alright now?"

"Yes, I'm fine. It was so hard to believe...I don't know why. After all the strange things we have encountered over the past six months...nothing should surprise me."

"Are you talking about those three men we picked up?"

"Well, yes...that's part of it. In addition...my dream, that they were in... all the strange creatures. And then the strange ship we encountered a week ago. It's all just so unnerving."

Jeffrey offered, "Well, hopefully getting underway will make you feel better. I've ordered our supplies. They will be delivered in the morning. We have until then to rest and set our minds to other opportunities."

"Yes, of course."

That night, Raven invited the three men they had rescued from the sea to join her, Jeffrey, and her captains to dine together. She hoped the activity would distract her from the events of the day. The eight of them sat around the table exchanging stories as Louis Hardy finished preparing their meal. Kupika and Michael Murphy, the new ship's boy, brought in platters of food and served Raven and her guests.

Kupika began setting the table with pewter plates and utensils. Michael brought in a keg of ale and began filling tankards for all the guests. Kupika and Michael then began serving platters of roasted vegetables and fresh fruit. Then Kupika entered the cabin, carrying a large platter that displayed a small, thirty-pound roasted pig. Kupika took out a large carving knife and fork to begin carving the meat away from the bone of the pig. The outer casing of the pig was crispy and snapped as she cut through it. She then pulled the meat away from the carcass in shredded chunks, placing them on each guest's plate. Michael moved from guest to guest, serving a honey and mustard glaze to each to eat with the pork. When everyone had had enough of the pork and predilections, Michael began serving plum tarts to the guests.

After dinner, Raven began questioning her guests, whom they had rescued so many days ago.

"Leftenant, I'm sorry we haven't had time to chat since all of you were brought aboard *Destiny*. Tell me...how did you manage to find yourselves drifting in the ocean in the middle of nowhere?"

"Well, Miss Ashworth..."

"Please, call me Raven, or Captain."

"Yes, of course, Captain. We were on air maneuvers flying over Bermuda. We were flying with five other torpedo bombers on a training mission. Our instruments malfunctioned, and we got lost, eventually running out of fuel. We had to bail out and hope someone would rescue us."

Raven turned to Jeffrey and asked, "Jeffrey, my love, would you mind pinching me, dear? I think I'm dreaming again. It's very similar to the dream I had before, without the dragons and rhino dinos."

"No, Raven. You're not dreaming. I'm hearing it too."

"Leftenant? What would you say if I told you I've met you and your men before?"

"Really? I'm sorry, I don't recall ever having met you. And excuse me for saying so, but I think I would remember someone as beautiful as you, Captain."

"Why don't I offer some information, and you tell me if I'm correct?"

"Sure."

"Alright. Your name is Charles Taylor, you are from a place called Tex-as..."

"Texas, ma'am."

"Right! Texas. You and your crew were flying sometime in the 1940s, I believe it may have been 45. When you talk about "bailing out" your ship, you don't mean that it was full of water. You mean, you had to jump out of it before it crashed. And, you used something called a para... para..."

"Parachute, ma'am."

"Right... to land safely in the water where you and your men climbed into a small boat you kept in your flying machine and then were rescued by my crew."

Taylor was shocked by how much Raven seemed to know about him.

"Captain? You're not really pirates, are you?"

"I beg your pardon?"

"What, are y'all makin' a movie out here or something?"

"What is a movie?"

"Never mind. How do you know so much about me, Captain?"

"Well, I was recently injured and unconscious for several days. I either had a dream or a premonition while I slept. I hope it was a dream, because I lost Jeffrey during that time. If it were a premonition, I'm afraid it might all come true. All three of you died as well. Killed by creatures on an island of mysterious beings. Giant carnivorous beasts. Flying reptiles. Hairy man-apes. Deadly vegetation. I hope I never visit that place again. In my sleep, or otherwise."

"I hope you're right as well. But…that doesn't explain how we ended up here, in the 18th century."

"No, it doesn't. However, I am discovering that there are strange, malevolent happenings in these waters. My crew and I witnessed what we believe to be a ghost ship about a week ago. My father and I talked with a man in a tavern who wasn't there. He was the ghost of a man who died over forty years ago. But he was as real as you are sitting in front of me now. You are real, aren't you?"

"I sure hope so, ma'am."

Raven replied, "Good."

"Well, ma'am, what should my men and I do while we're here on this ship?"

"You can join my crew if you like. You've all been trained to fight, have you not?"

"Well, yes, ma'am, but with guns and airplanes. Not swords and knives."

"It isn't all about fighting. Most of it is about sailing. Living on the open waters. Being free to be or do whatever you want."

Turner turned to his men, "Well, George, Walter? What do you think?"

George replied, "I'm with you, Lieutenant."

"Me too!" added Walter.

CHAPTER 7

Bridgetown slept in a hush of lamplight and waves, its cobbled streets gleaming with the damp shimmer of evening rain. The revelry of port life had dulled to a low murmur—the clink of a distant bottle, the fading laugh of a drunkard, the clatter of hooves on the cobblestoned street. *Raven's Destiny* swayed gently at anchor, her rigging whispering secrets to the wind as the tide pushed against her hull. Raven's banner flew high above, whipping against the wind.

Raven emerged from the captain's quarters just past midnight, her dark coat loose about her shoulders, boots silent on the well-worn deck. She nodded to Jeremy, who stood at the helm, holding the night watch. The dinner below had been pleasant enough—three new crewmates, all recently sworn to her Articles, had toasted her leadership with rum. They were loyal, or at least eager to appear so, and she appreciated the effort.

Still, something in her chest had begun to ache—an itch born of restless memories and the feel of land beneath her feet too long. She flashed to her dream—or was it a dream? A time she remembers vividly when she first met her three new men—the island. Segments of a nightmarish encounter with the island and all that it held came rushing back to her. Her body shuddered at the thought.

She needed air. Quiet. Stars.

She walked the port side rail and leaned, gazing toward the sleepy port. Bridgetown's harbor lamps burned low with amber hues. Beyond them, the narrow walkway between sea and stone was nearly empty—until a figure stepped into view.

Raven's breath caught.

The man was tall and narrow-shouldered, his coat too thin for the Caribbean night. A broad-brimmed hat shadowed his face, but she could see the high cheekbones, the long grey beard hanging from his jaws. He walked with purpose, though no destination seemed to guide him.

She narrowed her eyes, her heartbeat skipping like a startled bird.

"Geoffrey?" she whispered.

The figure paused.

Geoffrey Neely. Dead for more than forty years now, according to Faye, who served her at the tavern. Raven had spoken to his ghost once before—in *The Pelican's Roost*, the half-ruined tavern in town where spirits whispered over rum bottles and secrets pooled in dark corners. She and her father had spent the afternoon dining and speaking with him-or what was left of him. He had warned them of betrayal. Of a ship that sailed without wind. Of a name whispered in the water. *La Dama de Sangre.*

Now, the figure slowly turned its head. A pale glint showed beneath the hat's brim—eyes like dull glass, fixed on her. A small, cold smile tugged at his lips. Raven's hands fell to her sides, but she did not reach for a blade. It would've been useless.

She stepped onto the gangplank, the ship creaking beneath her. But when she looked again—

The dock was empty.

No sound. No footsteps. No shadow.

Only the soft knock of water on wood and the distant shriek of a gull, careening through the dark sky above.

Raven exhaled, slow and heavy.

He'd come for a reason. Ghosts did not wander without a tether to bind them where they remained.

And Geoffrey Neely had warned her of things to come.

Raven stood motionless for a long while, eyes fixed on the place where the figure had been. The wind tugged at her coat, and the sea below sighed like a creature unsettled in its sleep. Finally, she turned and descended to the lower deck, her boots silent on the planks.

She pushed open the door to her quarters.

Inside, a lantern burned low, casting soft amber light over the walls lined with charts and sea-worn books. Jeffrey lay asleep where she had left him on the narrow bed, one arm behind his head, the other resting across his chest.

Raven stood over him a moment, listening to the rhythm of his breath. It was steady. Rumbling.

Then she sat on the edge of the bed and laid a hand lightly on his shoulder.

"Jeffrey," she whispered. "Wake."

His eyes opened, slow at first, then sharper as he registered the look on her face. "What is it? Something wrong topside?"

She shook her head once. "Not exactly. I saw someone. Or... I believe I did."

He sat up now, swinging his legs over the side of the bed. "Who?"

"The man. On the docks. Tall, slight, walked with a limp." She paused. "It was Geoffrey Neely."

Jeffrey blinked. "Neely? That ghost you and your father met this afternoon—the one from *The Pelican's Roost*?"

"The same."

"Are you certain?"

"As certain as I can be of any man who's dead and walking."

Jeffrey ran a hand through his sleep-tousled hair, then reached for the flask beside the bed. He handed it to her first.

Raven took a sip, more for the ritual than the rum.

"I don't think he's just wandering," she said. "He looked at me...like he'd come with purpose. Like he had a message for me."

Jeffrey frowned. "Neely, about a ship with no sails."

"And a name whispered in the waves," she finished. "I remember."

"You think this ghost ship... it's tied to him?"

"I think," she said slowly, "this isn't over. I think whatever's been stirring out there—whatever's kept us from finding prey on the sea—it's bigger than coincidence."

Jeffrey was quiet for a moment, then reached for her hand. "What do you want to do?"

Raven looked at the lantern flame, flickering in the draft like a fragile life. "First light, we speak with Pharaoh and Alexander. I want to know if their men have seen anything. Strange lights. Whispers. Shadows."

"And if they haven't?"

She squeezed his hand. "Then we keep hunting. But with one eye on the horizon... and one on what's following us."

She lay beside him then, not to sleep, but to feel warmth, steady and familiar. Outside, the wind rose. The harbor creaked. And somewhere in the dark, unseen eyes watched the water, waiting.

When Raven awakened, Jeffrey was no longer by her side. Instead, Captain Billings had taken his place, snuggled up in her long, tangled curls. Raven rose, wiping the sleep from her eyes, feeling oddly refreshed after enduring such a harrowing night. For some strange reason, she no longer felt tangled in the web of ghostly secrets. Perhaps it had all been a dream, like the one about her island.

Raven disrobed, bathed, and then changed her clothes to begin a new day. A day of hope. Hope that might bring new adventure and possibly riches.

She exited her cabin and found Jeffrey and her papa standing together on the quarterdeck. The supply wagons had just arrived, and Jeffrey was preparing his crew to bring *Destiny's* share onboard.

Raven met Jeffrey as he stepped onto the gangplank. When he saw how rested she appeared, he smiled. "Looks like you slept well."

"I do feel rested. I don't know why, after such a strange encounter with the night."

Jeffrey asked, "Will you join me as I check the supplies?"

Raven looked around. "I was hoping to talk to Jeremy."

"John just relieved him at the watch two hours ago. I'm sure he's fast asleep."

"Of course, yes. Well then, I shall join you, then."

They walked together arm-in-arm down the gangplank and met the supply wagons as they pulled up to the docks. A voice called to her from east of her position. It was Pharaoh who walked toward Raven with Alexander by his side. Behind them were twenty young men, white, African, and Spaniards, all coming to help resupply the ships.

Six wagons pulled up to the docks, and Raven's men began unloading each of them so the supplies could be checked off Jeffrey's extensive list. Barrels, kegs, and sacks were laid out on the pier to be counted and inspected by the quartermaster before being shelled out to each of the ships. Flour, rice, cornmeal, oatmeal, fresh fruits, and vegetables were all meticulously inspected by Jeffery before being dispersed to the ships for storage.

Once every item had been accounted for, Jeffrey allotted barrels, kegs, and sacks to be dispensed to each ship. Jeffrey paid one of the delivery men for the supplies, then he and Raven walked back up the gangplank onto *Destiny*.

Raven was looking forward to getting underway once again. She had the feeling they would be successful on this voyage. She looked forward to leaving Bridgetown behind, and hopefully Geoffrey Neely as well. Her hopes were high, and her spirits were too. For the first time in a long time, she allowed a smile to reach her lips.

Days passed at sea with the steady rhythm of wind in sails and the slap of waves on oaken timbers. Raven stood often at the bow, scanning the horizon with her spyglass, the salty air tangling in her hair. The breeze whispered promises of riches, but so far, the sea had remained empty.

Still, something had shifted.

Her men moved with sharper energy. Even Pharaoh and Alexander's crews, hardened and skeptical veterans, began to show signs of renewed purpose. The strange quiet that had blanketed the Caribbean in recent weeks, like the sea was holding its breath, now seemed to break.

It was the seventh day when the lookout's voice rang down from the crow's nest like a cannon shot.

"Ships! Three points off the port bow. Sails on the horizon!"

Raven's head snapped up. She raised her glass, training it toward the glare just above the waterline. Her heart leapt.

There they were.

Three, no, four—vessels, low in the water, sluggish with cargo. Spanish galleons, unmistakable with their gold-gilded sterns and high masts.

Heading east.

Heading home.

The gold-laden ghosts they'd been hunting.

Raven lowered the glass slowly, a smile blooming across her face—triumphant, calculating. She turned to Jeffrey, who had already joined her at the rail.

"Do you see that?"

Jeffrey used her spyglass to have a look. Then handed it back.

"I do. Ripe for the picking!"

"Time to earn our keep," she said.

He nodded once. "Shall we rouse the others?"

But just as Raven opened her mouth to reply, a second voice came from the masthead. The tone had changed—sharpened, urgent.

"Another ship! Off their starboard side—can't tell her colors. Fast. She's gaining on the Spaniards."

Raven lifted her glass again. She gasped.

The new ship rode low in the water, sleek and dark. Blood-red sails, nearly ripped to shreds. No flag. The sea seemed to move strangely around it—unnaturally smooth, as if the waves dared not touch her hull.

It was as if the ship was gliding across the sea under some unknown power, not dependent upon the winds.

A shiver tickled Raven's spine.

Jeffrey leaned close. "What is it?"

Raven didn't answer at first. Her voice was a whisper when it came.

"*La Dama de Sangre.*"

The wind fell still.

And somewhere, far off on the water, a bell began to toll.

CHAPTER 8

N o one else had seen it yet—not Jeffrey, not the crew. But she felt its presence press against her like the weight of the deep.

No one heard the tolling of the bell. Only Raven.

And just as suddenly as it had appeared, it was gone—swallowed by the rising sun.

Raven stood motionless, heart pounding.

The Spanish ships lay ahead.

But something else was hunting the hunters.

The Spanish ships, burdened with the weight of the empire's riches, moved with surprising haste, their sails full and white against the azure skies. Raven's fleet—*Destiny* at the lead, *The Sea Witch* to her port, and *Royal Victory* trailing close—chased hard, but the wind had turned unpredictable, fickle as a cat.

Each hour stretched like a rope pulled taut. The galleons stayed just beyond reach, their shadows looming on the horizon. Raven cursed under her breath, standing next to Isaac, who was gripping the wheel alongside John. The sails sagged, snapping with frustration rather than force. Isaac struggled to catch the wind no matter what he tried.

"The wind fights us," Isaac muttered beside her. "As if it favors them."

She nodded grimly. "It's always that way when gold's afoot. The sea makes you earn every coin."

For two days, they pushed east, adjusting tack, trimming sails, even resorting to towing lines when the winds died entirely. Crewmen sweated and cursed, their backs aching from the labor as they were sent into the dories to pull the heavy ships manually by oar. The sun beat down mercilessly, and every barrel of water they drank made the prize seem more untouchable.

Then, just as they thought the Spaniards might vanish entirely into the haze, the wind returned, fierce and wild. *Destiny* surged forward, her sails straining against the renewed gusts. Pharaoh's *Sea Witch* followed, the black-painted hull cutting waves like a blade. *The Royal Victory* brought up the rear, with its gunports already opened and poised to fire.

By dawn the next morning, the Spanish galleons were within cannon range.

Raven stood at the rail, spyglass in hand. "Signal Alexander to sweep portside. Pharaoh can cut in from starboard. We can box them in."

Attila nodded and turned, pulling out his conch shell. He blew a signal with orders to place each ship in its place of pursuit.

Then came the thunder.

The first Spanish cannon fired a second too early, its ball splashing uselessly to port of *The Sea Witch*'s bow. But the second shot—deadly accurate—crashed through the forecastle, sending splinters and men flying.

Raven's jaw clenched. "All guns ready!"

Jeremy ordered his gunners to prepare for fire.

Destiny's starboard side roared to life as Isaac turned the helm to come about. Iron screamed across the sea, crashing into the nearest galleon and ripping away her stern gallery in a shower of timber and smoke. The Spanish replied in kind, and soon the air filled with smoke, flame, and the roar of battle.

Destiny rolled with each blast—first port, then starboard. Men shouted. Blood splattered the deck. A mast cracked on the *Victory*, toppling into the waves. Still, they pressed forward.

Through the gunpowder haze, Raven could make out the red and gold trim of the trailing Spanish vessel, *La Fortuna*. Her hull gleamed, splattered with fresh wounds, yet she did not slow.

Raven's voice cut through the chaos. "Prepare to board!"

But as grappling hooks were readied and cutlasses drawn, a shadow rippled across the water. Not a cloud—no storm. Something else. Something beneath the ship's wake, menacing and eerie.

Raven's breath caught. Jeffrey saw it too.

A swell rose between them and the Spanish ship, unnatural in its shape—long, smooth, as if something enormous stirred beneath the surface.

And from that dark trough, a sound rose—not the crash of cannon or the scream of dying men—but a whisper. Ancient. Hungry.

Raven looked back. No one else seemed to hear it.

But she did.

And she knew.

***La Dama de Sangre* was near.**

The waves crashed harder as the wind screamed like a choir of wailing spirits, pressing *Destiny* dangerously close to the closest galleon. Raven barked orders, her voice raw with smoke and urgency. Grappling hooks soared. Pirates surged across the narrowing gap.

"Board now!" she shouted, her cutlass high. "No mercy!"

Pharaoh's *Sea Witch* had already made contact with a second galleon. Flames licked up the rigging of the Spanish vessel, her crew retreating to the higher decks as steel clashed and bodies fell into the sea.

Alexander's *Royal Victory* limped in on the far flank, battered but still afloat. She let loose another broadside, splintering the hull of a third galleon that had tried to flank the pirates.

Raven was the first to leap to the enemy deck. Her boots struck with force. Her blade was already singing. The Spaniards rallied, desperate, disciplined—but the pirates were a tide of chaos, driven by hunger and a thirst for blood.

Jeffrey fought beside her, his pistol blasting one man in the face as his sabre caught another mid-thrust in his gullet. The deck pitched beneath them, slick with seawater and blood.

Then it came again.

That cold whisper.

Raven froze for half a breath. Around her, the noise of battle dulled, as though something vast had gasped for breath beneath the waves. She turned toward the sea.

And there, beyond the battle smoke, on the horizon—

A ship.

No sails.

No flag.

No crew on deck.

It glided silently, hull black as charred bone, its masts were broken stumps. And though wind and tide should've held it back, it moved forward... without resistance, as though the water itself parted before it.

"*La Dama...*" Raven whispered.

"Raven!" Jeffrey called, slicing down a Spaniard at her flank. "Eyes on the fight!"

Raven shook the fog from her thoughts. "Aye!" She drove forward, her blade flashing in the sunlight. But behind her, the chill never left the back of her head.

The Spanish captain met her blade to blade—a well-trained man with gold-trimmed epaulets and eyes full of fury. Raven fought hard, matching him stroke for stroke. But the moment she found an opening, she hesitated.

A whisper.

Right at her ear.

"Betrayer."

The Spanish captain lunged, but Jeffrey tackled him before the strike could land, knocking the man out cold.

Raven turned, pale now. Jeffrey grabbed her arm. "Did you hear that?"

She nodded. "It's here. Watching us."

Behind them, a sudden scream erupted from one of the pirate galleons—*The Sea Witch*. Men pointed to the horizon, faces pale with fright.

The ghost ship had vanished.

Not sailed away. Not drifted out of view.

Gone.

And where it had been, the sea churned like boiling water.

But there was no time to wonder. No time to fear.

The battle still raged.

And *La Dama de Sangre* had only just begun to remind them that she was real... and she was waiting.

The air burned with gunpowder and the stench of blood as the battle raged across the decks of the Spanish galleons. Screams rose with the smoke. Raven pressed forward, with bloodied blade and breath heaving, every movement a defiance of the weight that had rested on her shoulders—ghost or no ghost, she would not die here.

Jeffrey stayed close to her flank, his sabre now notched and his coat sliced in three places. Around them, *Destiny's* crew fought like madmen.

Pharaoh's boarding party had driven back the defenders on the second galleon, its mainmast sagging under the weight of cannon damage. Alexander, bleeding from a gash above his brow, had forced the surrender of the third Spanish ship, now flying a makeshift white flag of torn sailcloth.

But it wasn't over.

The flagship, *La Infanta*, still resisted. Heavily manned, thick-hulled, and defiant, she fired another brutal broadside that struck *The Sea Witch* amidships, tearing through the deck with a roar. The pirate ship groaned, then caught fire at the fore.

"Get those flames down!" Pharaoh bellowed from the gunwale. Buckets flew as men scrambled to douse the blaze.

Raven saw it: the tide was shifting. If *La Infanta* held them off just long enough, the tide might turn in favor of the Spanish.

"Bring her down!" she roared. "Take the flagship!"

She surged forward with a war cry, gathering a wave of *Destiny's* crew behind her. Together, they drove into the last Spanish line.

Amid the chaos, thunder rolled overhead—not from cannon, but from the sky. Clouds swirled unnaturally fast above them. The wind whipped cold and salty, sending loose canvas flapping like the wings of giant birds.

And then... it happened again.

La Dama de Sangre.

She appeared without warning—between the Spanish galleons and the horizon—her bow emerging from a sudden bank of fog, though no fog had been present moments before. No sound accompanied her. Just the sight of that water-bleached figurehead—*a woman weeping blood*—and her tattered, motionless sails.

The fighting slowed.

Men, pirates, and Spaniards alike froze in terror.

Even cannon crews stopped loading their gun.

The ghost ship glided silently closer, impossibly cutting through waves that should've capsized her. One of Alexander's Spaniards fell to his knees, crossing himself.

Raven stared, lips parting. *"She's come for the dying."*

A horrible creak echoed across the sea, like a coffin lid being opened far below. And then—*a scream*—from the water.

One of the Spanish sailors flailed, dragged under by something unseen. Another followed. A third slipped on blood and was sucked into the black waves without a splash. Panic broke across the remaining Spanish crew.

"Abandon ship!" one of them shouted.

"No!" Raven yelled, but it was too late.

Some jumped into the sea—only to vanish in bubbles and silence.

Others dropped their weapons and ran for the lower decks.

La Dama de Sangre stopped just beyond cannon range... watching.

Waiting.

"Enough!" Raven shouted, raising her blade high. "Take the ship before we all lose our minds!"

Her cry broke everyone's paralysis.

With a final, furious push, *Destiny's* crew stormed the quarterdeck. Jeffrey drove the Spanish first mate to his knees. Raven kicked open the cabin door and found the captain inside, pistol in hand. She fired first.

La Infanta was taken.

And only then... only after Raven's crew raised her flag high on her mast... did the ghost ship begin to slowly fade.

Not sail away.

Fade.

Like a breath lost amongst the wind.

Like she had never been there.

But Raven knew better.

She'd been marked.

And *La Dama* would return.

Raven's chest heaved as she gasped for the much-needed oxygen to enter her lungs. She looked around to inspect the damage done. All three of her ships would need repairs. But first, the galleons would be assessed to determine which, if any, was suitable to join her fleet. Raven coveted the flagship, *La Infanta*. She would be a prize indeed. Attila had waited patiently for his chance to captain a ship. Maybe now would be his chance.

Pharaoh's crew continued to extinguish flames that had ignited throughout the battle.

Alexander's crew cut away the rigging holding the broken mast from sliding into the sea.

Repairs were needed all around. But not here. They needed to get back to Barbados. But first, they needed to search the three captured ships for loot. Raven assigned each of the other captains to one of the captured ships. Attila would search *La Infanta* on behalf of *Destiny*. Alexander searched the hull of the third ship, *León Coronado*, while Pharaoh searched the second ship, *Pájaro de Fuego*.

As Attila boarded *La Infanta*, he discovered the damage was much worse than they initially believed. Her hull had extensive damage at both the starboard stern, just below the waterline, and the gold-gilded stern that was splintered. She would be unsuitable for Raven's fleet.

Attila explored below decks and found what they were looking for. Treasure. One hundred sea chests, each weighing about fifty pounds, were stashed inside a locked room below, at the lowest level on the ship.

Attila ordered his boarding crew, "Get these chests over to *Raven's Destiny* before this ship sinks."

Alexander searched the decks of the *León Coronado* with his crew. Aside from the shattered mast, her hull was in good shape. Alexander found the treasure waiting below. Another one hundred chests filled with treasure. His men scrambled to move the chests up to the main deck to be transferred to *Destiny*.

When Pharaoh climbed aboard *Pájaro de Fuego*, he found the ship to be relatively intact. There was very little damage to her. Twenty of her crew were found hiding below on the second deck. When they saw Pharaoh and his men, they raised their hands and cried out, "Rendirse! Rendirse! (Surrender! Surrender!)"

The twenty were taken up to the main deck where they could be questioned and their fates decided.

Another one hundred chests were discovered on the lowermost deck and brought topside to be turned over to *Destiny*, where Jeffery would distribute shares to the men of Raven's fleet.

Once Raven reconvened with her captains, it was decided that only Pájaro de Fuego was suitable to join her fleet. Raven turned the ship over to Attila with the instructions to change her name to the English version of her former name. "From now on, she will be *The Firebird*."

Then, Raven asked Jeremy to step forward, "Attila, Mr. Finch will be your first mate."

Jeremy was shocked at her announcement. Attila smiled as he looked at Jeremy, then at Raven.

"Aye, Raven. A wise choice."

All men and women present gave cheer to the sixteen-year-old first mate. Jeremy had served with Raven for four years and was certainly capable of leading under Attila's command. He had not, however, expected the honor to come so soon.

Jeremy looked at Raven, then at his father, Isaac, who was Raven's helmsman. He was a little sad to be leaving his father behind on *Destiny*. Raven saw his look of dismay.

Raven then said, "Helmsman Finch! You will be joining Attila as his helmsman."

Isaac and Jeremy smiled at each other, looking at each other, and thanked Raven for not separating them.

CHAPTER 9

T he sun hung low over the horizon as *Raven's Destiny's* crew bustled with preparations, ropes creaking and sails catching the wind in slow, lazy snaps. From her place on the quarterdeck, Raven watched the movement below, but her eyes were fixed on a lanky figure near the longboat — Jeremy Finch, newly appointed First Mate of the *Firebird*.

He stood with his back straight, trying to look older than his sixteen years. The red sash tied at his waist fluttered in the breeze, and his boots, freshly polished, still seemed a size too large.

Raven descended the steps and crossed to him, her long coat trailing behind her like a shadow.

"You've grown an inch since breakfast," she said, folding her arms.

Jeremy flushed, but a shy smile tugged at his lips. "Maybe two."

"Attila will need a proper log to keep track of your height," she said, teasing. "Or he'll start issuing orders to your kneecaps."

That earned a quiet laugh from him — short, soft, but genuine.

For a moment, Raven just looked at him. Gone was the quiet, wide-eyed boy who had first come aboard clutching a sailor's satchel and his father's sleeve. She remembered how he'd barely spoken above a whisper that first week. How Captain Billings, her mischievous monkey, had taken to curling up on Jeremy's shoulder like a barnacle. And how, once, after a brutal squall, she'd found Jeremy on the main deck in the dead of night, drying the monkey with a corner of his own blanket.

"I'll miss you," she said, softer now. "You've been more than crew to me, Jere."

He looked up at her, surprised by the old nickname.

"I wouldn't be what I am without you, Raven," he said, and his voice cracked just slightly on the words. "You saw me when I was no one."

She reached into her coat and pulled something from her inner pocket — a narrow strip of dark blue ribbon, worn at the edges.

"This was mine," she said, "when I first left England, when I became ship's boy aboard the *Destiny*. Tied it in my hair the day I swore I'd never let the sea break me."

Jeremy took it carefully and reverently, nodding.

"You won't be alone on the *Firebird*, Jere. And you won't stop being mine, either. Not truly."

Just then, Captain Billings scampered down from the rigging and hopped to Jeremy's shoulder with practiced ease, chittering as if to say goodbye in his own language.

"Seems someone else will miss you, too."

Jeremy reached up and scratched the monkey behind the ear, chuckling. "Take care of her, Billings. She pretends not to need it, but she does."

Raven raised a brow. "Oh, do I now?"

He smirked. "More than you let on."

She laughed and nudged his shoulder. "Now go, First Mate. Make me proud. But not so proud I have to steal you back."

"Aye, Captain," he said, and with one final glance over his shoulder, he climbed down to the dory.

Raven watched until he reached the edge of the *Firebird*, the ribbon still clenched in his hand like a thread tying the past to whatever came next.

The rowboat bumped against the hull of the *Firebird*, and Jeremy reached for the rope ladder, his fingers trembling just enough for him to notice. He took a steadying breath, then climbed, boots thudding softly against the timbers as he pulled himself up onto the deck.

She was a sleeker ship than *Raven's Destiny* — narrower, rigged for speed, with bright sails furled tight along the yard arms. The deck crew glanced up at him, a few offering brief nods. No greetings. No applause. Just the measured stares of men waiting to see if the new first mate could hold his place.

Attila stood near the helm, arms folded. The wind whipped through his hair and tousled it, but little. The African captain's skin grew darker in the lowering light of the evening, making him look like only a shadow standing on deck. He watched Jeremy approach with the expression of a man measuring grain before it's bought.

"You're late," Attila said.

Jeremy opened his mouth — then saw the grin beneath the gruffness.

"Only jesting," the captain said. "But don't make a habit of it."

Jeremy gave a quick nod. "No, sir."

Attila's eyes flicked over him, noting the polish on his boots, the crisp cut of his coat, the still-soft edge in his voice. "You know how to run a gunnery team, Finch. Raven swears by you. I've seen you work."

"She's taught me a great deal," Jeremy replied. "And I've been learning since I was twelve."

"Good," Attila said. "Because I need more than a good lad. I need a first mate. You'll be calling orders, checking rations, settling arguments, and keeping this deck from rotting out from under us. Are you up for that?"

Jeremy squared his shoulders. "I am, Captain."

Attila studied him for a beat longer, then gave a single nod. "Then take the watch. Show me what Raven sees in you."

Jeremy turned to the crew and took a few paces down the deck, the feel of the ship already beginning to register beneath his feet. Different than

Raven's Destiny — she was faster, less forgiving — like a whip instead of a hammer.

One of the older sailors, a grizzled man with a scar under his left eye, gave him a look that wasn't quite respect... but it wasn't disdain either—just curiosity. *Let's see what you've got,* it said without words.

Jeremy lifted his chin. "Hands to the main deck," he called out, voice ringing clearer than he expected. "We take inventory before dusk. Rigging checks after."

The men began to move. Slowly at first, then with more purpose. The *Firebird* creaked beneath their boots as Jeremy found his sea legs again — not as a ship's boy, not even as a gunner, but as first mate. He let out a breath and glanced toward the horizon.

This is where it begins, he thought. *Not the end of Destiny — just the start of something more.*

He didn't see Raven watching from afar, standing at the rail of *Destiny*, a small, quiet smile curving her lips as her little brother stepped into the storm of manhood.

The sun sagged toward the western horizon, bleeding orange and crimson over the *Firebird*'s sails. Below deck, the air was thick with sweat, pitch, and the scent of old salt. Jeremy moved along the gun deck with a ledger under one arm and a lantern swinging from his other hand.

He'd ordered the crews—split evenly between Spaniards and Africans—to work together checking powder kegs and tightening mounts. It had seemed straightforward. Necessary. But now the tension hung like wet wool in the air.

A loud *crack!* Stopped him cold. He rounded the gunport and saw two men squared off—one a wiry Spaniard with a trimmed beard, the other a tall, bare-chested African with a scar splitting one eyebrow. They shouted in two languages, faces flushed with heat and pride. Powder kegs had been kicked out of line. Someone's tools lay scattered.

The African, Jabari, shoved the Spaniard, who stumbled back a step before grabbing for a belaying pin.

Jeremy stepped between them, fast.

"Enough!"

The word echoed through the gun deck.

The men froze. All eyes turned to Jeremy, the boy first mate. Just sixteen. A whisper of peach fuzz on his chin and nerves riding just beneath his calm demeanor.

But his voice had cracked like a whip. And for that moment, it held.

Jeremy turned to Jabari. "What's the problem?"

"He says my men touch nothing. Says we only stand and stare."

The Spaniard—Luis—snorted. "Your men work like they're blind. No care for order. We could all blow sky-high from your laziness."

"Watch your mouth!" Jabari snarled, stepping forward again.

Jeremy raised a hand, and to his surprise, both men halted.

He looked around at the crew. "You think I care one little bit where you were born? On this ship, you're brothers or you're nothing. You don't fight each other—you fight for *this* crew. For *your* survival."

The men were silent.

Jeremy bent, picked up the scattered tools, and held them out. "You want to swing fists, you do it in the ring above deck, by the drum. You want to swing a hammer, then fall in and do it right."

He held the tools between the two men.

Jabari looked at Luis.

Luis looked at Jeremy.

Then, after a breath, they both reached for the tools. Jeremy didn't let go until their fingers brushed, and they both grunted in irritation.

"Good," Jeremy said quietly. "Now stow this deck before sunset. I'll be back to check it."

He turned on his heel and left them standing there. Behind him, the crew moved—slowly at first, then faster. The scrape of crates, the thud of rope, the ring of order returning.

Back above deck, Jeremy leaned against the mainmast and let out the breath he'd been holding.

A voice behind him said, "That could've gone badly."

It was Attila.

Jeremy straightened. "I handled it."

"You did," Attila said, stepping beside him. "You made them listen. You kept your hands steady. That's more than most men twice your age could manage."

Jeremy didn't smile, but a quiet warmth filled his chest.

"Don't let it swell your head," Attila added, a grin creeping in. "The sea'll do that for you soon enough."

Jeremy Finch was born in the seafaring village of Whitby, along England's rugged northeastern coast, where ships were built and legends were born. His mother, Margaret, was a weaver renowned for her soft voice and remarkable courage in stormy weather. His father, Isaac Finch, had saltwater in his blood—a helmsman by trade, who had sailed merchant routes from London to the Carolinas. Isaac's last voyage on a merchant ship was on the *Tryton*, a slave ship captured by Raven and her crew. The crew of the *Tryton* was given the choice of swearing allegiance to Raven and turning pirate under Raven's banner or taking their chances marooned on a nearby island. Isaac and Jeremy chose to remain with Raven, a choice neither of them ever regretted.

When Jeremy was twelve, a fever swept through Whitby. Margaret succumbed within days. With no kin left ashore and a boy too young to fend for himself, Isaac made the only choice a father could—he brought Jeremy aboard the *Tryton* and then *Raven's Destiny*.

At first, Jeremy scrubbed decks and ran messages—just another ship's boy among many. But his eyes were sharp, his hands quick, and his instincts uncanny. By fourteen, he was studying the gunnery charts and training alongside the artillery crew. Raven herself noted his precision during a cannon drill off the coast of Tortuga. By fifteen, he'd earned his place as a junior officer and gunnery mate.

Now sixteen, Jeremy stood taller, lean and wiry like his father, but with his mother's calm steadiness in his eyes. Raven had just promoted him to First Mate aboard *Firebird*, and though Jeremy knew the responsibility was immense, he bore it with a quiet pride. He still looked to Isaac for wisdom and to Raven for purpose, but he was no longer a boy afloat—he was a rising officer in the fleet. Raven's voice always remained in his head. When in doubt, he asked himself, *what would Raven do?*

What he didn't know, yet, was that his name would one day be spoken in the same breath as legends. For the sea was stirring with old forces, and Jeremy Finch had a part to play in the reckoning to come.

The sky had turned a greyish shade of blue, the sea calm in the fading light. Jeremy leaned on the weathered rail of the *Firebird*, watching the horizon stretch endlessly ahead. The sails creaked above him, and the crew moved below with the low murmur of a ship settling into its night rhythm.

Captain Attila was below, reviewing maps. For a rare moment, Jeremy was alone.

A footstep behind him broke the silence. He didn't have to turn to know who it was.

"You always did watch the sea like it held answers," came his father's voice—deep and familiar, like the creak of an old rope.

Jeremy smiled faintly. "Maybe it does."

Isaac Finch came to stand beside him. The wind lifted the long ends of his coat, salt-white at the edges. "You were twelve when you first stepped aboard the *Tryton*. Scrawny as a gull and but half as loud."

Jeremy chuckled. "And still you brought me."

Isaac's smile was quieter. "Wasn't much choice. Not after your mother passed." He paused. "I feared it might break you. But you bent with the wind. Like a good mast."

Jeremy was quiet for a moment. "Do you think she'd be proud?"

Isaac didn't answer at first. He looked out to sea, then back to his son. "She'd be terrified," he said with a half-smile. "But proud, aye. You've made more of yourself in four years than most do in twenty. And now first mate... on your own ship."

"Well, it's Attila's ship."

Jeremy looked down at his hands, calloused and scarred. "Feels strange, being so far from home. I barely remember the village anymore."

"The sea's your home now," Isaac said. "And make no mistake, boy—you've earned every knot you've sailed. Just remember... it can give, and it can take. Just like life."

Jeremy nodded slowly. "I'll remember."

Father and son stood side by side in the dusk, bound by blood, by storm, and by the great wild ocean that had taken them in.

The last light of day had just slipped beneath the horizon when the cry came down from the mast.

"Smoke! Aft port side!"

Jeremy was halfway across the quarterdeck when the second shout followed.

"Fire below!"

He didn't hesitate.

"Beat to quarters!" he bellowed. "All hands, move!"

Feet thundered on the planks as the crew scrambled into motion. Jeremy shot down the companionway, heart pounding, smoke already curling around the ladder. He could hear coughing and shouting below as men raced to form a bucket line.

When he burst into the lower deck, the heat hit him like a cannon blast. A storage crate had ignited—likely from a spark missed after gunnery checks. Flames licked up the wall, devouring canvas and rope, smoke billowing thick and fast.

"Jabari! Luis!" Jeremy barked, eyes scanning through the haze. "You're on the pumps—move!"

To their credit, neither man hesitated. Jabari pulled two men toward the pump handles while Luis organized the line to the water barrels.

Jeremy grabbed a bucket himself, his throat raw from smoke, eyes stinging. "Cover the powder crates first!" he shouted. "Soak the canvas around them—we lose this deck and the whole ship goes up!"

The crew fought hard, sweat pouring, boots slipping on soaked boards. The fire roared, coughed, and hissed as water slammed against its base. It seemed to resist them like a living thing, fighting to stay fed.

Then—at last—it faltered.

The flames choked, retreated, and hissed into blackness.

Jeremy slumped against the wall, soot streaked across his face, lungs burning. Around him, the crew stood panting, soaked, eyes wide.

Attila's voice came from the ladderway. "I had a report of fire. That confirmed?"

Jeremy turned toward him, still catching his breath. "Confirmed... and extinguished."

Attila took one look at the blackened timbers, the exhausted men, and Jeremy's smoke-covered face. He nodded once.

"Well done, First Mate."

Jeremy didn't reply right away. He looked at the men who had fought under his orders—Spaniard and African alike, shoulder to shoulder, buckets in hand, no time for old resentments.

Then he looked up at Attila and said, "It wasn't just me."

Attila smiled, one eyebrow lifting. "You're right. But it wouldn't have happened without you."

CHAPTER 10

Raven stood on the quarterdeck as the sun began its ascent into the cloudless sky. She glanced over to the *Firebird* and wondered how Jeremy's first few hours as first mate had gone. She realized she was now short one gunnery mate and one helmsman. Kifaru was her only remaining helmsman. Her papa was once a helmsman and would be a good teacher for anyone she chose to replace Isaac.

Raven glanced over to see Kifaru at the wheel, John standing next to him. She beckoned her papa to join her at the stern.

"Papa, we need a new gunnery mate and helmsman. Who do you think we should train?"

"I've been thinking about that myself. Kifaru does a good job at the helm, but not everyone on this ship is as ready to learn as he is. Seremala might work out, or even Simba."

"No, I don't want Simba as a helmsman. I need her beside me as a warrior. I was, however, thinking of making her the second mate since Hadari is now with Alexander on *The Royal Victory*. Do you think the men will follow her? Will they have trouble taking orders from a woman?"

"I think it depends on the woman. They seem to have no trouble following your orders."

"Yes, of course, but it came about sort of naturally. Many of them were with me from the beginning when I was only a girl. They were lost and confused and had no one to lead them."

"Aye. But I think they will follow Simba as well. If not, she can put them in their place. There's no one better with a blade or gun than Simba...other than you, that is."

"Aye, you're correct. However, that still leaves us with a vacancy at the helm. What do you think of the new men?"

"You mean, the three men who fell from the sky?"

Raven chuckled, "Yes."

"Possibly. What did you have in mind?"

"I think one of them might possibly be my next gunnery mate. They all seem to be familiar with all kinds of weapons. Maybe the other two could be trained at the helm."

John replied, "Why don't we ask them?"

Jeffrey joined them on the quarterdeck and missed most of the conversation, "Why don't we ask who, what?"

"Jeffrey, would you please instruct the three new men to join us on the quarterdeck?"

"You mean the men who fell out of the sky?"

Raven looked at John, and they allowed their lips to curl into a smile.

"Yes, please, my love."

Jeffrey raised his eyebrows at her pet name for him.

"Your wish is my command."

Jeffrey climbed down from the quarterdeck to search out the three new men who recently joined Raven's crew. Lieutenant Charles Taylor was near the bow, learning how to tie rigging on the foremast, while Walter and George were at the mainmast, learning how to sew the sheets to repair the sails.

Jeffrey walked past the mainmast to find Charles first.

"Mr. Taylor, the captain requests that you join her on the quarterdeck."

"Yes, sir, Mr. Hamilton."

Charles handed the rigging back over to Muziki, who had been teaching him, then followed Jeffrey across the deck. Jeffrey then stopped at the mainmast to collect Walter and George.

"Mr. Parpart, Mr. Devlin, would you please join the captain on the quarterdeck?"

"*Yes, sir, Mr. Hamilton.*" They both replied.

When they all arrived on the quarterdeck, they found Raven with her back turned to them, looking across the water.

Jeffrey announced, "Excuse me, Captain. The new men, as you requested."

Raven turned and eyed each man accusingly, examining their build and features. Each of them stood at attention, waiting for whatever order or accusation might be at hand. Being military men, each had received ridicule in the past. It was nothing new. However, this was a pirate ship. Unlike the United States Military, the captain of this ship could throw you overboard for anything or any reason.

"Relax, gentlemen. I'm wondering what to do with each of you on this ship. You all seem to have various talents related to your previous lives. I need to know how best you can serve on this ship. Have any of you ever fired a cannon?"

Charles spoke up, "Yes, Captain. My grandfather fought in the Civil War and had a cannon he, let's say, acquired after the war. He used to shoot it every Fourth of July to celebrate Independence Day. I learned how to load and shoot it from him."

George spoke up, "Captain, we all know a little about navigation, using maps, compasses, and such."

"How about you, Mr. Parpart?"

"Yes, Captain. I'm pretty good with a compass. However, our instruments are more modern than what you use now. But, I'm sure we can get the hang of doing things the old way."

Raven was a little confused by their unconventional use of the English language.

"Yes. I see. I think."

Raven nodded to John, who then said, "Mr. Taylor, you will begin training as our new gunnery mate. Mr. Parpart and Mr. Devlin, you will begin training as helmsmen. Training begins immediately."

John looked back at Raven, who then nodded and called Simba to the quarterdeck.

"Simba!"

Simba was working with Andrew Greer, inspecting the ship's condition after their recent battle. She looked back when she heard her name. When she recognized that she was wanted on the quarterdeck, she said, "Please excuse me, Mr. Greer. It seems I am needed on the quarterdeck by the captain."

"By all means, Simba."

Simba quickly walked to the quarterdeck and faced Raven, waiting to receive orders.

"Simba, there are a few changes that need to be made onboard *Destiny*. Since Hadari is no longer here to serve as second mate, I have a vacancy."

Simba looked at Mr. Taylor and said, "Aye, Captain. Mr. Taylor will make an excellent second mate."

Raven furrowed her brow, "Yes, maybe some day the leftenant will make a good second mate, but now is not his time."

Simba was confused. "Then, who will be taking Hadari's place?"

"You will."

Simba's insides shook with nervous excitement. "Me, Captain?"

"Yes, Simba. You are the most capable of all who serve on this ship at this time. Someday, you will make a great captain. But first, you need experience as an officer. Will you accept the position?"

"Aye, Raven. I only hope the crew will accept me as an officer."

"They will…if you lead. The men are like sheep. You can't force them to go where you want them to go. You have to lead them into your fold. When they see your example, they will follow. Don't force yourself on them. Lead."

"Aye, Raven."

"Raven then said, "Simba, call the men to all hands. Assemble on the main deck."

Simba pulled out a conch shell from her leather satchel and blew the signal for all hands. Each man stopped what they were doing and quickly stepped onto the main deck in front of the quarterdeck to receive instructions.

When all had assembled, Raven began. "All hands, listen. There are some changes that you should be aware of. First, Mr. Taylor will be training as your new gunnery mate. Mr. Devlin and Mr. Parpart will be trained as helmsmen. I expect all of you to treat these men with respect and give them aid should they have any questions for you. They are new to sailing, but very intelligent men. They should become able seamen in no time."

The crew stood by silently, seemingly accepting the news.

"One more change needs to be announced. Since Hadari is now first mate on *The Royal Victory*, we need a new second mate. I have chosen Simba to be our second mate."

A rumble of surprise rose through the crowd of men and women who stood on deck. Raven wasn't sure whether it was positive or negative.

"I expect all of you to treat your new second mate with honor and respect as you did with Hadari."

Raven was a bit surprised when the crew exploded with a cheer for their new second mate.

"Three cheers for Simba!"

Hussah! Hussah! Hussah!

Raven was pleased with the crew's response. She stood by and waited for the cheers to end, but relished it as much as Simba did.

"All hands, back to your stations!"

The sun broke through the clouds in long golden streaks as *Destiny* cut through the blue waters east of Barbados, her crimson sails full, her crew humming with the rhythm of morning duties. But among the veteran pirates, three men stood out—not for their inexperience anymore, but for the quiet determination with which they had embraced this impossible new life.

Lt. Charles Taylor, once a flight leader over the Atlantic, now stood at the starboard battery under the watchful eye of Raven's seasoned gunner, Bila Meno. The lieutenant's frame was taut, his movements clipped with military precision, but the lines of doubt that had furrowed his brow in those first days had eased.

"Hands off the breech until I say," Bila Meno barked, and Taylor nodded sharply, his fingers hovering just above the gunlock. When Samuel gave the order, Taylor stepped through the process smoothly, methodically, and in control. The shot boomed out over the sea and splashed clean into the target barrel they'd set drifting from the launch boat an hour before.

"Not bad for a landlubber," Bila Meno grunted, nodding in begrudging approval.

Across the deck, Walter Parpart and George Devlin were under John Ashworth's careful watch at the helm. The older helmsman, now first mate, barked orders in short bursts, testing their reaction time as the ship came about to practice maneuvers. The two men, once trained in aviation navigation, had taken surprisingly well to reading the sea's language.

"Trim the fore tops'l!" John called.

Walter didn't hesitate. "Aye, trimming now!"

Walter spun the wheel slightly, correcting *Destiny's* bearing as instructed. He was beginning to read the tug of the water, the mood of the wind, the lurch and lean of the great vessel beneath him—so different from the flight deck of a Grumman Avenger, and yet... not so different at all.

Raven stood at the quarterdeck rail, watching them with a thoughtful expression. Captain Billings clung lazily to her shoulder, tail coiled, his tiny black eyes blinking in the sun.

"They're adapting faster than I expected," Jeffrey said, stepping up beside her.

"They're soldiers," Raven replied. "Whatever time they came from... men like that are trained to survive. It's what they do."

Jeffrey glanced toward Taylor, who was now adjusting the elevation on another cannon with care. "It's eerie, isn't it? That storm, that sky. They came from a world that doesn't exist yet. Or maybe doesn't anymore."

Raven said nothing for a moment, only tapped her fingers along the rail. Then, softly, "Do you believe in fate, Jeffrey?"

He looked at her. "I believe in choices. And I believe some things don't happen by accident."

She nodded slowly. "Nor do I."

Captain Billings gave a soft chirp, as if to affirm it.

Below, Lt. Taylor looked up from the cannon, sweat on his brow, but a small, solid smile on his lips. He caught Raven's eye and gave a crisp nod. She returned it—nothing dramatic, just a subtle acknowledgement between leaders of men.

Behind her, the sails creaked and snapped. The sea stretched wide and waiting.

Raven turned back toward the wheel.

"We'll need every hand for what's coming," she murmured. "And perhaps, just perhaps... fate sent them here for more than just survival."

The wind was mild, the seas forgiving. *Destiny* glided across the waves toward Barbados, her hull in need of tending after weeks of pursuit and battle. The other ships also needed repairs. The clang of hammer and the scrape of pitch had paused for the evening. Lanterns hung low along the deck, casting warm shadows on worn planks and tired faces.

On the forecastle, away from the murmuring crew, Charles Taylor sat with his back against the gunwale, polishing a brass fitting more from habit than necessity. Walter Parpart lay nearby, eyes fixed on the stars above, while George Devlin slowly rolled a hand-rolled cigarette between his fingers, though the tobacco had long since run out.

Raven had given them this hour to themselves. She said the ship needed their bodies in shape, but she also knew their minds were still at war with the past.

"Those stars..." Walter finally said, lifting a hand to trace Orion's belt. "They look the same. That's the hardest part."

Devlin gave a low grunt. "They *are* the same. What's changed is everything beneath them."

Taylor didn't look up. "I still remember the storm. One moment, we were flying maneuvers, checking instruments, chasing our heading... the next, nothing made sense. Compass spun wild. Clouds swallowed the sun. Static on every channel."

"And the light," Devlin added. "That light. Like the sky tore in half."

They were silent a moment, listening to the creak of sails, the occasional flap of canvas.

"You think we're dead?" Walter asked. "That this is... something else?"

Taylor finally set down the brass piece. "If we are, then death has a wicked sense of humor. I bleed. I sweat. I work till my hands blister. That's not heaven."

"Hell, then?" Devlin muttered.

Taylor shrugged. "If it is, it's quieter than I imagined. No fire. Just wind, salt, and seas."

They all laughed softly, but it faded quickly.

"I dreamed last night," Walter said. "Dreamed of a television set. But it wasn't black-and-white. It had a color screen, as big as a suitcase. I was sitting in some living room—don't know whose—and there was a man on the screen. Said we'd landed men on Mars."

Devlin sat up. "You what?"

"I know it sounds crazy. But it felt real, like I *remembered* it. Rocket ships, computers... people talking through television screens. I even saw something called the *internet.*"

Taylor's eyes narrowed. "You dreamed of things that haven't happened yet."

"Maybe they *have*," Walter said slowly. "Just not *here.*"

Silence settled again, heavier this time. Somewhere below, the monkey, Captain Billings, gave a sleepy chirp.

"You ever think," Devlin said, "that maybe we weren't sent back in time... but sideways? Into another world?"

Taylor stood and walked to the railing, peering out over the dark sea. "If we were, there's a reason. Raven's not an ordinary woman. This isn't an ordinary ship."

"She believes us," Walter said. "Doesn't even question it."

"She doesn't have to," Taylor replied. "She's seen things. Things we're just beginning to understand."

Behind them, the lantern light flickered. A shadow moved between masts—too tall to be crew, too silent to be wind. Taylor turned, but it was gone.

He stared at the place where it had stood, then slowly sat again.

"Something's coming," he murmured. "I feel it."

Devlin lit the stub of his last cigarette with a shard of burning rope. "Let it come," he said. "We've already crossed the line."

Walter leaned back again, watching the sky for the next vision that might not be his own.

CHAPTER 11

The afternoon sun was slowly creeping toward the horizon, creating long, dark shadows growing along the streets near the wharf of Bridgetown. Four new ships rested against the docks of the port city, waiting for their repairs to be completed. Some of the repairs were extensive. *The Royal Victory's* mainmast had been shattered in the last battle and needed replacing. But her hull was in perfect condition.

Raven stood on the edge of the wharf, arms crossed, watching the progress. The repairs were going well, faster than she'd hoped. Still, she felt uneasy.

Jeffrey had taken a shore crew into town to procure new sails. Pharaoh and Alexander were overseeing the purchase of powder and munitions. Attila had sent Jeremy to see about copper sheets for *The Firebird's* hull. Even Captain Billings was content, sunning himself on a coil of rope with his tail curled over his nose.

But Raven felt something chilling in the air, even though the temperatures were warm and the humidity high. There was a stillness beneath the noise as if the very island was holding its breath.

Raven turned away from the docks, wandering past the timber piles and crates of oranges to a narrow lane that wound between warehouses. She remembered this lane. She passed through here weeks ago when she and her papa found The Pelican's Roost.

Now it felt narrower. Shadows clung to the walls despite the sun.

And there he was.

Geoffrey Neely.

Leaning against the brick wall, arms folded, his coat hanging in tatters. The broad-brimmed hat shadowed his eyes, but the same thin, menacing smile played on his lips.

"You're a hard man to forget," Raven said, her voice quiet.

"Aye," Neely replied, voice dry as old parchment. "And harder to out-run."

She stepped closer. "Why are you here?"

He tipped his head toward the harbor. "The sea's stirring. Old things are waking. You've crossed into deeper water, Captain."

"You warned me before. About *La Dama de Sangre*. She's real, isn't she?"

"As real as I was," Neely said, his gaze unreadable. "And as cruel."

Raven swallowed. "What does she want?"

Neely's smile faded. "She wants to sail again. And she's found the wind for it."

Raven's heart thudded.

"Your time's thinning," he said. "The threads between the world you know and what lies beneath it—they fray every time that ghost ship breaches the veil."

"Then tell me how to stop her."

"You can't." He stepped away from the wall, the air growing colder with each step. "But you *can* learn the shape of what's coming. Seek the *Coffin Reef*. Dive deep."

"Where?"

Neely's form flickered.

"North of Saint Lucia. East of charted water. A graveyard of ships and secrets. You'll find the bones of the first to curse her name."

"And then?"

He was fading now, like mist unraveling in the sun.

"Then," he said, voice barely more than wind, "you'll have to choose the kind of captain you mean to be."

And he was gone.

Raven stood alone in the alley, the air strangely still. Somewhere behind her, a cart rattled over cobblestones and a child laughed. The world returned in layers.

She turned and made her way back toward the docks, her boots slow and steady on the stones. Her mind churned with questions.

La Dama de Sangre was stirring. The ghost ship had power. Purpose. And if Neely was right, their next destination would take them farther from safe waters than ever before.

And Raven intended to sail straight into it.

Two days later, all ships had been repaired, and they pulled into the bay away from Bridgetown.

Later that night, there was a meeting in the captain's quarters aboard *Destiny.* A storm lantern burned low at the center of the table, its golden light casting long shadows across the weathered faces of those gathered. Raven sat at the head, her fingers interlaced under her chin. Around her sat Pharaoh, Alexander, Attila, John, and Jeffrey. Jeremy stood quietly near the door, not officially part of the council, but invited nonetheless—a sign of trust earned.

None of them spoke. Not yet.

On the table lay a chart, its edges curled, ink faded from sea air and fingers. Raven slowly unrolled a second parchment—an older, darker map. One she'd kept hidden until now. Its lines were inked by hand, with parts of the sea labeled only in riddles: *Whisper Shoals, The Drowned Path, Coffin Reef.*

"This isn't our usual hunt," Raven began, her voice calm but firm. "What I'm about to tell you... It's not easy to believe. But you've seen enough by now to know I'm not one to chase shadows without cause."

Alexander leaned forward, his dark eyes sharp. "Is this about the ship? The one from the battle?"

Attila nodded. "The one that appeared behind the smoke and vanished."

"You saw it too? Yes," Raven said. "But it didn't start there."

She told them everything about Neely at the Pelican's Roost, and again earlier this same day. His warnings. The ghost ship, *La Dama de Sangre.* A vessel that sailed without wind appeared through smoke and was tied to a growing force beneath the sea. She mentioned the ancient curse, the thinning between worlds, and the place he named: *Coffin Reef.*

"A ghost ship?" Pharaoh asked at last. "I've heard rumors. Old sailors speak of her in the rum houses in St. Felix. They say her crew drowned a hundred times, but still steer her under red ragged sails."

Jeremy spoke, hesitant but clear. "I saw her during the battle. Just a glimpse through the gun smoke. She was...wrong. Like a shadow cast, but backward...inside out."

Attila, ever practical, scratched his jaw. "So what do we do? We're not ghost hunters. We need Spanish gold and powder, not phantoms."

Jeffrey glanced at Raven. "But what if the two are tied together? We were lucky to find that last fleet of ships—storms were there that shouldn't be. Galleons rerouted, as if something's herding them. Maybe she's clearing the sea."

Raven nodded slowly. "Geoffrey said we'd need to dive deep. To find answers in the graveyard off Coffin Reef. North of Saint Lucia. No charts mark it, but I've heard whispers—reef spikes that snagged a dozen ships over the years. None returned."

Alexander stood. "So we sail into cursed waters?"

"We do," Raven said. "Because we're already caught in its wake. If we don't move first, it'll come to us."

The captains sat in grim silence. Then Pharaoh broke it, raising his cup.

"Well then," he said with a wry smile. "Let's make ready. If we are to chase ghosts, best we do it with powder dry and cannon loaded."

The others lifted their glasses in turn, each exchanging glances that mixed dread with duty.

Raven remained seated, eyes fixed on the map, her finger resting on the dark waters labeled *Coffin Reef*. She didn't smile.

Outside, the wind shifted. The tide pulled harder than before, as if it, too, sensed the change in course.

Three Days Later – North of Saint Lucia, the wind had gone strange.

It blew not steadily from east or west but in circling bursts—gusts that howled one moment and died the next, leaving sails slack and flapping like the wings of dying birds. The four ships—*Raven's Destiny*, *The Sea Witch*, *The Royal Victory*, and *The Firebird*—cut through the darkening sea, their formations tight, wary, and silent.

Raven stood at the prow of *Destiny*, one hand gripping the rail, her gaze on the horizon. The sun had dipped behind a curtain of clouds, and though it was early evening, the sea had gone darker than it should have. No stars, no moon. Only a violet-gray ceiling above and a sea that looked bruised beneath, dark and angry.

Jeffrey joined her at the bow. "It's too quiet."

She nodded. "Even the gulls are gone."

From the lookout, a cry broke the silence.

"Wreckage off the port bow! Floating wreckage!"

Raven and Jeffrey hurried to the rail as *Destiny* eased toward the drifting debris. Bits of charred wood bobbed in the swells—barrels, splinters of hull, and tangled rigging. A single masthead surfaced from a wave, grotesquely warped, its figurehead carved in the shape of a saint, now scorched and eyeless.

No name on the boards. No signs of life.

Then came the smell.

Jeffrey reeled slightly. "Booming barnacles... smells like burned flesh and rot."

Suddenly, a shout from *The Firebird*—Jeremy's voice, carried by the wind:

"Raven! Something is in the water!"

Everyone turned.

Behind the floating wreckage, something moved. Not a shape exactly—but a distortion. A ripple, a shimmer. As if the water itself bent unnaturally in a perfect ring. It pulsed outward... then vanished.

And just like that, the sea exploded.

From below came a sickening groan of timber. A massive suction formed near the wreckage, as though the deep had opened its mouth. Barrels and planks were dragged under like toys. Even *Destiny* rocked violently, her hull groaning as sailors grabbed rigging lines and braced themselves.

From the whirlpool's edge, something floated up—**a body**.

Face down. Arms spread. Bloated and pale.

Raven barked, "Hook it aboard!"

Two crewmen obeyed, casting a long gaff to snag the corpse. As they dragged it in, the men recoiled—one dropped the pole entirely.

The body wore the shredded remains of a Spanish officer's coat.

And carved into its bare chest, from collar to navel, were the words:

"*LA DAMA DE SANGRE*"

The body spasmed.

Just once. A twitch of a hand, a flutter of a foot—as if it had been waiting.

And then it disintegrated, melting into the black water.

Silence. Then, from far behind them, deep within the sea, a low moan rose like a beast's breath. Not thunder. Not wind.

A warning.

Raven turned to Jeffrey. "It's begun."

The Night Watch

The night hung heavy over *Destiny*, the sky slick with clouds that veiled the stars. A dull orange moon hovered low on the horizon like a smoldering ember, its light casting long, uneasy shadows across the deck. The waters near Coffin Reef were quiet, but aboard *Destiny*, sleep did not come easily.

Below decks, hammocks swayed with restless bodies. Walter Parpart lay with his hands behind his head, staring at the low beams overhead. The creak of timber and distant murmur of waves offered little comfort.

"You hear that?" he whispered.

Across from him, George Devlin stirred. "The gulls?"

"No," Walter said. "The whispering. It's like... wind through the sails, but the sails are still furled."

George listened, his breath catching. Somewhere in the woodwork of the hull, a low hum seemed to rise and fall, like a voice just out of hearing.

Above Deck

Simba stood near the stern, her back straight despite the chill that had settled over the sea air. She glanced toward the dark water, her unease growing. Her eyes wide. The night watch was quiet, but something pulled at her—a weight in the air. Her eyes drifted to the horizon.

Then she saw it.

A pale shape, far off at sea, just for an instant—tattered sails that moved without wind. A ship where no ship should be.

She blinked. Then it was gone.

Behind her, Raven appeared from the shadows, her coat wrapped tight, her face unreadable.

"You saw it too," Raven said.

Simba nodded slowly. "For a moment. The ghost ship."

"It's not a moment anymore," Raven said quietly. "It's a shadow we carry now. And some shadows stretch longer the closer you get to the truth."

Below Deck, Later – Raven's Cabin

Jeffrey stirred in his sleep, a sheen of sweat on his brow. He twisted under the blankets, trapped in a dream.

In it, he stood on an endless sea, the water black as tar. Behind him floated *Destiny*, still and lifeless. Before him: *La Dama de Sangre*. No sails. No crew. Just a ship of bones and blood-red wood, drifting toward him.

A voice spoke—not loud, but deep, and old. *"She must choose."*

Jeffrey jolted awake, gasping. Raven, now beside him, reached for his shoulder.

"You heard it too?" she whispered.

He nodded. "In my dream. A voice. A choice."

They sat in silence for a long moment, both staring at the flame of the bedside lantern. It flickered unnaturally, as if it were breathing.

Back on Deck

The watchman rang the ship's bell once, his hand trembling.

Far below, in the water, something was glowing. A slow-moving ripple of green phosphorescence passed beneath the ship's hull, swirling like a serpent, then vanishing into the deep.

From the crow's nest above, a sailor whispered a prayer under his breath. And far off, on the edge of the sea, a low horn blew. No ship. No wind.

Just the long, bone-chilling cry of something old… and watching.

The new ship's boy, Michael Murphy, had finally finished his duties. He approached the hatch to descend to his hammock but waited. Something spoke to him over the windless air.

"She must choose."

Michael looked around, expecting someone to be behind him. "Pardon? Who's there?"

The twelve-year-old boy shook with doubt and fear as the voice faded into the darkness.

"She must choose."

Michael quickly scrambled down the ladder leading to the mid-deck to find Sean O'Toole. Since they had joined Raven's crew together and both were from Dublin, they had grown close to each other.

"Sean!" Michael loudly whispered. "Sean!"

"What is it, me boy?"

"I heard something."

"Of course you heard some-ting, now. We're on board a ship. Dare are many sounds ye might be hearing."

"No, Sean. It was a voice. A voice that sounded like the wind. But there is no wind. The air is still up above."

"Well, what did it say?"

"It said, she must choose."

"Really, now? Dat's funny. I just now heard that in my dreams, as you woke me. Very strange indeed."

"Sean, I'm scared."

"It be alright now, Michael. Here...climb up into me bed and lay beside me. We'll face the voices together."

Sean could feel Michael's body shivering as the boy climbed into the hammock beside him.

"Dun worry, none. It be alright in da mornin'."

CHAPTER 12

The night hung thick over Coffin Reef, the moon veiled behind slow-crawling clouds. The waves were quiet—too quiet, and *Destiny* rocked gently at anchor, as if the sea itself were holding its breath.

Raven awoke with a start.

A strange silence had settled over the ship. No footsteps, no murmur of voices, not even the usual creak and groan of wood. She slipped from her bunk and climbed to the quarterdeck, eyes scanning the horizon. The air was damp, with a heavy taste of salt and something else —like old iron.

John met her near the helm, lantern in hand.

"Kifaru's missing," he said, his voice low.

"What do you mean, missing?"

"He had the last watch. Never reported in. His musket's still up top, but no one's seen him since the bell rang before dawn."

Raven's jaw tightened. Kifaru was not a green sailor—he didn't wander, didn't shirk duty. She moved swiftly to the starboard rail, scanning the dark waters below. The reef shimmered faintly in the dim starlight, jagged and sharp. No rowboat missing. No sign of a man overboard.

He hadn't fallen.

He'd been taken.

By first light, the mood aboard *Destiny* had grown taut as a pulled line. The other ships—*The Firebird, The Royal Victory,* and *The Sea*

Witch—remained quiet but watchful, their crews noting the strange stillness around the reef.

It was Charles Taylor who found the marks.

He'd gone over the side in the early light to inspect some minor hull damage and surfaced minutes later with a grim face. "You best come see this, Captain."

Raven leaned out with John and George Devlin as a dory was lowered to the waterline. The hull bore four long gouges—deep, blackened, and in places slightly glowing with a faint reddish sheen, like embers cooled under ash.

George frowned. "Those weren't here last night."

John nodded. "They look... burned into the wood."

"No fire did this," Raven said. "This was etched with purpose."

Walter Parpart added, "Two other ships—*The Firebird* and *The Victory*—they found similar scratches on their sterns. Always just above the waterline. Same number. Same depth."

Charles Taylor climbed into the boat, studying the marks with a pilot's keen eye. "It's a warning," he muttered. "These are placement symbols. Flight markers. But not any I've seen before."

"What kind of warning?" John asked.

Charles looked up. "That someone or something knows we're here."

By dusk, whispers had begun to spread. Some claimed to have seen shapes under the water, long shadows that moved against the current. Others spoke of voices in the wind — garbled words, hissing sounds just beyond understanding.

One of the Spaniards from *The Firebird*, a man named Varga, woke screaming from his sleep, shouting in a tongue even his crewmates didn't recognize. His eyes were bleeding—his fingernails, raw from clawing at his hammock ropes.

"It was red," he gasped later. "The water, the sky... the sails. *La Dama de Sangre.* She is coming."

Attila relayed this information to Raven.

She stood at the stern that night, lantern in hand, coat drawn tight.

Jeffrey joined her. "The men are rattled."

"They should be," she replied. "So am I."

He nodded toward the horizon, where lightning flickered in the distance, silent and pale. "Do you think Kifaru's still alive?"

"I think," she said slowly, "he saw something we weren't meant to see. And it marked us for it."

Jeffrey studied her. "You're thinking of Neely's words."

"*Choose what kind of captain you mean to be,*" she echoed.

Then she looked down at the scratches again, glowing faintly in the dark, as if something were watching.

"Because whatever's hunting us... it already knows what *it* is."

The Midnight Council

The bell rang twice — not for the watch, but a signal known only to the captains.

At Raven's command, a single lantern was lit on the quarterdeck of *Destiny*, shrouded in a thick canvas hood. The signal flickered low and steady, a call to gather without rousing the crews. A mist rolled off Coffin Reef like breath from the grave, curling across the decks in pale tendrils.

One by one, the longboats arrived in silence.

Pharaoh came first, eyes sharp beneath his feathered hat. Then Alexander, boots quiet against the wood. Captain Attila followed with a grim face and hands clenched behind his back. Each man brought a trusted second

— but left their blades sheathed. The fear didn't come from one another...
but from something far older.

They met in *Destiny*'s map room — the air thick with salt, sweat, and
unease.

Raven leaned over the table, her finger tracing the reef and surrounding
waters. "You all know what's been happening. The markings. Kifaru. The
dreams."

"And the ghost," Alexander said softly. "The one you saw."

Jeffrey looked up. "Geoffrey Neely. He's warned her before. And now
he's warning again."

Pharaoh grunted. "We're anchored over something cursed. This reef—it
is not natural. I had two men throw up black bile just rowing in."

Attila added, "My helmsman says the water here pulls against the rudder
like a current with no tide. And the compass spins for hours."

Raven exhaled, then opened a leather pouch and dropped a scrap of
parchment onto the table. It was a rubbing of the hull markings — the
same etched symbol found on all four ships.

Walter Parpart had copied it earlier, comparing it to strange shapes he
remembered from Air Force intelligence files. "This was a flight path once,"
he'd said. "Or a seal. Something locked in."

Alexander studied the sigil now, eyes narrowed. "What is this?"

Raven's voice was low. "A warning. Or an invitation."

Jeffrey looked to her. "We need to decide what comes next."

Attila's voice cut in: "Do we leave? Pull out before the tide turns?"

Pharaoh shook his head. "Leave, and we bring it with us. It followed us
from Burmuda. It marked us for stepping through time."

Raven's hands rested on the edge of the map. She stared at the parchment.

"We came here to repair. To recover," she said. "But the sea had other plans. I believe we're sitting above something — or someone — that does not want to be found."

She looked at each of her captains in turn.

"This thing we're chasing — the galleons, the ghost ship, the disappearances — it's all connected. And it's not just haunting us. It's watching. Testing us."

"And if we pass the test?" asked Alexander.

"Then we live," said Raven. "And maybe we understand why so many never made it out of these waters."

A long silence fell.

Then Pharaoh leaned in, his voice a growl. "Then what is your order, Captain?"

Raven looked out the porthole, where the moonlight broke through the clouds — just long enough to catch a single white shape far out past the reef, drifting on still waters.

A ship. Pale. Tattered sails. No flag.

"La Dama de Sangre," she whispered.

She turned back to her captains. "We make ready. Double the watches. We sail at dawn — not away from it... but toward it."

They all turned toward the ghost of a ship waiting in the night, and said nothing.

Because they all saw it too.

It began just after the third bell — well past midnight, when most of the fleet slept and the mist had thickened into a blanket across the water.

A scream cut through the fog.

It came from the *Sea Witch*.

By the time torches were lit and bells rang on the other ships, the flames had already begun licking up her rigging. Not fire, but a strange phosphorescence — blue-green and shimmering like ghost light. It did not burn wood, but spread like sea mold, glowing and pulsing along the ropes and railings.

Pharaoh's crew scrambled, shouting curses in Swahili and Spanish, buckets flying, muskets drawn. But there was no enemy. No ship had approached. No shadow in the fog.

Only... things.

Shapes. Wet and long-limbed. Some swore they had eyes like eels, others saw only flickers in the water — pale hands gripping ropes, shadows climbing silently from the sea. A Spaniard was dragged screaming over the starboard rail. Another vanished into the dark with a splash and a swirl of bubbles. No shots hit their marks. Blades sliced only air.

From *Destiny*'s deck, Raven watched in horror as *The Sea Witch*'s mainmast toppled with a sickening crack, its sail smothered in that eerie glow. Her voice rang out like a cannon: "Launch boats! Get them off that ship!"

Alexander and Attila responded instantly, sending dories toward the chaos.

By the time help arrived, half the crew had jumped or fled below deck. The strange light retreated as suddenly as it came, seeping into the seams and vanishing. The only sign of violence was the missing men—six in total—and the claw-like gouges along *The Sea Witch*'s hull.

No enemy was found. No trail to follow.

Just seawater. Cold and still.

And a sound… like distant singing. Faint and sorrowful. Coming from the east.

Where the ghost ship had been.

When dawn finally broke, it was a colorless sky.

The sun crawled above the horizon like an exhausted flame, casting pale gold across a sea slick with mist and memory. The sky held no blue — only ash and pearl. Not a breeze stirred.

Each of the ships was quiet.

Repairs were halted. The *Sea Witch* drifted slightly apart, her sails limp and her crew too shaken to speak.

Raven stood on the quarterdeck of *Destiny*, arms crossed, eyes on the horizon. The other captains joined her shortly after, none bothering with pleasantries.

"What in the name of Poseidon was that?" Alexander muttered.

"Not Poseidon," said Pharaoh grimly. "Something older."

Attila added, "We're being warned. That ship — the ghost — it doesn't want us near."

Jeffrey came up beside Raven. "And yet here we are."

Raven nodded. "And we're not turning back."

At her signal, the flags were raised.

The fleet would sail east, into open water, and into whatever waited for them in the silent zone beyond Coffin Reef.

As the anchors lifted and sails unfurled, a sudden gust of wind tore across the water, sharp and cold, nearly ripping Raven's coat from her shoulders.

From the crow's nest, Seremala cried out, pointing.

There, in the distance… *La Dama de Sangre.*

Drifting slowly along the horizon. No crew visible. No wake in the water. Just a presence — like an injury in the sea itself.

And as they watched, a flock of seabirds erupted from the reef and flew west, away from it.

Every single one.

Raven's jaw clenched.

"We go forward," she said. "Whatever awaits... we'll meet it head on."

And the fleet of pirates—cursed, loyal, hunted, and chosen—sailed east into the unknown.

The sea outside whispered like a warning.

Below, in Raven's quarters, a single lantern burned in the center of the wide oaken table. Around it sat Raven, Pharaoh, Alexander, and Attila — four captains, hardened by war and weather, now staring at shadows cast by things not of this world. John Ashworth and Jeffrey were also present.

The silence had stretched too long.

It was Pharaoh who broke it. "It is not hunting us. Not yet. It could have torn *The Sea Witch* apart — but it did not. Why?"

Raven leaned forward, elbows on the table, her fingers interlaced. "Because it's watching."

Jeffrey nodded. "Testing us. Marking who's strong. Who might serve it."

Alexander scoffed. "Serve it? That ship is cursed. Rotten with death."

Raven's gaze flicked toward him. "Maybe. But it has rules. Ghosts always do. There's a pattern here... it's not striking randomly."

Attila frowned. "You think it's waiting for something?"

"I think," she said slowly, "it's judging us. Like Neely said — we'll have to choose what kind of captains we mean to be."

Pharaoh's brows rose. "What did he mean by that, Raven?"

She hesitated, then answered. "That there's more than one kind of power at sea. The kind that commands men by fear... and the kind that earns loyalty. Neely knew something about both. Whatever *La Dama de Sangre* is, it's tied to that choice."

Jeffrey leaned closer, his voice low. "You think it wants us to take a side."

"Not just us," Raven replied. "All the ships. All the captains. Maybe even the sea itself."

Silence again. This time heavier.

Attila glanced at the small map spread before them — the jagged outline of Coffin Reef, and beyond it, uncharted waters.

"We go deeper," he said. "And it will follow."

"We're already marked," Pharaoh added.

Alexander looked uneasy. "Then maybe we should turn back."

"No," Raven said flatly.

She stood, pushing the chair back with the scrape of boots on planks.

"We came here for gold, for glory — for prey. But there's something greater now. A reckoning. And if that ship wants answers..." Her eyes flashed. "It'll get them."

Jeffrey stood beside her. "Then we sail at dawn?"

Raven nodded. "With cannon ready. Eyes sharp. And hearts prepared."

"Prepared for what?" Alexander asked.

Raven looked to the lantern, flame flickering inside the glass like a restless spirit.

"To become the kind of captains we were meant to be," she said. "Or the kind this sea will swallow whole."

CHAPTER 13

The sea whispered.

It was not the hiss of wind over water or the creak of lines in the dark — Pharaoh had known those sounds since he was a boy, and they never set his nerves so sharp.

This was something more profound. Older.

Like breathing through teeth. Like a promise not yet fulfilled.

He stood alone at the starboard rail of *The Sea Witch* after their meeting, his fingers curled around salt-slicked wood, his eyes fixed on the black horizon. *La Dama de Sangre* had disappeared with the sunrise, but its presence lingered — like the feeling of chains long gone, but never truly forgotten.

Pharaoh had once worn real chains.

He closed his eyes, and the night opened his memory.

He'd been just a boy—no older than Jeremy was now—when the slavers came to the coast near his village. They'd descended like smoke, quick and choking, with fire and iron. He'd fought, and bled, and screamed until his voice was gone. They'd beaten him, bound him, and shoved him onto a ship that smelled of blood and misery.

That first voyage... he'd thought the Devil lived in the belly of every European ship that the sea itself had sold its soul.

It had taken only days to reach Madagascar — Port St. Felix. There he was sold like meat, branded with hot iron, given a number instead of a name. He remembered kneeling in the dirt, his wrists aching, as he watched coins pass from hand to hand.

Then, the boy, not more than twelve, with bright red hair and fierce blue eyes. Richard Ashworth. Young and reckless and bold, even then. Smart as the flick of a whip.

The boy had stared at Pharaoh as if he were a man, not a purchase.

And when Pharaoh dared to meet his gaze, Richard had smiled.

Later, Pharaoh learned that the boy had bargained with his captain, not for a servant, but for a crewman. "A sailor," the boy had said. "He's too proud to be anything else."

And so it began.

Freedom came slowly, in the shape of friendship first. Then trust. Then a quiet moment below decks after slaves had been off-loaded at the port of Charles Town. When the boy placed a set of keys in his hand and said, "You're not mine, you're not anyone's, I want you to sail with me because you choose to."

That was the day Pharaoh began to believe that chains—even old ones—could break.

And now...

He opened his eyes. The sea was still dark. But not silent.

This ghost ship, this cursed presence — it made him feel that way again. Bound. Hunted. Watched.

It wasn't just a phantom vessel. It was *something more*—something perceivable. Testing them, herding them like animals in a pen.

And he didn't like how that felt.

Behind him, he heard soft footfalls on the deck. It was Zachery Thacker, his special aide and interpreter, silent and observant as always.

"You can't sleep either?" the young man asked.

Pharaoh didn't turn. "The sea is full of noise tonight."

Zachery stepped up beside him. "Do you think the ghost ship is following us still?"

Pharaoh exhaled slowly. "No. I think it's *leading* us."

Zachery frowned. "To where?"

"That," Pharaoh said, his voice low, "is the question I fear the most."

He clapped a hand on Zachery's shoulder and squeezed gently. "But we'll face it together, my friend. We've both seen dark things... and lived to sail again."

Zachery left Pharaoh and returned to his duties. Pharaoh returned to his previous thoughts. Pharaoh often thought about those early days. He remembered the day Batimkoo was captured by the white men and brought to the island of Madagascar to be sold. He thought about the young boy who had befriended Batimkoo and taught him how to speak English and how to become a sailor. Where would he be, and what would he be doing if he had never met Richard Ashworth?

Batimkoo had never seen a boy with fire in his hair before.

The red-gold strands caught sunlight like copper flashing as young Richard Ashworth perched atop a barrel, legs swinging, a leather-bound book in one hand and a mango in the other. The boy chewed, pointed at the page, and said firmly, "Ship."

Batimkoo blinked. His wrists still bore the raw marks of the iron around his wrists and ankles. His stomach growled with hunger, but his pride was louder than his hunger, so he just stared.

Richard took another bite of the mango, wiped the juice on his shirt sleeve like any ordinary lad would, and pointed again.

"Ship," he repeated, slower.

Batimkoo said nothing.

Richard frowned, then softened. "Look, I know you understand me, a little. You watched me argue with Papa. You knew I wasn't bartering with the captain for a servant."

Batimkoo looked away.

Richard flipped the page in the book and ed again.

"Water," he said, pointing to the picture.

Then: "Sky."

Then: "Free."

That one made Batimkoo turn his head.

He didn't say it, not yet. But his eyes met Richard's. The boy smiled.

That was the beginning.

"You will be free, Batimkoo. I will make sure of it."

The *Destiny* rocked gently in port, the smell of pine tar and rotting cotton mingling with the ocean breeze. On the wharf, vendors shouted over each other, their voices lost beneath the shuffle of crates and the groan of beasts of burden. Inside the captain's cabin, voices were quieter—but sharper.

"No," said Captain Billings, scowling beneath a salt-stiff hat. "He was *cargo*, Richard. The manifest lists him. I could sell him in less than an hour—"

"I'll pay for him."

Billings laughed. "With what?"

"With my wages," Richard said.

Billings raised a brow.

Richard stood taller. "He won't be a servant. He'll be a sailor. Your crewman."

Billings grunted. The captain had a soft spot for Richard—Richard was intelligent and bold.

"And if he runs?" Billings asked.

"He won't."

Billings sighed. "Does your father know?"

"He will," Richard replied. "He's proud when I stand my ground."

That was true.

Finally, with an exasperated wave of his hand, Captain Billings said, "Fine. He's yours. But mark my words, Richard Ashworth—buying a man's freedom doesn't mean he owes you anything."

"I know," said the boy. "That's the point."

Later that day, Batimkoo sat beside Richard under the awning, the sun slanting warm across the planks. He looked down at the papers Richard had given him — documents with seals and signatures that meant nothing to him but everything to the world.

"I am... free?" he asked, slowly, in the English he'd spent months learning from the boy.

"You always were," Richard said. "Now everyone else has to admit it."

Batimkoo turned the papers in his hands, then looked at the boy beside him.

"You give me... new name?"

Richard smiled. "How about Pharaoh?"

"Pharaoh," Batimkoo said, tasting the word.

"It means a king," Richard said. "One that doesn't bow to anyone."

Batimkoo nodded slowly, then smiled for the first time since his capture.

"Yes," he said. "I am Pharaoh."

Then, Pharaoh thought back to the days after the wreck. A hurricane had sunk *Destiny,* taking Captain Billings and his officers down with her. Richard had taken his freed Africans below decks to release as many of the chained captives as they could before the ship succumbed to the depths.

The sea had gone quiet in the way it does after fury. Not peaceful—just hollow. Like the world itself had taken a breath and hadn't yet decided to let it out.

Pharaoh floated on a splintered mast, one arm hooked loosely around the girl he had thought was a boy.

He hadn't even realized he was still calling her Richard in his mind, even after everything. It didn't seem to matter then. Survival was louder than questions.

The wreck of the *Destiny* bobbed in the distance like broken teeth on a bruised mouth. All around them, others floated — Nero, Alexander, Attila, Caesar — once slaves, now survivors. And nearly a hundred more, African men and women who had been packed like cargo now clung to barrels, doors, planks... anything.

A storm-torn sky smeared the world in ash and orange. The smell of salt and death was thick. Sharks sought out the injured and bleeding.

Pharaoh's fingers were numb, but he kept hold of the mast, kept hold of Richard—no, not Richard. Not anymore.

Because in the lull between waves, her torn shirt had opened.

And Pharaoh had seen.

There was no mistaking the curve of her chest beneath the shredded linen, no denying the truth that had hidden beneath the boy's voice, the clever mouth, the bold eyes.

He didn't speak at first. He just looked at her, and she saw the change in his gaze. He removed his shirt and wrapped it around her to hide her nakedness.

"I'm sorry," she whispered, chest heaving from exhaustion. "I never meant to lie. I just—if they knew I was a girl, they wouldn't have listened. They wouldn't have let me lead."

Pharaoh nodded slowly. "I know."

She looked away. "My father said it would be the only way we could be together after my mother died. But that's not who I am. Not anymore."

A wave rocked them gently, and the creak of drifting wood filled the silence.

"I'm Raven," she said at last. "Raven Ashworth."

Pharaoh looked at her—at the way her hair clung to her cheeks in bloody coils, at the fierceness still burning behind her exhaustion. His lips curved slowly into a weary smile.

"No," he said. "I think you are The Red Raven."

She blinked.

He lifted her tangled curls in his hand. Curls the color of sunrise fire.

"The storm tried to take your name. But you are still flying."

She smiled then, despite everything.

They floated on, the sea gently claiming the last pieces of their old lives. Together, they drifted toward the silhouette of a distant island rising in the mist—unknown, unwanted, but alive.

A sudden gust of wind pulled at Pharaoh's coat.

He blinked, eyes shifting from the horizon to the deck of *The Sea Witch*. The scent of salt air and lantern smoke brought him fully back. The past slipped away like seawater between his fingers.

Someone was calling his name.

"Pharaoh!"

It was Zachery, urgency in his voice as he jogged across the deck, boots thudding on the wet planks. "Raven needs—all of the captains. Now."

Pharaoh nodded, shaking off the weight of memory. The mast. The wreck. Her name—Red Raven. It all lived inside him, but now was not the time for ghosts of the past. Now they had newer ones to face.

He rowed back to Destiny and crossed the deck swiftly, passing Jeremy and Charles Taylor, speaking in hushed tones near the helm. A strange light flickered beneath the waves off the port side—there and gone like a blink. He paused only a second to watch it vanish, like a warning pulled back into the deep.

The captains were already assembled in the captain's quarters. Raven stood at the map table, her red hair tied back with a ribbon and her eyes storm-dark with thought. Jeffrey was at her side, arms folded, gaze fixed on the door as Pharaoh entered.

"You all saw it," Raven said before Pharaoh could speak. "That ship didn't just vanish. It *slipped*—like a blade through cloth. Like it was waiting for us."

Attila grunted. "A ghost doesn't wait. It haunts."

Alexander leaned forward. "Then maybe we're not just being haunted. Maybe we're being *led*."

The lantern light flickered, as if agreeing.

Pharaoh took his place at the table and cleared his throat. "We've followed shadows and signs, crossed storms and blood for this fight. But this...

this is different. That ship's not just an omen. It's a test. Maybe for *her*—" He nodded to Raven. "—or maybe for all of us."

Raven met his gaze, a question unspoken between them. He gave her a nod.

He hadn't told her about the memory. About the wreck. About the girl with fire in her hair who gave him a name and a future. But he knew this: the Red Raven would not be broken by ghosts, nor would he.

And whatever lay ahead, they would face it together.

CHAPTER 14

T he wind died just before dawn.

Not the usual hush of early morning, but an unnatural stillness—like the world itself was holding its breath. No gulls cried. No waves lapped the sides of the ships. Even the creak of the ships had fallen silent, as if they too feared to make a sound.

Destiny's lanterns flickered low as pale grey light edged over the horizon. Fog hovered over the reef, curling like cold fingers over the water, thick and heavy.

Raven stepped out onto the quarterdeck, the hair on her arms rising despite the warmth. Pharaoh, Alexander, and Attila were nearby, each on their own ship, their eyes cast toward the sea.

"What is it?" she asked softly.

Jeffrey was beside her now, jaw tight, staring ahead.

It was *there*, just beyond the edge of the reef, where the rocks jutted out like broken teeth into the surf.

A shape.

It bobbed, just once, then settled. Something pale.

A bundle?

Jeffrey raised his spyglass, then quickly lowered it, his face going white. "It's a sail," he said. "But it's... wrong."

They all watched as the fog thinned, and more shapes came into view.

Sails. Dozens of them. Tattered, waterlogged, and drifting like funeral shrouds. Broken masts bobbed among them—some snapped clean through, others bearing old rigging tangled with seaweed.

And among the sails floated something worse: a figurehead. A woman, carved in blackened wood, her eyes hollow, her mouth twisted in a silent scream.

Raven's heart sank.

"La Dama de Sangre," Pharaoh whispered.

Then, the tide turned.

Every floating sail, every broken mast, began to drift inward—*toward* the anchored fleet. No wind moved them. No current pulled. They simply glided, steady and slow, as if summoned by an unseen will. Possibly something towing them from below the surface.

Walter Parpart stumbled back from the rail. "The sea's giving us *ghosts*," he muttered. "They're coming to climb aboard."

"No one touches them," Raven barked. "Cut anything that gets close."

All the crews scrambled to obey, swords drawn to sever any line or grapple that reached any ship's hull.

And still, the sails kept coming.

As the fog thickened once more, the floating wreckage faded—but the sea remained silent, like it had swallowed its secret again. Only one thing was left behind, caught on the anchor chain of *The Sea Witch*:

A sailor's skull. Wedged in the iron links. Its empty eye sockets turned toward the ships.

Raven stared at it as the sun finally broke over the horizon, casting bloody gold across the reef.

"We leave now," she said, voice sharp. "Whatever haunts this place won't let us rest again."

And so, with hulls and masts repaired but nerves frayed, the fleet made ready to leave Coffin Reef.

But no one—*not one soul*—spoke above a whisper as they raised their sails and turned their ships toward the open sea.

The fleet slipped silently away from Coffin Reef, sails billowing weakly in the fickle morning breeze. The eerie calm of dawn still clung to the air, pressing down on every man and woman aboard the ships like a heavy shroud.

Raven stood at the prow of *Destiny*, her eyes narrowed against the salt spray. The haunting image of *La Dama de Sangre* lingered in her mind like a dark omen. No one spoke above a whisper, and an uneasy watchfulness replaced the usual chatter of a fleet underway.

Hours passed with little wind. The ships drifted in a sluggish procession, creaking timbers groaning under the weight of anticipation.

Then, without warning, a chill swept through *Destiny*—an unnatural cold that seeped beneath the decks, snuffing lanterns and causing the crew to shiver despite the midday sun.

On the quarterdeck, Charles Taylor stood rigid, his gaze fixed on the horizon as if something unseen was calling out to him. Raven approached quietly, placing a steadying hand on his shoulder.

"Something wrong, Leftenant?" she asked.

He turned slowly, eyes shadowed but alert. "This cold...it's like a warning. A memory I can't place, but it feels old—too old for these waters."

Raven nodded, sensing the weight behind his words. "Whatever it is, we'll face it together."

Charles gave a faint smile, the ghost of a pilot from another time, ready to navigate mysteries no compass could chart. He had already seen so many things since joining Raven's crew after being rescued from the sea. Even before...his torpedo ship getting lost in the skies above Bermuda.

Their compass going haywire. Their radio only broadcasting static. But now...traveling through haunted waters was almost more than he could bear.

The chill deepened, creeping through *Destiny's* timbers like a living thing. Even though the noon sun had advanced above, the skies were darkened like an eclipse. Lanterns flickered violently, casting erratic shadows that danced and twisted against the sails and rigging.

The crew murmured uneasily, glancing around as if expecting to see a ghost materialize on deck. Hands instinctively reached for cutlasses and pistols, though none dared speak above a hushed whisper.

Suddenly, the air thickened with the scent of brine and something else—something metallic, like blood. They could smell it in the air. The temperature dropped further, frost forming along the railings and spider-webbing across the wooden deck.

From the fog-shrouded sails emerged a spectral glow—a pale, ghostly light that shimmered and pulsed like the heartbeat of the sea itself. Shapes took form in the mist: pale faces with hollow eyes, translucent figures clad in tattered uniforms from centuries past.

A hush fell over the crew as the ghostly apparitions drifted silently among the masts, their eyes fixed on the living with sorrow and accusation.

George's grip tightened on the wheel. "This is no mere haunting," he said grimly. "This is a warning. The past is reaching out to us—and it won't let go easily."

Raven stepped forward, voice steady though her heart pounded. "Whatever binds them here, we need to understand it—before it drags us down with it."

The ghostly light flickered once more, then vanished as suddenly as it had appeared, leaving behind a biting silence and the distant cry of a lone gull.

The crew exhaled collectively, but the weight of the encounter settled deep within their bones.

The captains met again onboard *Destiny*. They gathered around the large oaken table in Raven's cabin. Charts were still scattered about on the table from previous meetings. As usual, Jeffrey joined the captains in their conference.

Raven spoke, "Let's analyze what we're dealing with here. We know it is something otherworldly... whether a ghost or something else. Why is it attaching itself to us?"

Alexander replied, "Yes, what have we done that it continues to find us and haunt us?"

Pharaoh asked, "What did your ghost friend...Geoffrey Neely tell you about *La Dama de Sangre*? Do we know the whole story?"

"I only know what I was told. A ship called *La Dama de Sangre*. She was captained by an Admiral Mendoza who had spared the life of a witch who had been tortured during the Spanish Inquisition. He told her she would remain under his protection as long as she protected his ships. A storm came upon them one night and destroyed all the ships but one. That ship barely made it home with a half-mad crew onboard, screaming about a ship with red sails glowing in the night. Its crew was all dead, but their bodies walked the decks during the night."

Attila asked, "So, we don't know what happened to the witch?"

"I can only assume she went down in the storm. She must have been on the ship with the dead crew whose bodies walked the decks at night."

Alexander added, "This witch was supposed to keep the ships safe in exchange for her life. So what happened? Neither the ship's crew nor the witch survived. And now, she haunts other ships? I don't understand."

Raven said, "I just remembered something else. When we attacked one of the fleets and took their treasure, I heard a voice whisper in my ear, 'betrayer'."

Pharaoh asked, "Who? Who was she calling the betrayer? You, or the captain?"

"I don't know. Maybe we should find the answer to that question. Did she think I betrayed, or someone else? And, if it is me, why did she call me a betrayer? Who did I betray?"

Jeffrey interjected, "Raven, I don't much like the idea of you having another conversation with your ghost friend, but...maybe that's exactly what you should do. Ask him if he knows who the betrayer is."

The sea was calm, but it wasn't peace they sailed through.

The water stretched like black glass beneath *Destiny's* keel, wind skimming the sails in uneven breaths. It felt as though the sea were holding its tongue, watching. Judging.

Raven stood at the bow, gloved hands gripping the rail as the coastline of Barbados slid into view. Bridgetown loomed ahead—familiar, but changed. The sky hung low, bruised with storm light. Seabirds wheeled above the rooftops but made no sound.

A knot had settled in her chest and refused to loosen.

Behind her, boots scraped. John Ashworth, her papa, stepped up beside her.

"Almost there," he said quietly.

She nodded.

They had seen many strange things together. Survived them. But this was different.

Raven glanced sideways at him. The lines in his face seemed deeper today, his eyes shadowed. He'd heard the whisper, too—*The betrayer is among you*. And he'd looked at her after. Not with suspicion... but with something worse.

Recognition.

"You heard it too," she said.

He didn't look at her. Just nodded once. "Aye."

"You know who it meant?"

A long pause. Then, with a tight breath, he said, "We'll ask the ghost."

She didn't press further. Not yet.

They made landfall with no fanfare. No greetings from the docks. Bridgetown had grown uneasy in their absence.

The once-bustling waterfront felt deserted. Shop windows shuttered closed. Stray dogs wandered the alleys. A tavern window swung open and shut with a broken hinge, tapping like a finger against glass. Even the harbor breeze smelled wrong—brine laced with something scorched.

Jeffrey left the ship first to investigate the closed feeling of the town. He returned after half an hour to report to his wife. He met John and Raven at the dock. "Locals say the place burned. Just like the dreams."

Raven stiffened. "What dreams?"

He looked at her, hesitant. "They say a man in a captain's coat walks the ruins at night. Cards in one hand. Something dripping from the other."

Raven narrowed her eyes. "Blood?"

Jeffrey swallowed. "Ink."

"Let's have a look."

John, Charles, and Jeffrey followed her through the streets winding past closed shops and boarded-up buildings—each one with an untold story. Finally, they found what used to be The Pelian's Roost.

The tavern ruin stood like a charred skeleton at the edge of Bridgetown's old quarter.

Charred timbers jutted upward like snapped bones. Soot-blackened stone clung to the earth, still streaked with fire scars. No birds. No insects. Just the crackle of long-dead embers that shouldn't still be burning.

They stepped into the ash.

John, Jeffrey, and Charles spread out silently, weapons close at hand. The ruins creaked, though no wind blew.

Then the smell came.

Salt.

Rum.

And ink.

Raven turned. The shadows had thickened.

And then, with a hiss of breath, he stepped forward from the dark: **Geoffrey Neely**, just as she remembered him, though thinner, sharper, like time had sanded him down to essence. There was no longer any mistaking him for a live man. His coat hung in spectral tatters. His eyes gleamed with wet black.

"You came back," he said, voice like wet parchment. "Good."

Raven stood her ground. "You whispered to me. In the middle of a battle. You called me *the betrayer*. Why?"

Geoffrey's smile was cold. "I said no such thing."

Raven's mouth went dry. "It was your voice."

"No," Neely said, "it *borrowed* my voice."

He looked past her to John and the others.

"I told you once, Mr. Ashworth: the sea remembers. And she doesn't forgive."

John stepped forward, eyes flinty. "Who spoke through you, Neely? Who's reaching out?"

The ghost's expression flickered. "She was old when the oceans were young. She lies beneath Coffin Reef still. But she stirs. Because of *you*."

He pointed—not at Raven, but at her father.

"You know her name. You heard it once in the dark. And you never told her."

Raven turned sharply. "What's he talking about?"

John's face was stone.

The air grew heavy. The ghost shimmered. A low, droning whisper rolled through the scorched beams—too many voices overlapping. *The tide turns. The debt returns. The blood must answer.*

"Tell her," Neely rasped, eyes locked on John. "Before she hears it from the dead."

And with that, the ghost dissolved—ink bleeding into air, vanishing like smoke.

Silence fell.

Only the crackle of distant surf and the flap of a torn sail in the harbor filled the space he left behind.

Raven stared at her papa. "Tell me. Now."

John looked at the ruined hearth where Neely had stood and closed his eyes.

"When you were born," he said slowly, "your mother heard a voice through the waves crashing against the wharf, through your first cry. It said you'd carry a name forgotten by men. A name that sank long ago but still draws breath."

Raven whispered, "La Dama de Sangre?"

John nodded once. "But that wasn't the ship's name. That was *hers*. The one bound inside it. She's calling to you, Raven. Through Neely. Through the reef. Through blood."

A gust of wind whipped through the ruins, scattering ashes.

The voice—faint but unmistakable—rose again on the air.

"The betrayer walks the deck again..."

Raven's heart pounded.

She didn't know what it meant.

But the sea wasn't done with her yet.

CHAPTER 15

It was a stormy birth.

Rain lashed the shutters of the cottage overlooking Bristol. Wind howled like the dead outside, and waves pounded the rocks with furious rhythm near the docks where merchant ships were moored. The sea had risen with the labor.

Inside, the fire barely held against the wind's breath. The midwife worked by lamplight, sweat on her brow, sleeves soaked to the elbow. On the floor beside the bed, a black cat crouched, fur bristling, green eyes wide. It hadn't moved in hours.

Margaret Ashworth gripped the headboard, breath ragged, face pale. Her dark curls clung to her temples. John knelt at her side, hand in hers, his own knuckles white.

"You're doing fine," he said, though his voice cracked. "You're almost there."

She met his gaze, only for a moment. "Something's wrong," she whispered.

"No," he said quickly. "It's just the storm."

She shook her head, sweat rolling down her cheek. "No. The sea's listening. I can feel it."

John was confused by her words, but before he could answer, the child came.

The wail rang out like a lightning strike—precise, sharp, fierce.

But beneath it... something else.

For one breath, one heartbeat, the sea answered.

Not with wind.

Not with waves.

But with words.

A voice—old, vast, feminine—rose from the streets below, not spoken aloud, but heard *inside* them. A voice that had traveled across the sea and through the walls of their little flat. In the stone. In their blood.

"The bloodline calls. The name returns. The heart shall bear the sea's forgotten face."

Margaret gasped—not from pain, but from recognition. Her eyes went wide, fixed not on the baby, but on the *window*.

Lightning lit the storm-tossed sea—and for one impossible moment, the ocean seemed to gather right outside their window. It rose toward the second-story flat like a black wave bearing a woman's face.

Then it was gone.

The midwife hadn't heard it.

The baby, swaddled and bawling, lay in Margaret's arms.

But Margaret was trembling, tears streaking down her face.

John wiped her forehead. "You're all right," he whispered. "She's perfect."

Margaret held the child tighter. But her voice was distant. "She has a name already," she said.

John frowned. "We haven't—"

"No," Margaret cut in. "She already *had* it. It's older than mine. Older than yours."

She looked down at her daughter, Raven's eyes already open, wide, unblinking.

"She's been claimed."

From that night on, Margaret Ashworth never spoke of what she'd heard.

But sometimes, in the dead of night, John would find her standing at the window, staring out across the dark waters, lips moving silently.

As if listening for a voice that had spoken only once…

…and was waiting to speak again.

The fever had been burning for days.

In the bedroom of the Ashworth flat, the air was thick with salt, sweat, and the sharp stench of boiled herbs. Outside, the sea murmured constantly, as if waiting. The healer had come and gone twice, shaking his head with each visit.

Twelve-year-old Raven sat quietly by the tiny stove, carving lines into a driftwood scrap with her sailor's knife. She hadn't spoken in hours.

John Ashworth kept vigil with his wife constantly.

Margaret lay propped against a nest of pillows, her face pale, lips cracked, eyes staring at the ceiling beams like they held secrets only she could see. Her hair, once thick and dark, was soaked and clinging to her temples. Every few breaths, she murmured things John couldn't make out.

Then, suddenly, her eyes found him.

"John."

He leaned closer, taking her hand. "I'm here, Maggie."

She blinked slowly, a strange calm settling over her. "Don't let her go to the sea."

His grip tightened. "It's too late for that. She *is* the sea. Always has been."

Margaret shook her head, sharp for the first time in days. "No. You don't understand. She was *called*—not born. The night she came into this world, something else came with her. I heard it from the water."

John nodded slowly. "You told me before. The voice. The name—Raven."

Margaret's gaze grew glassy. "That wasn't the name. That was *our* name for her. A shell. A disguise."

John felt a chill crawl up his spine.

"She had a name before that," Margaret whispered. "Older than storms. I didn't say it out loud, not even to you. But it's in her blood. You've seen the way the sea moves around her. How the compass reacts. How the winds bend."

John said nothing. He *had* seen it.

Margaret's voice turned hollow. "She dreams of waves she's never sailed. Sings in languages she's never heard. She hears things when the fog rolls in." Her fingers curled tightly in his. "You must protect her...from the name. From the ship."

John swallowed hard. "What name?"

She hesitated.

Then, barely audible:

"Anaíra."

The wind pressed against the windows like a breath held too long.

John whispered it again: "Anaíra."

Margaret's body went rigid. Her pupils dilated.

"Don't let them find her."

A long silence followed. The waves beyond the cliffs crashed in slow, heavy rhythm, like a heartbeat fading.

Finally, Margaret closed her eyes. "I hear her voice again," she said. "In the tide."

Then she was still.

Three days later, John stood alone at the sea's edge, Raven's hand in his. She hadn't cried. She hadn't spoken. Just stood there, wind in her red hair, staring out to sea.

John looked at her.

"You'll come with me," he said. "Ship's leaving in two days. You'll dress in boys' clothing. Your name will be Richard."

Raven didn't blink.

Suddenly, a thought entered her mind. "Because she's coming?"

John stiffened. "What did you say?"

"The woman in the water," she said quietly. "She wants me to remember something."

John knelt beside her, heart pounding."

"What woman in the water?"

"She whispers to me sometimes.

"If she ever whispers to you again," he said, "you don't answer. Not until I say."

Raven nodded.

But out at sea, where the moonlight danced on shifting waves, something watched.

And it remembered her true name.

Aboard the original *Destiny*
One year after Margaret's death

The wind had died at sunset.

The sails hung limp in the masts, barely stirring. Even the gulls had vanished from the sky, leaving behind only the slow groan of the hull and the rhythmic slap of water against the planks. It was Richard's watch—middle of the night, moon full and high.

He crouched on the main deck, scrubbing dried salt from the quarter railing with a chunk of rough canvas; his hands were raw and red. The rest of the crew dozed in hammocks or played bones below. Only the helmsman, Andrew Crane, and the stars kept him company.

And the sea.

Tonight, it felt too quiet.

Richard paused, frowning, and glanced over the rail. The water was black glass—flat, endless: no foam, no wave, no ripple.

Then he heard it.

A whisper. Soft and low, like a breath drawn through water.

"Anaaaiiira..."

He froze.

There was no one nearby—only the night wind and the still sea.

"Little girl..."

"You wear his name like armor."

"But I know your true name."

Richard stood slowly, hands trembling. He looked around, then up, toward the crow's nest. Empty. No movement, but the moonlit shadows swaying in the rigging.

He backed away from the rail.

"Come closer," the voice urged, with a lullaby soaked in brine. "Say it, and I'll tell you what you are."

"Anaíra..."

Richard's breath caught in his chest. The name vibrated in his bones.

He'd never heard it before. But it *knew* him. It felt like it belonged to something just beneath his skin—something old, deep, and terrible.

He clamped his hands over his ears. "No. No, that's not my name."

"Isn't it?" the voice asked. "You've always known. You've always heard me."

He turned to run—but stumbled, falling to one knee.

At that moment, the sea beside the ship shimmered.

Something was rising—no splash, no ripple. Just *rising*.

Moonlight touched the surface—and for the briefest instant, he saw her.

A woman. Pale and long-limbed, hair streaming like kelp, eyes wide and black as the deep. She floated just beneath the water, upside-down, mouth open—not gasping, but *singing*.

He squeezed his eyes shut.

"RICHARD!"

A voice, real, human, cut through the trance.

It was the first mate, Mr. Faulkner, stomping onto the deck with a lantern swinging. "Boy! You sleepin' on your feet?!"

Richard gasped, heart slamming in his chest.

Faulkner frowned at him, taking in his face. "You look like you've seen a ghost."

Richard looked over the rail again, but the water was empty.

Still. Black.

"I...I thought I heard something," he mumbled.

"Best you stop thinking, then," Mr. Faulkner said, slapping the railing. "You get haunted out here, you'll end up overboard."

Richard nodded shakily and returned to scrubbing the rail.

But as Mr. Faulkner turned and walked away, Richard risked one last glance into the deep.

And though nothing stirred the water's surface...

...the whisper still echoed in his mind:

"Anaíra..."

Aboard *Raven's Destiny*, Raven Age 16
Location: Open waters, Gulf of Guinea
Nightfall

The sea was quiet again.

Too quiet.

Raven stood alone at the stern rail, the moon was high and pale above her, its reflection trembling against the dark water. A light wind tugged at the sails, but the night felt... wrong. Heavy. Expectant.

Behind her, the deck of *Raven's Destiny* creaked with the weight of a crew that was finally sleeping. Pharaoh had taken the second watch, leaving her a brief moment of peace. Or at least what passed for it these days.

She gripped the railing, fingers tightening on the salt-worn wood. Something tugged at the edges of her memory—something old. Something she hadn't thought of for years. Unsettling. The kind of thing that hid in dreams and came back to you only when you were alone.

Then the whisper came.

"Anaíra…"

She gasped softly.

It was the same voice. The same chill, like cold water sliding down her spine. But this time, it wasn't faint. It wasn't just in her head.

It was in the *air*.

"You've grown bold, little storm. But you still wear your borrowed name."

Raven turned sharply, scanning the water, the sails, the masts, and the decks.

Nothing.

But her heart thundered.

Sixteen now. Captain. In command of her own ship. She'd buried Richard with the wreckage of the old *Destiny*. She'd carved her name—**Raven Ashworth**—into the helm. And still the sea remembered something else.

Something older.

"Do you remember the last time you heard me?" the voice said, soft as surf on stone.

"You were twelve. You bled salt and shadows that night. Dressed as a boy, as I recall. Trying to forget who you are, maybe?"

And she *did* remember. The voice had come when she was scrubbing the rail. When she was pretending to be someone she wasn't—someone small. Someone safe.

That night, she'd seen the woman in the water—the one with black eyes and streaming hair.

"Say my name," the voice beckoned. "Set me free."

"Why?" Raven whispered, fists clenched. "Why me?"

No answer.

Only the sound of the waves. But the question lingered, hanging in the dark.

Then a boot step behind her.

Raven turned fast, blade half-drawn.

Pharaoh stood there, holding a tankard. He didn't flinch.

"Didn't mean to spook you, Raven," he said calmly. "You were staring into the dark like it owed you money." He said with a concerned smile.

Raven exhaled slowly, sheathing the blade. "Just... thinking."

Pharaoh studied her a moment, then handed her the tankard. "Night's too still. Wind's gone sour. I don't like it."

She took the drink, nodded. "Neither do I."

She took a small sip.

Pharaoh leaned on the rail beside her. "You used to get that look. Back when you were young. Like you were listening to something the rest of us couldn't hear."

Raven glanced sideways. "Maybe I was."

He met her eyes. "You hearing it again?"

She hesitated. Then nodded. "It knows my name. The real one. The one my mother tried to keep secret."

Pharaoh didn't blink. "Are you going to tell me?"

"No," Raven said firmly. "Not tonight."

He grunted. "Good. The sea's got enough dead things talking. We don't need to give them company."

They stood together in silence for a while, watching the moon shimmer on the water.

Far below the surface, unseen hands stirred the deep.

And in the darkness, the name waited.

Anaíra.

CHAPTER 16

ABOARD RAVEN'S DESTINY: MORNING, JUST AFTER SETTING SAIL

The sails of the four ships billowed gently as they slipped out of Bridgetown's harbor, the morning sun casting long, golden shadows on the sea. Raven stood at the helm, one hand on the wheel, the other shading her eyes as she watched *The Firebird*, *The Sea Witch*, and *The Royal Victory* fall into formation behind her.

They were headed south—back into dangerous waters.

She hadn't spoken since they left the harbor mouth. Not since Geoffrey Neely's voice echoed like a cracked bell in that forgotten cellar below the chapel. Not since he told her the name whispered in her ear during the last battle wasn't meant as a warning, but a summons.

"The sea remembers its own," the ghost had said.

"And the Betrayer walks in your shadow."

Her shadow.

Not her father's. Not John Ashworth's.

Hers.

The deck creaked beneath her boots as the ship rocked into open sea. Wind curled through the rigging and seabirds circled above, but it felt too quiet for the beginning of a voyage, as if something was waiting.

She was still replaying Neely's final words when a voice pulled her back to the present.

"Cap'n?"

She turned. Sean O'Toole stood a few paces back, hat in his hands, thinning red hair tucked behind his ears. He'd been aboard for six months now, quiet mostly, but reliable. He looked like he'd aged twice in half the years the sea gave him—but there was strength in him still. And sorrow.

"I dent mean to intrude on ya, now," he said, nodding toward the bow. "But if I might have a word wit ya?"

Raven motioned him closer.

Sean stepped up beside her and leaned on the railing, gazing out over the water. "I heard duh ghost spoke to yuh in Bridgetown."

"He did," Raven said carefully.

Sean nodded, lips pressed into a thin line. "Then I s'pose it's no sin to tell yuh now what I've kept quiet since I signed on."

She waited, silent.

Sean took a long breath, eyes far away.

"Years ago—long before dis ship, afore I was ever in the Indies—I sailed out of Galway aboard a cutter named *Sable Jane*. She were fast and cursed, same as most good ships." He chuckled grimly. "We wuz off the coast of Portugal when we foun'er. Or maybe she fount us."

Raven raised an eyebrow.

"She be a wreck. Burned and splinnered, drifting with no crew aboard. Just one body—a woman, tangled in duh shrouds. Looked half-drownt but freshly dead. Her hair was black as pitch and her eyes..." He paused. "They wuz open. Starin' right at me, though she hadn't breath in her chest."

He swallowed.

"Cap'n ordered her body buried to sea, but before we could cut her loose, I leaned in—dunt ask me why. Sometin' pullin' me. And she—" His voice broke for a moment. "She spoke."

Raven turned sharply. "What did she say?"

He met her gaze. "She said, *'Tell Anaíra the tide remembers.'* Then she smiled and slipped into the sea like a stone."

The name hit her like a wave.

Raven gripped the railing, her breath catching. "You're sure she said that name?"

"Clear's a bell," Sean whispered. "Didn't know what it meant then. Thought it was the fever. But when I heard you shoutin' in the storm the other night—when you said *no* to something no one else could hear—I knew. The sea's marked you, Miss Raven."

Raven turned her face toward the wind, jaw tight.

"Why now?" she muttered. "Why is it all coming back now?"

Sean looked out over the water again, eyes hard. "Maybe it's not coming back, Cap'n. Maybe it never left."

A gull cried somewhere above, but it sounded distant—muted, like a bird calling underwater.

Raven's gaze drifted to the horizon, where the sun struck gold off the waves. Somewhere ahead waited the truth. A name. A curse. And the woman in the water.

She straightened. "Thank you, Sean."

"If the sea speaks again," he said, stepping back, "don't wait too long to listen. The sea don't whisper forever. One day, it roars."

She nodded, already turning her eyes to the east.

Below her, *Destiny* surged forward, and the fleet followed close behind.

Whatever waited beyond the horizon, Raven would face it.

Even if it called her by a name she'd never chosen.

Clouds had gathered by mid-afternoon two days later, thick and low, flattening the light and casting the sea in a dull gray wash. The fleet sailed in formation, their sails slack in the listless air. Not a sound echoed but the occasional groan of timber and the hollow flap of canvas.

Raven stood on the quarterdeck of *Destiny*, squinting toward the horizon where the water looked strangely still. Too still.

"Something's wrong," Pharaoh's voice crackled from *The Sea Witch* across the waves. He stood high on the rigging, his long coat streaming behind him like a shadow. "You feel it?"

Raven nodded. She felt it in her gut—tight and coiled.

A bell rang aboard *The Firebird*, sharp and quick. Attila's voice called from the rail, his spyglass pressed to his eye. "Starboard side! Something in the water!"

Crew gathered at the rail, murmurs rippling like nervous wind. Raven moved to the edge of her ship and raised her own spyglass.

She froze.

A ring of white lilies floated on the water.

Dozens of them. Perfect, pale, unspoiled. Their petals bobbed with unnatural calm, forming a perfect circle the size of a longboat. In the center floated a silver pendant, spinning slowly, catching the weak sunlight like a lure.

Raven's blood turned cold.

"Lilies?" Sean O'Toole said behind her, stepping forward, his voice low. "No wild bloom like that grows out here. That's... that's a funeral ring."

"A message," George muttered. "Or a trap."

Alexander's voice crackled from *The Royal Victory*, rough with disbelief. "Raven, are you seeing this? That pendant—have you ever seen anything like it?"

Raven didn't answer right away. Her fingers closed around the spyglass tighter.

Yes. She'd seen it before.

Around her mother's neck.

Margaret Ashworth owned very little. But she owned a silver necklace and pendant that had been passed down through her family for generations. Raven remembered seeing it when she was five years old. The pendant had been silver, shaped like a teardrop, etched with a curling script no one in the family had ever been able to read.

She lowered the glass.

"Bring it aboard," she said.

The crew hesitated.

"No ropes," she added. "No grapples. Just a net. And gloves."

Three men did the task, holding their breath as they drew the pendant from the lilies and brought it on deck, placing it gently on a stretch of canvas.

The moment it touched wood, a wind exploded outward from the ring of lilies on the water.

All four ships reeled with the force of it—masts groaning, sails snapping taut in sudden motion. The lilies scattered across the waves, vanishing into the sea like foam.

Then... silence.

The pendant gleamed.

No one spoke.

Raven stepped toward it, but Sean reached out, stopping her.

"I seen a sailor touch a token like that once," he said quietly. "He forgot his own name by sundown."

Raven studied the pendant but didn't lift it.

Instead, she looked toward the sea. The wind now blew in a steady whisper, and as she listened, she thought she heard it—

A voice, just below hearing.

"Anaíra..."

She stepped back. "Lock it below. In the strongbox. I don't want anyone near it."

"Aye, Captain," Sean said, handling it as if it might bite.

Raven turned back to the sea, heart hammering. The omen had been clear.

Her past was circling closer. Her name wasn't just something forgotten. It was something summoned.

And the woman in the water—whoever she was—had just laid the first piece of bait.

The sun pierced the clouds for a moment, casting an eerie gold sheen across the fleet.

In that flash of light, Raven saw a shape in the sea—a flicker of black hair and black eyes—before it vanished below the waves.

"She's watching," Raven whispered.

"And she's getting closer."

Pharaoh's voice came across the water again, more solemn this time.

"What do we do now?"

Raven took a breath.

"We sail on."

And as the fleet cut through the waves once more, the pendant in the hold shimmered in the darkness—waiting.

Raven's Cabin, midnight

The ship creaked and sighed like an old animal in sleep. A low swell rocked *Destiny* gently, as if the sea herself were breathing slow and deep.

Raven lay next to Jeffrey in their bed, one arm slung over his chest as she lay on her side. The pendant was locked far below in the strongbox. But it didn't matter.

It had already followed her.

She slipped into dreams like falling through dark water—no resistance, no breath.

She stood ankle-deep in a **mirror-flat sea**, the water as still as glass, stretching to the edge of the world. The sky above was black and heavy with stars, but they didn't twinkle. They watched her.

Raven was barefoot. The hem of a long red coat floated around her like blood in the water. Her hair hung loose, clinging to her shoulders.

And before her stood the woman.

The same woman she'd glimpsed in storms and whispers. The one who had stared from beneath the waves with eyes too dark, too old, too knowing.

Even though she was ancient, she was beautiful in the way storms are beautiful—untamed, aching, and deadly. Her long black hair floated as if in slow motion, her skin pale and almost luminous. Seaweed wrapped around her arms like living jewelry.

And in her hands...

The **pendant.**

It spun slowly, hovering between her fingers. Etched upon it was that same curling script, glowing now with faint silver light.

Raven took a step back. But the water did not ripple. It clung to her like glass.

The woman tilted her head.

"Why do you run from your own name?"

Her voice was both a whisper and a wave, ancient and intimate, like the sea speaking when no one else is listening.

"You have worn so many names," she said. "Richard. Raven. Captain."

"But this is the one the sea remembers."

She held out the pendant.

"Say it," she murmured. "Say what you are, and I will open the way."

Raven shook her head. "I don't know it."

"You do."

The woman took a step closer.

"The name is not something you learn. It's something you awaken."

The pendant drifted toward Raven, spinning, glowing brighter now. The etched script pulsed faintly with every beat of her heart.

Raven wanted to reach for it.

Her fingers twitched.

"I don't trust you," she said.

The woman smiled.

"You don't have to trust me. You only have to become."

Behind the woman, the stars shifted.

One by one, they fell from the sky like sparks from a dying fire—plunging into the sea with no sound. The sky darkened. The ocean began to swirl.

"Say it," the woman whispered again. "The sea is listening."

And just for a moment, Raven remembered.

A flicker of a name—just at the edge of thought. Not spoken aloud for centuries. Not human.

She opened her mouth.

A rush of wind exploded through the dream like a cannon blast, and she gasped—

—awake.

Her bed rocked violently as the ship shuddered in its moorings. Outside, the wind screamed.

She sat bolt upright, drenched in cold sweat.

Jeffrey awoke. "What's the matter?"

From belowdecks, there was a sound. A metallic thump. The strongbox.

Raven grabbed her coat, boots half-laced, and stormed down the narrow stairs.

"Raven? Where are you going?"

Lanterns swung wildly, casting mad shadows on the walls.

She reached the hold and yanked open the hatch.

The strongbox had shifted. The pendant lay half-spilled from its velvet lining.

And glowing—softly, steadily—was the script carved into its face.

Raven stared at it.

A name burned there. Not in English. Not in any language she knew.

But she understood it.

Anaíra.

She whispered the name aloud.

Nothing happened. Not immediately.

But the sea, outside the hull, suddenly calmed. The wind dropped away in a heartbeat. The whole ship went still.

Too still.

Raven exhaled.

"Not yet," she whispered. "Not... yet."

And carefully, she closed the strongbox.

CHAPTER 17

In the early morning hours, Raven sat cross-legged on her bunk, hair still damp with sweat, a blanket wrapped around her shoulders though the night was warm. The lantern flickered low beside her, casting golden pools over the maps and sea charts rolled across the floor.

Jeffrey stood in the doorway, boots in one hand, eyes searching her face.

"You didn't come back to bed," he said softly.

She looked up, startled. "Didn't mean to wake you."

"You didn't." He crossed the room, dropped his boots with a quiet thump, and crouched in front of her. "But the wind's gone again. I could feel something was wrong."

Raven studied his face. That steady calm he always carried, the way his jaw tightened just a little when he was worried. She wanted to tell him everything, and at the same time, wanted to protect him from it.

But he'd followed her through storms and worse. If there was one person she could trust with this—

She exhaled. "I had another dream."

Jeffrey sat beside her, arm brushing hers. "The woman in the water?"

Raven nodded. "She spoke to me again. She was holding the pendant... and she asked me to say my name."

Jeffrey tensed. "Your *real* name?"

"She said I already know it." Her fingers curled into the blanket. "I didn't say it in the dream. But when I woke up... the pendant—it was out of the box. Glowing. Like it knew I'd been near it."

He glanced toward the locked chest in the corner of the cabin.

"And the name?" he asked. "Did you say it?"

She hesitated. Then, quietly: "*Anaíra.*"

The name felt ancient and wild on her tongue. It made the lantern flicker again.

Jeffrey turned to look at her fully. "Is that you? Is that who you were—before?"

"I don't know. It feels like it. Not just a name, but a...weight. Like I've been carrying it without knowing. Like it's... alive somehow."

Jeffrey reached for her hand. "What happens if you say it again? Out loud. With intent."

"I think the sea will answer." She looked down. "And I don't know if I'll come back from whatever answers me."

Jeffrey was quiet for a long moment.

Then: "Do you want to say it?"

Raven blinked. "No," she said. Then, softer: "Yes. Part of me does. The same part that wants to dive into a whirlpool just to see what's at the bottom."

He smiled faintly. "I married a madwoman."

She smirked. "And a pirate."

"I like the pirate more." He leaned forward and kissed her forehead, then rested his against hers. "Whatever this is, we face it together. If that name comes with danger, we'll meet it. If it comes with power, you'll decide how to use it."

She let out a breath she hadn't realized she was holding.

"Thank you," she whispered.

He nodded. "Just don't say it three times in a mirror."

She chuckled—genuine and short-lived.

But somewhere below deck, the wood groaned.

And outside the cabin window, the sea murmured.

Like it was listening.

The sea was glass. Endless and silent.

Sails hung limp on every mast, the rigging groaning now and then with the weight of stillness. Overhead, gulls circled once or twice before drifting inland, as if the open sea offered no promise. The sun glared off the water like polished steel, blinding and relentless.

Pharaoh stood at the helm of *The Sea Witch*, his face shadowed beneath his wide-brimmed hat. Sweat glistened on his brow. He hadn't slept properly in days. None of them had. The unnatural calm was fraying every nerve.

No wind.

No ships.

No sign of Spanish gold.

Only the sun. Only silence.

Below decks, voices rose—sharper than they should've been.

He turned to Ricardo de la Cruz, his first mate. "Go check on the stores. And tell Mateo to get those men to quiet down before they bring a storm none of us wants."

Ricardo nodded and disappeared down the companionway.

But it was too late.

Shouts rang out—Spanish voices, angry and fast, spilling out onto the deck with boots and blades.

A dozen men pushed their way topside, sunburned and restless, eyes flashing. At their head was Luis Ortega, a lean, scarred man who had only been with the fleet a few months. A survivor from the captured Spanish galleon, *Royal Victory*, spared by Raven and taken aboard for his knowledge of trade routes.

Now he stood on Pharaoh's quarterdeck, uninvited.

"We've been adrift too long," Luis spat in Spanish. "Weeks without prey. The sea does not move. You call this the path of a captain? In my country...we do not follow women. They are too emotional."

Pharaoh's hand drifted near his sword hilt, but he didn't draw. Not yet.

"This fleet moves when the wind moves," he said calmly. "Same as it always has. And, if you think The Red Raven is just any ordinary woman...I suggest you go over and say it to her face!"

"Maybe your Red Raven has angered the sea," Luis growled. "Maybe *she* carries a curse. A woman with no past, no name—dragging us deeper into death while gold-laden ships vanish!"

There were murmurs of agreement. Others stepped forward, shoulders squared.

Pharaoh's eyes narrowed.

"She brought you out of chains," he said coldly. "You call her cursed now because the wind rests for a few days?"

Luis laughed bitterly. "It's not just wind. It's an omen. Every ship we follow disappears. The waters boil behind us. Storms rise when she whispers. No prayers work anymore. This isn't command—it's witchcraft!"

The word hit like a match to dry tinder.

Several crew members crossed themselves. Others tightened their grips on cutlasses. Pharaoh knew this tension well. He'd seen it on slave ships—right before revolt.

He raised his voice, deep and commanding.

"She is the reason any of you still draw breath. She has fed you, armed you, freed you. You want to mutiny now, over superstition and ghost stories?"

Ortega sneered. "Maybe we'd rather follow a man who answers to God, not voices from the sea."

That did it.

Steel rasped from sheaths.

Before the first man could lunge, Pharaoh drew and moved like a storm. The flat of his blade cracked across Ortega's jaw—hard. The man staggered, blood spitting from his lip. Another rushed Pharaoh from the right, only to be slammed backward by Ricardo, who'd reappeared with two more loyal crew.

In seconds, the deck was chaos—yelling, shoving, curses shouted in Spanish and English.

Pharaoh slammed his blade into the deck boards point-first and roared, "ENOUGH!"

Silence crashed down.

He turned a glare on Ortega, now held upright by two crewmen.

"You think you know curses? I once lived in chains. I've *lived* through real nightmares." His voice dropped low and hard. "If the sea wants something, we don't challenge it—we listen."

He stepped closer. "You want to leave the fleet? Be my guest. But step off this ship, and you'll be setting out in a rowboat... with no wind."

Ortega spat at the deck.

Pharaoh nodded once. "So be it."

He turned to the others. "Get these cowards below. Lash them to the hold until The Red Raven decides what is to be done."

The men dispersed slowly, unease still curling through the air.

As Ricardo helped secure the mutineers, Pharaoh turned toward the still horizon.

And far off, almost imperceptible—a shape broke the water.

Not a ship.

Not a wave.

Something *watching*.

Pharaoh didn't blink.

He just whispered, "If it's you again, sea… then speak plainly."

Location: Aboard *The Sea Witch*
Time: Nightfall, same day as the attempted uprising

The winds had not returned.

Lanterns swung on motionless air, casting dim light across *The Sea Witch's* main deck. The rest of the fleet bobbed nearby—silent, shadowed outlines in the moonlight. The sea was dead calm, yet the air hung heavy with something sharp and expectant.

Raven stood at the base of the mast, flanked by Pharaoh and Jeffrey. Her long coat stirred only slightly, as if from some wind no one else could feel. Her face was carved from stone.

She had been summoned to *The Sea Witch* by way of a conch shell. Because the winds were absent and useless, she and her entourage rowed over in a dory to meet with Pharaoh.

The crew had gathered. Dozens of them. Tense. Watching. Whispering.

Before her knelt Luis Ortega and three others—hands bound, shirts torn, bruises blooming along jawlines and ribs. One mutineer, young and wide-eyed, had already wept himself hoarse. Another stared at her with open defiance.

Ortega, blood crusted at the edge of his mouth, kept his head high. Proud. Foolish.

Raven's voice, when it came, was soft—but it carried.

"Do you know how many winds I've waited for?" she asked. "How many still nights I've sailed through with no food, no gold, and no hope—except the men beside me?"

She stepped forward.

"These men and women have followed me through fire and storm. Some of them wore shackles before they wore swords. Some have watched their homes burn. Some—" she looked at Pharaoh, at Alexander, at Attila's dark silhouette on *The Firebird*—"have followed me because they *believe*."

She turned her gaze on Ortega.

"You... you think still waters mean I've lost the sea? You think the silence is proof of my failure?"

Her voice dropped into something colder.

"Silence is not mercy. Silence is a *warning*."

A gust of wind hissed suddenly through the rigging—a single breath, as if the ocean had inhaled.

A murmur rose among the crew.

Raven knelt before Ortega. "You blame me for what you do not understand. You raise blades not against your enemy—but against your salvation."

Ortega spat again. "You are cursed," he said. "A woman playing at command, whispering to things beneath the waves."

Raven smiled—but it was not kind.

"Good," she said. "Because curses don't beg. Curses don't *kneel*."

She stood and turned to the crew. "These four betrayed us. They spread fear when unity was needed. They jeopardized every ship in this fleet."

Jeffrey spoke then, voice grim: "What's the sentence?"

Raven looked around at the gathered faces—Spaniards, Africans, Britons, former soldiers, escaped slaves. All hardened by sea and battle. All waiting.

"Let them choose," she said.

Pharaoh raised a brow. "Choose what?"

She faced the mutineers. "The boat... or the brand."

A gasp rippled through the deck.

One of the younger men whimpered. "Please... no—please, I didn't mean to—"

"You didn't mean to draw steel?" Raven asked coldly. "You didn't mean to curse my name and spit on your captain?"

Silence.

Then Ortega grinned, mouth bloody. "I'll take the boat," he said.

Raven nodded. "Then you'll have it."

She looked to the others. Two of them begged for mercy. The third, still staring defiantly, chose the brand. So did the boy.

The brands were brought. A simple mark: an "R" in the shape of a raven's wing. Not for punishment—but for *reminder*. Those who bore it once before had done so as a pledge. These would carry it as a scar of near-betrayal.

Ortega and the other man were rowed out at dawn with no supplies and no compass. Raven watched them go without expression.

But later, as she stood alone at the bow of *Destiny*, watching the horizon burn with first light, she whispered something the wind barely carried:

"Silence is not mercy. And next time, it won't be silence that answers them."

And somewhere, beneath the still waters, something listened.

CHAPTER 18

LOCATION: BELOW DECKS, THE SEA WITCH
TIME: TWO NIGHTS AFTER THE UPRISING

The lantern flame sputtered in its cradle, casting twisted shadows across the cramped crew quarters. Mateo Alvarado, one of the mutineers who had chosen the brand, lay wide-eyed in his hammock, the raw skin on his chest still blistered where the raven-wing "R" had been seared into his flesh.

The pain wasn't what kept him awake.

It was the water.

He heard it.

Even now, though they were far from any shore and the sea lay still as glass, he heard it lapping softly against the hull—too softly. It sounded... wrong, like whispers beneath the surface, not waves.

He sat up.

Other men were asleep, snoring or tossing in their hammocks. But not he. He felt it again—an ache behind his eyes like a word was being carved into his mind from the inside.

Then he heard her.

A woman's voice. Liquid, distant, yet intimate—as if she were breathing against his ear.

"You touched her name..."

"...but you do not *know* it..."

"...you branded yourself with lies..."

Mateo stumbled from the hammock, sweating despite the chill. He staggered toward the small hatch leading to the lower hold—drawn there by the sound, by the pull.

The moment he set foot on the steps, the lantern went out behind him. Darkness.

The whisper grew louder.

"She resists me. But *you*...you have no name worth keeping..."

Something brushed past his ankle.

He froze. Water.

The bilge was dry when last he saw it. But now... water lapped at his boots. Icy. Tinged with salt and something foul.

He tried to step back, but the hatch behind him slammed shut with a thunderous *crack*.

In the pitch black, he began to see her—*not with his eyes*, but in the wet red flashes of his mind.

A woman rising from the sea. Hair like kelp trailing behind her, eyes like barnacle-rimmed hollows. A mouth full of sea-glass teeth that didn't move when she spoke.

"She must speak it..."

"The name I left with her mother... the name that unlocks the vault of the drowned."

Mateo screamed. But no sound left his mouth. Only bubbles.

He clawed at his throat. Water—*inside* him now. Filling his lungs. His vision dimmed.

Then—nothing.

Mateo was found at dawn, slumped beside a barrel in the lower hold, soaking wet but alive.

When they tried to rouse him, he only murmured in a rasping voice:

"She's waiting in the deep...
For the girl with the name she cannot say."

And burned into his palm—no one knew how—was a mark none could read.

Twisted, etched, ancient.

Raven's name. In the same script found on the driftwood omen, days before.

Onboard *Destiny*, later that morning, a knock came just as Raven finished binding her hair, braiding it tightly behind her head.

Jeffrey opened the door without waiting. His face was pale, lips pressed into a hard line.

"It's Mateo," he said.

Raven's stomach dropped. "What happened?"

"He's alive. But barely. Pharaoh sent word—he wants you on *The Sea Witch*. Now."

She was already striding past him. She approached the port side where a dory had already been prepared for her. Mdago and Muziki were already at the oars, waiting for her.

As she walked across the deck, she turned to Walter and said, "Mr. Parpart, you're with us."

"Aye, Captain."

Walter quickly and adeptly followed her and John over the side and climbed into the dory. The oarsmen quickly rowed them over to The Sea Witch, where Pharaoh's crew was waiting to help Raven come aboard with John behind her.

Raven looked back over the side and said to Mdago and Muziki, "Stand by. I won't be long."

"*Aye, Captain.*"

As Raven followed Pharaoh to the hatch leading to the lower decks, she noticed everyone carefully watching. Pharaoh noticed, too.

"All of you...back to work!"

Everyone slowly returned to their duties.

Raven, John, and Walter climbed down the steps to the second deck, where they found Mateo being attended to.

The smell of salt, sweat, and something *wrong* hit her the moment she stepped into the hold. Mateo lay on a cot surrounded by crew. He was soaked, though the hold was dry. Shivering, muttering, eyes wide but unseeing.

Pharaoh stood nearby, arms crossed tightly. His face was grim.

Raven knelt beside the cot. "Mateo."

His eyes flicked to her, recognizing her—but not fully. He whispered hoarsely:

"She waits... in the deep...
for you to speak..."

Raven's blood turned to ice.

She took his hand gently and saw it.

Burned into his palm was the same twisting mark from the driftwood etched with her unknown name. It shimmered faintly under the lantern light, not carved, not inked. Branded by something unseen.

She stared at it, heart thundering. Her fingers trembled.

Pharaoh crouched beside her. "I saw the driftwood. I didn't want to believe it. But now this?"

"She's growing stronger," Raven said softly. "She doesn't just want me to hear her anymore. She wants them all to."

John stood in the hatchway, watching her. "Do you think he spoke it?"

"No," Raven said, but her voice shook. "If he had... he'd be gone. Taken."

Pharaoh looked at her, searching her face. "You know the name, don't you?"

She didn't answer.

Instead, she closed Mateo's fingers around his own palm, hiding the mark.

Then she stood.

"We double the watches. Nobody goes below alone. If the sea stays calm again tonight, we row if we have to—but we don't stop moving."

"And if the voice comes again?" Pharaoh asked.

Raven's jaw tightened. "Then I remind her I'm not hers. Not yet."

She turned to John.

"Set course for the edge of the Forgotten Shoals. There's an island unmarked on any charts. Captain Billings once told me, It's where sailors go when they dream of drowning."

Walter blinked. "You think we'll find answers there?"

Raven's eyes darkened. "No. But I think we'll find someone who remembers the question."

Back onboard *Destiny* later that evening, the seas were unusually calm.

The sea was the color of old pewter—flat, sullen, and smooth as polished stone. Not a wave broke. Not a seabird cried.

The masts creaked uneasily as *Destiny* pushed forward under oar and the last threads of sail. The other three ships flanked her, silent silhouettes on the horizon. No one sang. No one laughed.

Raven stood at the stern rail, staring out at the setting sun bleeding red into the sea. The color reminded her of something she'd seen once in a dream—and in the water, when the woman spoke.

She didn't turn when she heard her father's boots behind her.

"Papa," she said quietly, not looking.

He wondered how she knew it was he.

"You knew about the name," she continued, her voice even. "Did Mother?"

John's breath caught. He stepped up beside her, hands resting on the rail. "She did."

"Did *you* hear the voice?"

"No. But she did. Margaret... was always the one they whispered to first." He paused, then added, "You were too young to remember the first time. You were just a baby. She thought the sea would leave you alone."

"But it didn't." Raven turned to face him. "You heard Mateo. You saw the mark. This is no sailor's superstition. This is blood-deep. She's not calling to just *any* girl—she's calling to me. And she's been doing it for years."

John's jaw worked silently before he answered. "There's a name you were never meant to speak. Your mother forbade it. She said if it were ever spoken aloud, it would open something we could never close again."

"She said *that*?"

"She said it would come with a price—even if the reward seemed like treasure. Riches, power... or memory. Something too great to resist. But once it was spoken, you'd belong to the sea."

Raven looked away, voice a whisper. "Did she say what the name *was*?"

John nodded. "She whispered it. Just before she died."

Tears escaped his eyes.

"She claimed it was *given* to her." He hesitated. "By the sea itself."

Raven's heart thudded—the woman in the water.

"Why didn't you *tell* me?" she asked, her voice cracking. "After she died, you made me go to sea. You put me right in the path of whatever this is."

"I didn't know how else to keep you safe," John said. "Or *near*. I felt I could shield you if I were beside you."

Raven turned, walking a few paces away. "You don't protect someone from the sea by putting them in a boat, Papa."

There was silence between them as the sky darkened to bruised purple. The sea below remained unnaturally calm.

Then Raven said, softer now, "What if speaking the name is the only way to end this?"

John looked at her sharply. "Or the way to *start* something worse."

A gust of cold wind whispered suddenly through the rigging—unnatural in the stillness.

Both of them looked up.

On the horizon, black rock rose like teeth from the water. No island had been there minutes before.

It loomed ahead now...craggy and jagged, cloaked in mist, unmarked on any map.

Raven narrowed her eyes.

"She's leading us," she said.

John's voice dropped low. "Or luring us."

Raven turned toward the bow. Her voice was sure, but not without fear.

"Either way, I'm done running."

By midnight, *Destiny* lay at anchor in the shadow of the island along with Raven's three other ships.

No name marked the island. No map claimed it. It hadn't existed on the horizon until they were nearly upon it—and even now, the mists coiled so thick around its jagged cliffs that it seemed to slip in and out of reality with each blink of the eye.

The dory scraped against black sand as Raven leapt ashore, boots sinking slightly in the wet, grainy grit. Pharaoh, Jeffrey, Sean O'Toole, and two others followed behind, blades drawn, eyes wary. Even the ever-defiant Alexander had stayed behind, unwilling to risk too many officers at once.

The beach stretched in both directions, hemmed by sharp cliffs and pale rock twisted like driftwood petrified by fire.

Sean O'Toole murmured, "I've seen lands in the New World that dinnae look this... old." His Irish brogue was thick with unease. "Dis island feels like a place duh sea forgot to drown."

They pressed forward.

No birds. No insects. Only the slap of waves and the crunch of their boots over ancient shells.

A narrow path wound up the slope, half overgrown with strange moss that shimmered under the lantern light. The air grew cooler as they ascended, thick with a scent like salt, stone... and something faintly sweet—decay dressed in perfume.

About halfway up, Pharaoh held up a hand. Everyone froze.

Ahead, half-buried in the hillside, rose a stone monolith. Ten feet tall, cracked down the middle, worn by centuries. Carvings covered its surface—weathered symbols spiraling inward around a single, central shape:

A woman.

Arms outstretched, hair flowing around her like seaweed, her eyes closed, her mouth open as if whispering a name.

Beneath her feet, a line of ancient script curled like waves.

Raven stepped forward slowly. Her breath caught.

"It's the same script," she whispered. "The same as the driftwood."

Jeffrey knelt by the base of the monolith, brushing moss aside. The stone was warm to the touch, pulsing faintly.

"She's waiting," Raven murmured. "This whole island—it's her altar."

Pharaoh stepped back, sword raised, as the shadows seemed to ripple across the ground. "We shouldn't be here."

"No," Raven said. "We *have* to be here."

She reached out and placed her palm on the stone.

Instantly, the wind rushed back.

The mist surged, coiling up around them like hands. The lanterns guttered—then flared with an unearthly blue fire.

And from the trees behind the monument came a *voice*.

Low, melodic. Familiar.

"Speak the name, daughter of salt and sorrow. Speak, and be claimed."

Raven's hand dropped away from the stone. Her chest heaved.

"I... can't," she whispered.

The wind hissed—displeased. The mist retreated only slightly.

But the monolith no longer felt dormant. It hummed beneath her feet like a drumbeat under skin.

"We leave," she said, breathless. "We've seen what we came for."

As they turned back, Sean glanced one last time at the carvings. "She was here once. The woman. Not just a ghost. Not just a voice."

Raven nodded.

"She *is* the island."

And the island had let them leave—for now.

CHAPTER 19

That night onboard *Destiny*, the water was eerily still.

The island remained visible even in the dark—its jagged cliffs outlined in a faint, unnatural glow. No moonlight shone. No stars pierced the sky—just the low pulse of blue light at the summit where Raven had touched the monolith.

Aboard *Destiny*, the crew moved quietly and reluctantly, voices hushed. The usual sounds of a ship at anchor—clinks of chain, creak of rigging, hum of men's chatter—had been replaced with silence, as though the ship itself held its breath.

Raven stood at the stern, watching the island.

She hadn't spoken since returning. Not to Jeffrey. Not even to her father, who watched from the shadows near the helm.

She could still feel the heat of the stone—the beat beneath it, like a second heart.

Below deck, lanterns flickered even though no draft stirred.

Sean O'Toole sat at a table in the galley, a flask in hand. "I've sailed five of duh seven seas, seen a man struck blind by lightning without a storm in sight," he muttered to a nearby sailor, "but never has I felt eyes on me duh way I does now—and they're not human eyes, I tell ya."

Above them, in Raven's cabin, the air had turned thick and heavy.

She lay restless on her bunk, eyes wide open, the ceiling above seeming too low, the wood too close. Every breath took effort.

The whisper began softly, like wind through reeds.

"You felt it, didn't you? The truth beneath the stone. The name lives in you. Let it out. Let *her* out."

Raven bolted upright, drenched in sweat.

She wasn't alone.

A figure stood near the porthole—a shape of a woman, long hair floating as though underwater, her form hazy and wavering like light seen through deep waves.

Raven reached for the dagger beneath her pillow.

But the voice didn't threaten.

"The name is not a curse. It is a gift."

Raven stood, breathing hard. "Why me?"

The woman stepped closer. She was translucent—her face eerily similar to Raven's own, but older, ageless—a twin from another age.

"Because you were born from a promise made long ago. One your mother heard. One your father feared. But you...you carry it still."

Raven clutched the dagger but didn't lift it. "What promise?"

The woman's voice grew fainter, as if pulling away into water.

"Speak it... and you will remember. Speak it... and all you seek will be yours."

She vanished, melting into the shadows.

Raven stood alone in the dark.

Outside, the sea lapped once—only once—against the hull. The first sound the ocean had made in hours.

And then she heard another sound.

From the deck above: a scream.

She rushed up the ladder, blade in hand, just as John met her halfway.

"A man's missing," he said. "One of the Spaniards. No one saw him leave. But there's water in his bunk, and a trail of salt to the railing."

Raven's blood went cold.

"Seal the decks," she said. "Double the watch. No one alone. Tell the other captains to do the same."

John nodded grimly. "Aye, Raven."

Raven looked back toward the island.

It hadn't moved. But she knew it was watching.

And she knew something else, too:

The sea didn't just want her to *remember* the name.

It wanted her to *speak* it.

The lanterns swayed as Raven and John descended into the crew quarters, their light casting long shadows against the timber walls. Behind them trailed Jeffrey and two trusted hands—armed, alert, and grim-faced.

The air below decks felt wrong. Thicker somehow. Moist and tinged with brine.

"Here," said Jeffrey, pointing to the far bunk. "Juan Sánchez. Quiet one. Been with us since we captured *The Sea Witch*. Kept to himself."

The hammock swayed slightly, empty.

The boards beneath were soaked in seawater—too much for a spilled bucket or damp boots. It pooled in the seams of the wood, and tiny bits of seaweed clung to the edges like the ocean had crept in and made itself at home.

Raven crouched beside it. She touched the water. It was freezing cold. "The sea was calm tonight. No way this got here by a leak."

John studied the hammock, frowning. "Salt crust on the edge. And here." He pointed to a handprint—bare, water-marked—on the beam above the bunk. "He left it climbing out."

They followed the trail.

Faint drips. A smear of salt on the railing. One sandal caught in the netting near the stern.

"Why would he come up here barefoot?" Jeffrey murmured.

Raven didn't answer.

She was already moving to the rail, eyes narrowing.

It was there again. That same humming silence. Like the moment before a storm—but no wind, no skyfire. Just pressure.

Raven leaned over the rail. The sea reflected no stars.

Then John hissed, "There. Look...on the water."

Something floated, just beyond the reach of the lantern light.

A body?

No—it moved too gracefully. Too slowly.

A figure.

Juan.

Drifting face-up, eyes open, but blank—mouth parted as if in awe.

He was floating without sinking. Cradled by the sea like a child in its mother's arms.

Then, before anyone could react, *something* rose around him. Dark, flowing tendrils. Not seaweed. Hair. A woman's long, black hair.

And then she was there.

The exact figure Raven had seen in her cabin, now rising from the water like mist becoming flesh. Her eyes glowing faintly, not with malice... but with longing.

Mateo didn't struggle.

He smiled.

And then the sea took him.

The water closed over them both, soundlessly. No splash. No ripples.

Just gone.

Raven turned to John. "Blow the conch. Quiet, three times. All ships. Let them know we're not alone tonight."

John didn't argue.

As the conch blew into the night, Raven stood at the railing, watching the sea shimmer unnaturally, just for a moment.

Behind her, Jeffrey whispered, "What did he see?"

Raven didn't answer.

But in her mind, she heard the whisper again:

"*He has no name left to give.*
But you do."

The low, hollow *moan* of the conch shell echoed across the still waters like a cry from another world.

One long note. Three short. A signal known to every sailor in Raven's fleet.

Not danger. Not battle. Something worse.

"The Sea Has Taken One."

On *The Sea Witch*, Pharaoh stood at the bow, eyes scanning the black water. Lanterns on deck cast flickering reflections that refused to stay still. His crew—half restless Spaniards, half loyal Africans—muttered in their own languages.

When the conch sounded, all fell silent.

Pharaoh turned to his bosun, hand on the hilt of his cutlass. "Double the watch. Torches lit fore and aft. No man alone on deck. And if anyone hears a woman's voice...he doesn't answer. He *runs*."

Some men laughed nervously. Others crossed themselves.

One of the older Spaniards spat over the rail. "She's *La Sirena*. The sea's cursed us for turning our sails away from gold."

Pharaoh's voice was iron. "You think *gold* will help you when the sea swallows your soul?"

Aboard *The Firebird*, Attila stood tall at the quarterdeck, wrapped in his greatcoat, eyes narrowed.

The conch's cry had stirred even the deepest of sleepers. The junior officers scurried to stations as Attila paced to the rail.

"Another taken," he muttered, staring toward *Destiny*.

Beside him, young Jeremy Finch clutched the conch's twin, lips pale.

"She's real, isn't she?" the first mate asked. "The woman in the water?"

Attila didn't answer directly.

"I've seen storms that came from clear skies. Ships vanish without a trace. Men go mad in calm waters. I always thought it was fear, or hunger, or the wind playing tricks."

He looked at Jeremy.

"But this...this is something else. Keep the powder dry. No lights belowdecks. Tonight, we wait."

Aboard *The Royal Victory*, Alexander lit a single lantern in his cabin. The conch's signal had roused him from a restless sleep.

He stood over a map of the Caribbean, but his eyes weren't focused on any port or passage. They were fixed on the tiny symbol Raven had etched onto the chart just hours ago: the island—the one they'd found with the stone that pulsed beneath her hand.

Behind him, his first mate, Hadari, entered. "Word from the deck, sir. Nothing seen, but the men are nervous."

Alexander nodded, jaw tight. "They should be. Fear keeps them cautious. Let it."

He turned back to the chart, one hand resting on the point where *Destiny* now lay at anchor.

"We're in waters charted by none and haunted by many. Let's pray the sea finds us unworthy of her attention."

Back on *Destiny*, Raven stood near the helm, Jeffrey at her side.

The conch still echoed faintly in her ears, like a memory that hadn't faded.

"I saw her," Raven whispered. "She took him gently. Like he was hers already."

Jeffrey's expression was unreadable, but his hand found hers.

"You think she wants you next?"

"No." Raven's voice was cold. "Not next."

She looked out toward the black horizon.

"She wants me *last.*"

Later That Night... Each ship bristled with light—torches, lanterns, even firepots kept ready. No one slept deeply. Songs were not sung. Dice were not thrown. Rum was not poured.

And beneath every hull, something stirred.

Sometimes it was just the current, brushing along the keel.

Sometimes it wasn't.

Far below, where sunlight never touched, the woman in the water waited, arms spread wide—her hair drifting like seaweed, her eyes glowing softly, and her lips moving soundlessly as if singing a lullaby only the dead could hear.

Late in the afternoon of the next day, the winds remained slack as *Destiny* drifted slowly toward the shadow of the island. The sea was too calm. Even the gulls that usually harassed the rigging had vanished.

Raven stood at the bow, spyglass to her eye, studying the craggy coastline. The jungle beyond the rocky shore was dense and black-green, unnaturally still. Not a breeze stirred the canopy. Not a bird cried.

Behind her, the other three ships followed in tense silence, their crews wary, weapons close at hand.

Then George's voice broke through the quiet.

"Something on the water, Captain. Port side."

Raven lowered her glass and turned. It was there, just off their flank.

A shape. No, *several*. Half-submerged. Not drifting wreckage. Not sharks. Not boats.

"Bring us closer," she ordered. "Slow and quiet."

As *Destiny* eased through the still water, the shapes resolved into clarity: statues—dozens of them. Rising from beneath the waves, clustered around a reef that wasn't on any chart.

They were humanoid, but weathered, eroded. Some were missing arms, while others were missing heads. All of them faced inland, toward the island.

Each figure knelt in the water, as if frozen mid-prayer. Seaweed clung to them like ritual garb. Coral sprouted from their eyes. Barnacles crusted their backs.

The water around them shimmered faintly, as if lit from beneath.

Jeffrey came to her side, brow furrowed. "How deep is the reef?"

John answered from behind. "We've got ten fathoms at least. These... shouldn't be standing."

"They're not standing," Raven said. "They're *waiting*."

Suddenly, from the center of the ring of statues, something gleamed—metal, partially buried in the coral shelf.

A disc. No, a *shield*.

Raven motioned. "Launch the dory. I'm going down."

Jeffrey grabbed her arm. "You don't know what's down there."

"Exactly."

Raven dived from the small boat, lungs full, knife strapped to her thigh.

The water down here was colder than expected—*far* colder than expected. It bit into her bones.

She swam toward the gleaming shield. As she neared, she saw the etching on its surface: the same ancient script carved into the stone tablet on the island. The same one that had written her name, though she still couldn't read it.

Except... now, something was changing.

The letters *shifted* under her gaze. Like they knew she was coming.

She reached for the shield.

A *pulse* tore through the water, slamming into her chest.

And then she *heard* it.

A woman's voice—*not in her ears but in her mind*:

"Speak the name.
It was given to you.
It will set you free."

Raven screamed—bubbles tearing from her mouth—and kicked upward.

Jeffrey hauled her up, and she coughed hard, lungs burning.

"I heard her again," she gasped. "She was waiting down there."

"What was she waiting for?" he asked quietly.

Raven turned toward the statues.

"She's waiting for me to speak my name."

The crew fell silent as a sudden breeze stirred for the first time in days, rippling across the surface like a breath from something ancient, exhaled from the heart of the island.

Behind them, *The Royal Victory* signaled with blasts from their conch shell:

"Shall we land?"

Raven stared at the dark trees beyond the reef.

"Yes," she said, voice low. "It's time we walked ashore."

CHAPTER 20

J ust before dusk, on the shoreline of the uncharted island, the surf hissed softly as the longboat scraped against black sand. It wasn't the white or golden sand of the Caribbean—this beach was ashen, like it had once burned and never healed.

Raven jumped out first, boots sinking slightly. The air was hot and still, but thick with the earthy scent of rot and blossoms. Behind her, Jeffrey, John, and a half-dozen armed crew disembarked, weapons ready. George remained in the boat, holding it steady.

The jungle loomed just ahead, impossibly dense, with each tree twisted as if it had grown in pain.

"Papa," Raven said, scanning the treeline. "Post two at the boat. I don't want to leave it unguarded."

"Aye."

As they pushed forward, the air grew damper, heavier, soaked with silence. No birds. No insects. Just the distant, rhythmic sound of dripping water.

Then, the jungle *breathed*.

The undergrowth *shivered*—not from wind, but movement.

The crew froze.

Raven flashed back to her dream of the lost mysterious island that was filled with dangers and creatures the likes of which she had never heard of before. Hopefully, her dream had not become a reality.

She drew her cutlass slowly. Jeffrey's hand dropped to his pistol.

"Something's ahead," he whispered.

A narrow trail revealed itself, vines slowly pulling back as if inviting them forward. It wasn't natural. Not even animal-made.

It was *deliberate*.

John muttered a prayer quietly to himself. One of the Spaniards whispered, "Brujería..." which meant witchcraft.

They followed the trail single-file. Trees leaned overhead like arching ribs. Moss dangled like the remains of rotted sails. A mile in, the trail opened into a clearing, and there it stood.

A monolith.

Black stone. Taller than a man. Covered in carvings that spiraled around it like a snake coiled around prey. At its base, more of the script Raven had seen underwater—etched deep, as if with burning fingers.

Raven stepped closer. The carvings whispered in her mind, words she could hear, but they were just out of reach.

She pressed her palm to the stone.

It *shuddered*.

Behind them, a scream—cut short.

The crew spun around. One man was gone. Vanished. No sound of struggle. No rustling of leaves. Only a single boot, still steaming, sat where he'd stood.

Jeffrey swore and raised his pistol.

"Back to the beach," John barked.

But the trail they came through... was *gone*.

The vines had sealed it.

More whispers now—faint and feminine—surrounding them in the mist.

"The name... the name... the name..."

A wind picked up, though the canopy remained still.

The monolith glowed faintly with bluish veins like lightning caught in stone.

"Draw in close," Raven commanded, eyes never leaving the carvings. "Swords out. No one leaves the circle."

The trees pressed closer.

And deep beneath them, the ground rumbled, soft and distant. Not enough to panic. But just enough to warn them..

Raven's voice was tight. "She knows we're here."

Jeffrey met her eyes. "And she's waiting for you to answer."

The wind was still, but the trees *listened*. The monolith's blue glow pulsed faintly like a heart buried in stone, casting flickering light across the stunned faces of the landing party.

John crouched beside the boot that remained of the vanished sailor. He touched it lightly, then rose, face grim.

"No blood," he said. "No sign he struggled. It's like he... dissolved."

Raven stepped forward, her palm still tingling from touching the stone. "This place isn't cursed. It's alive."

Jeffrey stared at the spiral carvings. "What kind of place breathes? What kind of stone remembers who you are?"

Raven didn't answer. She was staring at the base of the monolith. Something was *changing*.

The ancient writing... was *rearranging itself*.

Carvings twisted, reshaped, one glyph at a time, until a word emerged in letters she still didn't understand—but *recognized*.

Her name. Her *true* name.

Unspoken. Unspeakable. Not Richard. Not Raven. Something *older*.

Her breath caught.

"Say it," the woman's voice whispered again.

"Free me. Free yourself."

The monolith cracked slightly—just a thin line from top to bottom—a sliver of darkness within.

Jeffrey moved beside her, voice urgent. "Do you see it? That writing? It's shifting. It's responding to *you*."

"I see it."

"Do you know what it says?"

"I think it's waiting for me to say it out loud."

"Then don't."

The ground rumbled again. The crew formed a tight circle, blades out, guns drawn. John's eyes swept the jungle.

Then something emerged from the trees.

Not a beast. Not a person.

A *reflection*.

Shimmering and shifting like heat on stone—an echo of Raven, stepping silently out of the forest. She wore no clothes, only seafoam and shadow. Her hair floated as if underwater. Her face was Raven's... and not. A little older. Eyes deeper. Mouth bruised by secrets.

The crew stepped back.

"Don't move," Raven warned.

The figure stared at her with hunger and longing.

Then it *spoke.*

"You're not whole. Not yet. But soon."

It turned and walked into the monolith's crack—vanishing into the stone like mist into glass.

The fissure glowed red now. From within came a sound like distant chanting. Ancient. Syncopated. Female voices in layered harmony.

Jeffrey grabbed Raven's wrist. "We need to leave. Now! I don't care what we learn here. We leave."

"I agree," John said. "Even evil has a rhythm, and this is building to something."

Raven gave the monolith one last look.

"I'm not ready," she whispered. "Not yet."

The fissure dimmed.

And behind them, the path reopened.

The jungle breathed again. The songs of the birds returned. A single parrot squawked from above and flew past.

"Let's go," Raven ordered.

They ran for the shore.

They each ran with a panic to their gaits. They gasped for air, unaware of their surroundings. Their only concern was to reach the shore.

Finally, they broke through the brush that had hindered their pathway back to the beach.

The Beach. The place that meant safety to them. They each sighed between each gasps of new air entering their lungs. Their bodies folded over. Only their hands resting on their knees kept them from falling to the ground.

The longboat was still there, the guards wide-eyed and pale.

"You saw her, too?" one asked. "The reflection in the trees?"

Raven didn't answer.

They shoved off fast, paddling toward *Destiny*. The moment their boat cleared the surf, a strong wind returned, as if the sea had exhaled in relief.

But Raven sat stiff and silent.

Jeffrey leaned close to her. "You didn't say it."

"I wanted to," she admitted. "Every part of me wanted to."

He nodded. "But you didn't."

Her eyes stayed fixed on the monolith, now half-hidden by foliage and shadow.

"No," she whispered. "But I will."

The wind picked up as the dory neared the ship. Sails fluttered. Lines creaked—the comforting sound of a living vessel under tension.

But no one came to greet them.

Not a call. Not a conch.

No faces over the rail. No boots on the stairs.

Just stillness.

Raven stood first, cutlass already drawn, as she climbed the ladder.

The *Destiny* was too quiet.

She stepped onto the main deck and froze. Behind her, Jeffrey and John climbed up—then stopped as well.

The crew was there.

All of them.

Standing in rows. Silent. Eyes wide. Every man and woman aboard.

Their lips moved, but made no sound.

Kifaru stood at the helm, eyes glassy, his hands limp on the wheel. Beside him, Walter Parpart stared at Raven with tears rolling silently down his cheeks.

"What—" Jeffrey began, but Raven held up her hand.

"Listen."

Only then did they hear it.

Not from the mouths of the crew.

But from *below*.

From the hold came a single sound. Soft. Constant.

A woman was humming.

A lullaby. Ancient and wordless.

And then—a voice.

From everywhere, but nowhere.

"You brought her closer. You brought *yourself* closer. Every choice carves the path. Every breath feeds the flame."

Raven's blood went cold.

Jeffrey whispered, "She was onboard."

"No," Raven said. "She *is* onboard."

The ship gave a slight jolt, barely perceptible. But to Raven, it was unmistakable.

"She's in the hull," she said, voice like flint. "Inside the timbers. In the ballast. In the water barrels."

John walked slowly among the frozen crew. Some blinked. Others wept silently. None spoke.

"She didn't kill them," he said. "She *showed* them something."

Raven turned and walked toward the stairs leading below.

Jeffrey grabbed her arm. "Don't."

"She wants something," Raven said. "And until I know what, none of us is safe."

"Raven—"

"She's not going to stop just because I look away."

She descended into the dark.

The humming grew louder. The hold was dim—lanterns flickered, though none had been lit.

Saltwater lapped in the bilges, though the hull was sound—no leaks. The scent of the sea mixed with roses and decay.

In the corner, a barrel had burst open. Water trailed from it in spirals. At its center lay a bundle—a bundle wrapped in seaweed.

Raven stepped closer.

It was the missing sailor's coat.

Inside it—his pistol, his other boot... and his *tongue*.

No blood. Just salt.

As Raven stared, the carvings she had seen on the monolith began to rise on the wooden ribs of the ship, etching themselves into the beams as if the *Destiny* herself had become a scroll for some ancient script.

Jeffrey appeared behind her, his breath catching at the sight.

The last line finished burning itself into the hull. It was still glowing, faint blue.

Raven touched it with her fingertips.

"Say the name," the woman's voice whispered. "Let the sea remember you."

But Raven closed her eyes. Her voice was steady, quiet, firm.

"No."

The humming stopped.

And the lights went out.

On the main deck, the light suddenly returned.

The crew gasped, blinking, clutching each other as if waking from a terrible dream.

Kifaru collapsed to his knees. Walter cried out and ran toward the stairs, calling.

"Raven! Raven!"

She emerged slowly, pale and damp, her eyes distant.

John caught her arm. "What did she do?"

Raven looked up at the sails. The wind had shifted again.

"She's getting closer," she said. "And the next time I say no... I'm not sure she'll listen."

Five days after *Destiny* cut slowly through silver seas, wind light but steady, sails taut with purpose. Yet below the rhythmic groan of timber and rope, something else traveled with the ship.

Silence.

Men and women who had always been jaunty were now quiet. Reserved.

A deep, unsettled silence that clung to every crew member like fog.

Conversations were short. Eyes lingered too long on shadows. Laughter—once abundant—had fled entirely.

Kifaru had not returned to the helm.

He slept most of the day now, waking only to eat in silence, then returning to his hammock as though the weight of the ghost-woman's gaze still pressed on him. He muttered in his sleep. Raven heard it one night when she passed below deck:

"She sees me. She *knows* I ran..."

Walter, young and brave, had changed too. He no longer spoke to Raven unless spoken to. He avoided the sea rail and refused to go near the lower deck, where the carving had appeared. He clutched a small St. Christopher's pendant of his mother's and whispered prayers when he thought no one watched.

Even John, solid as ever, had grown quieter. More watchful.

"Men start to doubt the chain of command when the things they see don't make sense," he told Raven, over a map he hadn't touched in days.

"Some of them think you brought this down on us. Others think you're the only thing keeping it at bay."

"And what do *you* think, Papa?" Raven asked him.

John looked up with a dry smile. "I think if she wanted you dead, she'd have taken your breath instead of Mateo's."

They both went quiet at the name.

Mateo.

His bunk remained empty. His boots still sat beneath it. But no one dared remove them.

On the *Sea Witch*, the Spaniards who had tried to mutiny now worked in subdued silence. Two had taken to wearing rosaries. One whispered prayers in Latin each dawn and dusk. Another had sworn to silence until they left the cursed waters, communicating only through gestures and drawings.

Some swore they saw the woman's reflection in the water when they leaned too far over the side.

Others reported hearing her hum in their dreams.

One night, Raven woke to find Sean O'Toole outside her cabin, sitting cross-legged with his back to the bulkhead, pipe unlit, staring at nothing.

"You alright?" she asked him.

He nodded. "Aye. Just... thinkin'."

"About what?"

Sean looked up, face lined and distant. "About how it is, the sea asks questions we're not ready to answer. And how sometimes, the wrong answer is the only one that fits."

Raven didn't ask what he meant. She already knew.

CHAPTER 21

Mdago's call came from the crow's nest just after midday on the seventh day. Sharp, urgent, and filled with hope:

"Sails! To the east! Big ones—galleons!"

Every crew on all four ships jolted to life.

On *Destiny*, Raven stormed up to the quarterdeck with Jeffrey and John close behind. She raised her spyglass, heart pounding. Sunlight flashed off distant white sails—at least eight, maybe more—crisp and fat like merchant ships, trailing banners of crimson and gold.

"Spanish," John said. "And heavy."

"They're crawling with treasure," murmured one of Charles Turner's young gunners, breathless.

Excitement exploded across the fleet like fire through dry powder. Drums beat on *The Firebird*. The drums were answered on each ship by other drummers. On *The Sea Witch*, the conch shell blew a call to arms. Men shouted and rushed to position—loading cannons, sharpening blades, checking powder.

"They haven't seen us yet," Jeffrey said, scanning the horizon.

"No," Raven muttered, lowering her glass. "But we've seen them."

She hesitated a moment—something in her blood humming.

But the hunger in the crew was undeniable.

"Give chase," she said.

The ships surged forward, sails trimmed for speed. The wind, blessedly strong, bore them like hounds on the scent of a fox. Hours passed as the distance closed—barely. The galleons always seemed just at the edge of reach, always just over the next wave.

Raven stood firm next to Walter at the helm, eyes locked on the shimmering fleet.

"They're running," someone said.

"No," said John softly. "They're *not*. They haven't changed tack once."

The air grew thick.

The sea began to shine too brightly.

The galleons loomed now, massive and slow—but no detail would come into focus. Their hulls were oddly featureless. Their sails didn't flap. And as *Destiny* crested a swell, Raven saw something that twisted her gut—

A wave passed *through* one of the galleons.

Then another.

They weren't ships. They were shadows.

Reflections.

Mirages.

Raven's blood turned to ice. "Pull back," she said. "Back to the line—now."

John's brow furrowed. "They're almost within cannon—"

"They're *not real!*"

He turned.

And then the *Sea Witch's* port-side gunner let loose a warning shot. It sailed clean through one of the galleons—

And vanished.

No splash. No hit. Nothing.

The air shimmered. The illusion rippled, as if stirred by an invisible hand, and then—

The fleet dissolved.

Not slowly.

In an instant.

Dozens of galleons turned to mist, and the mist vanished into the sea. Only open water remained.

The crews stared in stunned silence. All that was left was the gleam of the sun and the distant roll of a deepening fog.

And then a voice—soft, female, almost kind—echoed across the decks of *Destiny*.

"Closer now..."

Raven flinched.

She wasn't the only one who heard it. Mvuvi dropped a line. George backed away from the rail, pale as a bone.

"Conch," Raven rasped.

Muziki raised it and gave a sharp blast.

Bwooooh.

The haunting sound rolled across the waves, a signal to the others: *Retreat.*

But the sea did not calm.

The water shimmered beneath their hulls, whispering as if speaking through the timbers.

Raven closed her eyes and whispered a single word: No one heard her speak it.

Anaíra.

Then, she spoke aloud, "She's testing us."

Jeffrey stood beside her, eyes fixed on the horizon. "Or luring us in."

Behind them, the *Sea Witch* lowered her sails.

One by one, the other ships followed.

The hunt was over.

But no one aboard believed the chase had truly ended.

Raven's Destiny drifted in uneasy silence.

The crew spoke little as they trimmed the sails and adjusted course. The horizon lay empty, as if mocking their chase—no galleons, no treasure, only the memory of illusions and the strange hush that followed.

The water beneath them shimmered unnaturally, disturbed by more than wind or current. Raven stood near the stern rail, one hand gripping the polished wood. Her other hovered near the hilt of her sword.

That voice still echoed in her skull—soft, seductive, and ancient.

Then came the cry.

"Something's in the rigging!"

Raven turned sharply as young Michael Murphy pointed up to the mizzenmast. Something tangled in the lines fluttered faintly, like a torn sail or a jellyfish caught on the ropes.

Jeffrey climbed quickly, his boots thudding against the ratlines as he scaled toward the shape. He reached it in moments, then froze.

"Raven!" he called down. "It's... it's not cloth."

The crew below looked up as he carefully untangled it and began to descend.

He dropped to the deck with the object in hand.

A silence settled again as all eyes fixed on what he held.

It was a length of sailcloth, brittle and salt-stained. Stitched into it with dark, nearly black thread was a symbol—a spiral twisting into an open eye. Ancient, unfamiliar. But unmistakably intentional. Beneath it, faint gold thread traced delicate lines of script that shimmered with a hint of phosphorescence—letters not from any known alphabet.

Raven stepped closer, heart hammering.

"It's her," she said softly.

Jeffrey looked at her. "The woman?"

Raven nodded. "That script... I've seen it before. In my dreams. On the stone."

John peered over her shoulder. "It looks old... older than anything that should float."

Pharaoh, who had just come over from *The Sea Witch*, bent and touched the fabric. He recoiled instantly, hissing under his breath.

"It's cold. Like metal left in snow."

Raven reached down, bracing herself, and touched the cloth.

The moment her fingers met the stitchwork, a voice whispered—not aloud, not in her ears, but deep inside her skull.

"The name is close. It waits beneath the surface."

She staggered back.

Jeffrey caught her.

"What is it?"

Raven took a moment to steady her breath. "It wants me to speak the name. But not just any name. *Mine.*"

Pharaoh glanced uneasily from the sailcloth to the sea. "The fleet was never meant to be captured. This... this was the real message."

At that moment, a gust of wind stirred for the first time in hours. A single feather—white, pure, and waterlogged—fell from the sky and landed on the deck beside the sail fragment.

Raven looked up.

But there were no birds.

No clouds.

No explanation.

Only sky, sea, and the long shadow of the woman in the water.

The rain beat softly on the roof of the small house at the edge of Bristol. Raven—twelve years old and newly motherless—sat cross-legged on the floor of the upstairs flat, the scent of lavender and old wood thick in the air.

Her mother's chest had been tucked beneath the eaves, long unopened. John Ashworth had said it contained only Margaret's "girlhood things," but today, as grief gnawed a hollow in Raven's chest, she opened it.

Inside were silk scarves wrapped in waxed cloth, a small locket with a miniature painting of Margaret and a man Raven didn't recognize, a sachet of dried herbs, and—

—a book.

Bound in leather, the color of dried blood, the cover bore no title. Raven hesitated before picking it up. It was oddly warm to the touch despite the chill of the loft. She opened it slowly.

Most of the pages were blank.

But near the middle, pressed flat as if someone had once stared at it long and hard, was a single sheet inked in fading sepia.

There it was.

The *symbol*.

A spiral twisting into an eye, almost pulsing beneath her fingertips. Below it, that same flowing script, curved lines that reminded her of waves and wind and bones. Raven stared at it, her young fingers tracing the unfamiliar lines.

The moment she touched the ink, her vision blurred. The loft melted around her. She smelled salt. Heard waves.

And then—**a voice.**

"She is called, though the world would keep her silent."

The sensation passed as quickly as it came. Raven blinked and looked around. Everything was as it had been. Except—

The ink on the page was fresh.

She snapped the book closed and tucked it deep into the folds of her cloak, her breath coming fast.

She didn't tell her papa. Something inside her said not to. Whether out of fear or reverence, she didn't know.

But the first night on *Destiny*, curled up in her hammock for the first time, she dreamed of the ocean. A woman's voice whispered beneath the waves. She woke with the taste of salt on her lips—and a name on her tongue that she couldn't remember by morning.

And now, standing years later on the deck of her ship with that same symbol in her hands, she understood:

This had never been about chasing gold.

The sea had been chasing *her*.

Morning broke in hazy bands of silver across *Raven's Destiny's* deck. The air was still thick with the memory of vanished ships and strange cloth caught in the rigging. But Raven's mind was elsewhere—buried in the folds of a dream that hadn't felt like a dream at all.

The book.

The symbol.

Her mother's voice, whispering just beneath the surface of sleep.

"She is called, though the world would keep her silent…"

Raven found her papa at the stern rail, his hands clasped behind his back, watching the sea roll on without wind.

"Papa," she said quietly.

He turned with a half-smile. "You slept little."

"I dreamed," she said. "Do you remember the old trunk in the loft? Mama's things?"

His smile faltered. "I remember."

"I found a book there. After she died. You told me not to touch her things, but I—"

"I know," he said gently. "I knew you had."

She paused. "There was a page in it. A spiral and an eye. With strange writing. I didn't understand it then. But I saw it again yesterday—in the sailcloth. The one caught in the rigging."

John went still. The air between them seemed to tighten.

Raven swallowed, voice barely above a whisper now. "Papa… was Mama a witch?"

John turned away and looked out at the sea for a long time. The wind barely stirred his hair. His silence spoke volumes more than any words could.

Then at last, he spoke.

"She wasn't a witch," he said softly. "Not in the way people mean it. She didn't curse or conjure storms. She didn't brew poisons in the night."

"But she *knew* things," Raven said. "Things no one should."

He nodded slowly. "Yes. She did. Your mother was… touched by something old. Something that lives in the tide, between waking and sleep. She came from a line of women who listened to the sea—and sometimes, it whispered back."

Raven's breath caught. "She heard the woman too, didn't she?"

John looked at her then. His eyes were tired, sad, but steady. "Yes. And she feared for you from the moment you were born. Not because you were cursed, but because the sea *recognized* you. Like it once did her."

The deck creaked beneath them. Somewhere aloft, a conch shell sounded—one of the other ships signaling a course correction.

"I should have told you long ago," John said. "But I hoped… if I didn't speak it, maybe it would leave you alone."

Raven shook her head slowly. "It won't. She wants me to say my name."

John paled. "You mustn't."

"She said I would be rewarded."

"And she will lie," he said fiercely. "Raven, she will *always* lie. That voice belongs to something that's been drowning women like your mother for a thousand years."

Raven looked away, jaw clenched. "I think Mama wanted me to know. Why else leave that book where I'd find it?"

John exhaled, the weight of too many years pressing down. "Maybe she did. But if she did… it wasn't to lead you to the sea. It was to help you *resist* it."

A silence passed between them, heavy as the waves below.

Then Raven nodded once.

But in her heart, the voice still echoed.

Say your name.

Later that evening, the sky bled hues of bruised lavender and iron. *Destiny* sailed slower than usual—partly because the wind was reluctant, partly because her captain had not yet given the order to push her harder.

Below the quarterdeck, in Raven's cabin, the storm was already gathering.

A different kind of storm.

"You should have told me," Raven said, her voice sharp but not yet raised. "All those years I asked about her—about why she walked alone on the cliffs, about why she sang to the sea at night. You gave me *stories*. Pretty ones. Safe ones."

John sat stiffly in the chair across from her desk, arms folded like a soldier braced for cannon fire. "You were a child. She *was* dangerous."

"No. She was *scared.* And she was trying to prepare me for something I didn't even know was coming."

He stood abruptly, pacing to the wall where an old map of the Windward Islands hung, curling at the edges. "What was I supposed to do? Tell a twelve-year-old girl that her mother drowned in her own dreams? That the sea still *calls* to her through you?"

"Yes," Raven said bitterly. "You were supposed to *tell me the truth.*"

John turned back to her, jaw clenched. "The truth would've taken you from me faster than the sea ever could. I thought if I kept you close, if I raised you on the decks of a ship we sailed on together, I could protect you."

"I'm not yours to protect anymore, Papa. I'm not a girl hiding as a boy in trousers with salt in his hair. I'm the captain now. *Of four ships.*"

"And still just one daughter," he snapped.

The silence that followed rang louder than a cannon's roar.

Raven stepped back, breath caught in her throat. John's eyes softened as soon as he said it, but it was too late.

"I know that," she said quietly, almost to herself. "I've *always* known that."

She crossed to the cabinet near her bunk and pulled the old leather-bound book from its hiding place. She dropped it on the table between them with a solid thud.

"She left this for me. Not you. Me. And I think deep down, you always feared that more than anything—that one day I'd open it."

John's shoulders sagged. "I feared it would *change* you."

Raven's eyes glinted with something too old for her face. "It already has."

He stepped forward, reaching for her shoulder. "Raven—"

She pulled back. "Not tonight, Papa."

He hesitated, then nodded once, stiffly. "As you wish, Captain."

She winced at the word. It felt like a blade in place of a name.

John turned and left without another word, the door clicking shut behind him.

Raven stood in the silence for a long time, staring at the book, the symbol burned into the cover like a wound that wouldn't close.

Finally, she sat at the desk, opened it, and began to turn the pages.

The spine creaked like an old hull under pressure as Raven opened the leather-bound book.

The pages were aged but cared for—edges frayed, ink faded in places, but no sign of mildew or sea-wear. A preservation that felt... intentional. As though the book had been protected not just from weather...not from water, but from time.

Raven had flipped through it before, skimming sea shanties and herbal remedies, markings of constellations, even a few lullabies she half-remembered hearing Margaret sing when she was very small. But this time, something shifted.

There, toward the back. A page that hadn't been there before. Or perhaps... hadn't been *visible*.

The script shimmered faintly in the lantern light, written in a delicate, looping hand that wasn't ink—it was something more like silver ash. As she angled the page, words surfaced like shipwrecks rising from the deep.

Anaira Ashworth.

If you are reading this, the sea has already whispered your name.

You heard it, didn't you?

Raven's breath caught. *Anaira*—a name never spoken aloud in her life. The name buried in that strange dream. The name etched into the stone beneath the clearing. The name she had begun to suspect... was *hers*.

Her mother's handwriting continued:

I wanted to tell you. I begged for time. But your father feared what I had become, and feared more what you might be. He loved us both in different ways—but he feared me more than he could admit.

The sea speaks to women in our line. We do not worship it—we remember it. We are part of it. Not witches, as men call us. We are something older.

You must not speak the name until the time is right. Not in anger. Not in desperation. You'll know the moment when it comes. And when you do... the tide will turn.

Raven's hand trembled as she reached the bottom of the page. There, in even more faded letters, barely legible:

I will wait for you on the other shore. Not in death. In awakening.

She stared, the flame in the lantern crackling suddenly, flaring as if the page had breathed.

A soft knock came at the cabin door.

Jeffrey's voice. "Love? Are you all right?"

Raven shut the book quickly but gently, as if afraid to lose the spell.

"Yes," she called. Then softer: "No. Come in."

He entered, eyes immediately searching hers. "You've been crying."

"I haven't," she lied. Then added, "But I might."

Jeffrey crossed the room and put his arms around her. For once, she didn't resist. Her cheek rested against his chest as the weight of generations pulled heavy in her bones.

"She knew," Raven whispered. "My mother. She *knew everything*. And she tried to tell me."

"What did she say?"

Raven closed her eyes.

"She said the sea isn't done with me. And I don't think it ever will be."

CHAPTER 22

Raven leaned into Jeffrey's embrace, her mother's book still warm from her hands. The candlelight played against the wall like dancing shadows, as if the sea itself had crept into the cabin to listen.

Jeffrey's hand brushed a lock of her hair behind her ear. "You've been different ever since that ghost spoke your name. And now this..." His voice was low, cautious. "It's like the wind's blowing through you, and I'm afraid I won't know who you are when the storm hits."

Raven pulled away enough to look at him. "Do you think I'll change? That I'll... become something else?"

"I don't know," he admitted. "But I've seen it in your eyes lately. Something is *calling* you. And I can't follow you there—not all the way."

She took a deep breath, steadying herself. "I'm not sure I want to follow it either."

"But you will," he said gently.

They remained quiet for a moment. Then his hand found hers, rough fingers curling around calloused ones.

"I'm not afraid *of* you," Jeffrey added. "I'm afraid *for* you because the sea doesn't give back what it claims. And if it's your name it wants..."

He stopped himself, jaw clenched.

Raven nodded slowly. "It *is* my name. My true name."

He swallowed hard. "Then, when the time comes—when you speak it—I'll be at your side. No matter what it brings."

"You can't promise that," she said, half a smile breaking through the ache. "You're a sailor. You *know* not to sail into storms."

"I do," he replied. "But I married the storm."

They remained quiet again.

Raven let out a shaky laugh. "Fool."

Jeffrey kissed her temple. "The biggest."

She leaned into him again, the book closed on the desk beside them, silent, but still humming with unspoken words. Outside the hull, the sea was quiet. Too quiet.

But it wouldn't stay that way.

Mr. Hardy approached Raven the next day.

"Cap'n, we're running low on supplies. Ye might want to think about finding a harbor for us to supply up."

Raven looked to the eastern sky, then to the west.

"Alright, Mr. Hardy. We'll find the nearest settlement to resupply all the ships."

Raven looked back toward the quarterdeck where John was standing. Things were still a little tense between the two of them, but each was able to conduct themselves in a professional manner anyway.

"Mr. Ashworth?"

"Aye, Captain."

"Please set a course for Grenada. Mr. Hardy says we need to resupply."

"Aye, Captain."

"Be sure and have Muziki blow the signal to the other ships, please."

"Aye, Captain."

By the next morning, Raven's fleet arrived at Port Royal.

The harbor at Port Royal shimmered under a molten sun, its jade-blue waters deceptively calm. Palm trees swayed lazily in the breeze while gulls cried overhead, circling above the masts of the anchored fleet. Locals moved along the docks, hauling crates and shouting in Creole, as the smell of salt, citrus, and roast pork drifted over the bay.

It was almost peaceful.

Too peaceful.

Raven watched the crew unload barrels from *Destiny's* rowboats onto the quay that had been carved from ancient stone. *The Sea Witch, The Royal Victory*, and *The Firebird* were docked nearby, their flags fluttering faintly. Resupply was long overdue—fresh water, salted meat, rope, powder, rum. All of it being loaded in and accounted for.

Pharaoh was already bartering with a port merchant over limes, Alexander had vanished into the nearest tavern with his coat flaring like a hero from a stage play, and Attila was barking in three languages at a man trying to overcharge him for canvas.

Jeffrey stood beside Raven on the sun-warmed stone of the wharf. "It almost feels like a holiday."

"Almost," she said.

She didn't trust it. The sea had been quiet too long. And her mother's book still lay in her cabin, wrapped in oilskin as if it might burn the ship down from within.

Raven turned toward the shadowed edge of the pier—an alley where a breeze shouldn't have existed... yet one stirred her coat all the same.

A whisper.

Her name. Not "Raven." The other one. The one that still tasted like blood and saltwater when she heard it in her sleep.

Anaíra...

She stepped toward the alley. Jeffrey followed, frowning. "What is it?"

"Stay here," she said. "Just for a minute."

She turned the corner.

And there he was.

Geoffrey Neely.

Dressed in the same soaked and rotting navy coat he'd died in—buttons tarnished, eyes hollow, one boot still squelching as he stepped forward like a man half-drowned. He didn't look *frightening*, exactly... but he looked *wrong* against the sunlit market behind her.

"Ye came," he said, voice like wet rope dragging through a grave.

"I didn't come for you," Raven said.

Neely grinned, teeth shadowy and uneven. "Ye never do. But I'm always waitin'."

"What do you want?"

"Same thing as last time. To warn ye."

"Warn me of what?"

Neely's grin faded. He looked toward the sea, then back at her.

"They're stirring."

"Who?"

"The dead beneath the water. The ones who sleep in coral and bone. The ones she's been gatherin'. There's a tide coming, girl. And it's not made of salt and foam—it's made of *names*."

Raven's jaw tightened.

"You heard it again, didn't ye?" he rasped. "The woman. The voice. Beggin' you to speak it."

"I haven't," she lied.

Neely shook his head. "The sea doesn't ask twice, Raven. It *waits*. And the longer you resist, the more she'll take from ye. Bit by bit. Men first. Then ships. Then memory. And at the end of it... your soul."

She glared. "Why do you care?"

He looked at her for a long, quiet moment. The way a drowned man might look at someone still standing on the shore.

"Because I didn't speak my name when I should have," he said. "And now I belong to her. But you...you might still be *free*."

The alley behind her brightened—Jeffrey calling her name.

Raven turned back, just for a second.

When she looked again, Neely was gone.

Only water ran along the cracks of the cobblestone now—a thin trail leading back toward the sea.

It took the ships two days to resupply. Everyone's hearts seemed to lighten as they spent time on shore.

Charles, Walter, and George explored what to them was an ancient port city, with its cobblestone streets, stone buildings, and vendors on the streets who hawked their wares to passersby.

Sailors were disappointed when the call came that their ships would be out to sea again.

They reluctantly strolled back to their respective ships and began the work of preparing their ships to move back out into the open seas.

The wind sighed low through the rigging, and the warm scent of sea salt and wood oil filled the cramped cabin. Raven stood at the chart table, her hand pressed flat against the leather-bound journal she had taken from her mother's chest—the one hidden beneath false boards in her father's bedroom.

John Ashworth watched her from the shadows, his arms crossed over his chest, jaw tight. The lines around his eyes were deeper tonight, carved from years of silence.

"You knew," Raven said. Her voice was quiet. Not accusing—yet. "You knew there was more to her than you ever told me."

He didn't answer right away. The ship groaned softly, as if it, too, were straining under the weight of the truth.

"I knew," he said finally. "But I hoped it would die with me."

She opened the journal, pages fluttering to the one that mattered—the one with the **symbol**, etched faintly in her mother's hand. The same symbol they'd seen etched on the stone near the woman in the water. The same symbol that was now burned into Raven's dreams.

And beneath it, in ink faded by time and salt air:

"Anaíra. The name must remain hidden."

"I remember hearing it once," Raven whispered. "She called me sometimes, when she thought I was asleep. And this... Anaíra... this is what the sea calls me."

John turned away, his hand gripping the edge of the porthole frame. "Your mother was part of something older than any chart, older than these islands. She didn't often speak of it. Said it was dangerous. Said the sea remembers."

"Was she a witch?" Raven asked again, heart pounding.

He turned slowly. "You've asked me that already. No. Not in the way men mean when they spit that word. She was a daughter of the deep. As was her mother before her. They bore names the sea could not forget. And when they spoke their true names, the sea gave them power—and cursed them for it."

Raven swallowed hard. "Why didn't you tell me?"

"Because Margaret made me swear I wouldn't," he said. "Said it would come for you soon enough. Said if you spoke the name before you were ready, it would own you." His voice broke slightly. "I lost her trying to keep you safe."

She stared down at the page again. *Anaíra.*

"I don't feel owned," she said quietly.

"Not yet," he said. "But the sea is patient."

A long silence stretched between them.

"Do you know what it means?" she asked. "The name?"

He shook his head. "Only that it's older than English. Maybe older than words. Your mother said it was *a key and a chain.* I never understood what she meant."

Raven closed the journal slowly.

"I need to understand it," she said.

"I know," he replied. "Just promise me you won't speak it. Not until you're sure you're ready to pay whatever price it asks."

Raven stepped toward the door, then paused, glancing back. "And if I never speak it?"

He looked at her then, truly gazing at her. "Then you'll always be a captain. But you'll never be a queen."

The sky was velvet black later that night, scattered with stars that shimmered like shattered glass. The sea was calm, a vast mirror stretching to the horizon, with the ships swaying in the water as they headed eastward. Lanterns burned low across the fleet, their glow soft and steady.

Raven stood at the quarterdeck rail, elbows resting against the weathered wood, eyes fixed on the water below. She didn't look up when she heard footsteps behind her. She knew them—knew the quiet confidence of her husband's stride.

Jeffrey stopped beside her, silent for a moment.

"Your father's sleeping now," he said quietly. "Looked like he'd aged ten years when he came below."

Raven let out a breath. "He's been carrying it a long time."

Jeffrey didn't ask what. He just waited.

Raven's eyes never left the sea. "My name isn't Raven," she said. "Not really."

Jeffrey turned to her slowly, brows drawn.

"My mother called me something else," she said. "A name she never meant me to hear. And my father confirmed it tonight. Anaíra."

He let the name settle between them like a stone dropped in deep water. "It sounds like something the sea would whisper," he said.

"It *was* the sea," Raven whispered. "I've heard it before. Dreams. Whispers. I used to think I imagined it. But now... I don't know. My mother came from something older than anything I understand. She was part of it. And I might be too."

Jeffrey nodded slowly. "Do you believe it?"

"I do," she said. "Not just because my father finally admitted it, but because it *feels* true. Like something buried deep in me has always known it."

He took her hand gently. "What does it mean?"

"I don't know," she said. "My father said it's a key and a chain. That to speak it aloud might bind me to something, or unlock something. Maybe both."

"Are you going to say it?"

Raven shook her head. "Not yet. I'm not ready to be owned by the sea. Not until I know what it wants from me."

Jeffrey leaned in closer, lowering his voice. "And if the sea wants a queen?"

She turned to him, eyes dark and unreadable. "Then it'll have to wait until I decide whether I want the crown."

A gull cried softly in the distance, and the sails creaked overhead. For a moment, it felt as though even the stars leaned in to listen.

Jeffrey squeezed her hand. "Whatever happens, Anaíra or Raven or Red Queen of the Sea—you're still the woman I married."

She gave a small, tired smile. "Then you're braver than I thought."

He shrugged. "I married a pirate. Madness was part of the deal."

They stood together in silence, watching the stars dance over the still water, the name *Anaíra* echoing silently in the spaces between the waves.

CHAPTER 23

It was midnight on the open sea. The moon had long since dipped behind thick clouds, casting the sea into deep shadows. Most of the crew was asleep below, their dreams restless after weeks of haunting winds and empty waters. Only a skeleton watch manned the rigging, quiet as ghosts themselves.

Raven sat alone on the foredeck beneath the bowsprit, knees drawn up, cloak pulled tight around her shoulders. The stars were hidden behind the clouds, but the water shimmered—just faintly—with a silver gleam, as though reflecting light that wasn't there.

She stared out at the waves, her mind turning over the name again and again: *Anaíra.*

A whisper stirred.

It didn't come from the sails, or the crew, or even the sea breeze. It came from *beneath* the water.

Soft, yet coaxing.

"Anaíra..."

She froze.

The air around her changed. Grew thick. Heavier. The sound of the sea grew muffled, as if she were listening through cotton. The hull of *Destiny* groaned, a low, deep vibration that pulsed beneath her fingertips.

Then... a splash.

But not a single one.

Hundreds.

She leaned forward, gripping the rail, peering over the edge.

Below, rising from the depths, came lights—small, pulsing spheres of bluish-white glow. Dozens of them, maybe more, drifting upward like fireflies in water. They gathered beneath the bow like an audience. And in the center of them, a shape.

A woman.

Her skin was pale like moonlight. Her hair flowed black in the current. Her face was obscured, but her presence felt unmistakable, familiar, and ancient.

She raised one hand, palm open toward Raven.

And though her mouth did not move, Raven heard her again.

"Speak your name. Take your place."

Raven's breath caught in her throat. Her hand trembled at her side.

"Anaíra," she whispered—not fully, not yet aloud, but the syllables escaped her lips.

The woman's eyes—impossibly blue—flared bright beneath the surface.

Then, suddenly, the lights scattered like startled minnows. The woman dissolved into foam and shadow. The sea went black again.

Behind her, Jeffrey's voice broke the silence, quiet but urgent.

"Raven? Are you all right?"

She turned. Her eyes shimmered.

"I saw her," she said. "And she saw me. She's waiting for me to finish the name."

Jeffrey moved to her quickly, wrapping his arm around her shoulders.

"And will you?" he asked.

Raven looked back out at the dark waves.

"I think... the sea is waking up, Jeffrey. And it's remembering me."

As morning dawned, the eastern sky bloomed with a bluish lavender and orange hue, but the horizon remained strangely indistinct, as if the world had forgotten how to draw its edges.

Raven stood beside Jeffrey at the rail, her eyes bloodshot from a night without sleep. Below, the crew stirred, sluggish and bleary-eyed, yet alert. Something had shifted in the night. Even those who'd slept had felt it—an unshakable presence pressing down on their dreams like a tide.

From *The Sea Witch*, a conch shell blew—a single, low note that drifted over the water like a funeral bell.

A lookout aboard *The Firebird* shouted something unintelligible.

Then, from *The Royal Victory*, a sharp voice rang out.

"Captain! To starboard!"

Raven turned her spyglass.

And the breath caught in her chest.

There, just beyond the edge of the morning fog, a fleet floated silently—not Spanish, not English. Ghostly. Colorless. Ships with no banners, no sails catching wind. Their masts rose like skeletal fingers from decks slick with sea rot. Lanterns burned on their prows with blue flames that did not flicker.

But it wasn't the ships that chilled the blood.

It was what floated above them.

A shape hung in the sky like a tattered flag—a veil, translucent and rippling in the windless air. Upon it was a symbol, drawn in some script none could read, but one Raven *recognized* from her dream, from her mother's old belongings.

The same twisting mark—circular, ancient, like a serpent biting its tail.

The air grew cold. The water stilled.

Then the fleet was gone.

No splash. No wind. No fading into mist. Just... gone.

Raven let her arm fall, spyglass hanging limp at her side.

The rest of the captains hailed across the water. No one shouted. The crews spoke in low tones, heads turning to their captains like children seeking comfort.

Pharaoh's voice carried across from *The Sea Witch*.

"That was no trick of light, Raven. I saw them too."

"So did I," said Alexander from *The Victory*. "That mark in the sky—I've seen it carved into stone. In old ruins. Always worn away."

Attila stood at the stern of *The Firebird*, both hands clenched on the rail. "They want something."

Jeffrey turned to Raven, his voice quiet. "They're calling for *Anaíra*, aren't they?"

Raven didn't answer. Her heart thundered in her chest like a storm against the timbers.

Instead, she looked west—toward the open sea, toward the deep—and whispered, *"Not yet."*

The morning fog never fully lifted.

Though the sun climbed high, it cast no warmth, only a pale glow that seemed to bleach color from the sails and drain life from the sea. The crew of *Destiny* moved quietly, glancing often at the sky or sea with sidelong eyes, muttering prayers in whispers.

Some scraped barnacles from the hull just to keep their hands busy. Others sharpened blades they wouldn't need that day.

In the galley, Mr. Hardy's cookpots sat cold—no one had an appetite.

Raven stood with Pharaoh, Attila, and Alexander in her cabin, a map of the Lesser Antilles spread before them. Her finger hovered over a dark patch of water no one had ever dared to chart.

"They're drawing us toward something," she murmured.

"They?" Alexander asked.

"The woman. The ships. The mark in the sky." Her eyes flicked up. "You all saw it."

Pharaoh gave a slight nod. "It looked like something I once saw carved into a reef stone off Madagascar. The elders there said it was a curse mark. A warning."

Alexander leaned back. "My Spaniards told me, in Spain, the Church burned women for drawing signs like that. They said it called the sea's daughters."

"They weren't wrong." Raven's voice was low.

A knock came at the door.

Jeffrey entered, followed by Sean O'Toole, the older Irish sailor with sea-gray eyes and wind-worn hands.

"Captain," Sean said, twisting his cap in his fingers. "Beggin' yer pardon, but... I tink I know dat mark."

Raven's brow rose. "How?"

Sean pulled a scrap of oilcloth from inside his vest. He laid it on the table. Faded ink, nearly gone, but just visible—a spiraling symbol with pointed ends, nearly identical to what hung in the sky that morning.

"I was a wee lad aboard *The Wexford Queen* when we anchored near an island not found on any map. It had a circle o' stones at its heart, and dis mark on every one o' dem. The captain said to steer clear, but..." His voice faltered. "One night, we heard singing in duh water."

Pharaoh leaned forward, intrigued. "And?"

"We left men behind. Men who followed duh voice. They walked into duh surf like it be calling dare mother's name. The rest of us... we sailed like duh devil hisself was chasing."

He looked Raven square in the eye.

"Dat was near twenty-five year ago. But I never forgot dat symbol. It's a summoning mark, Captain. Calls to someting old. Hungry."

A silence fell over the room.

Jeffrey reached for Raven's hand. "What do you want to do?"

Raven stared at the symbol. It wasn't inked on paper anymore. It burned in her dreams. It shimmered in the morning sky. And she remembered now—*her mother* tracing that same pattern on her back when she was a little girl, humming a lullaby that made the air hum.

"They're drawing closer," she said. "And I think it's because I'm getting closer to saying it."

"Saying what?" Sean asked.

"My name," she said. "My true name."

Three days later, the sea was too still.

Even the gulls had vanished from the sky. Only the soft moan of the wind across the rigging gave any hint that the world still breathed.

A call came from *Destiny's* crow's nest.

"Ships ahoy! I make them to be Spanish galleons."

Raven stood atop *Destiny's* quarterdeck, the long spyglass raised to her eye, its lens fixed on the horizon. Behind her, Jeffrey waited silently. Aboard the other ships—*The Sea Witch*, *The Royal Victory*, and *The Firebird*—the crews watched too, their gazes drawn not to the glassy sea, but to what loomed beyond it.

A wall of darkness.

It rose like a mountain from the ocean, churning with angry clouds and streaked with forks of blue fire. The leading edge was a knife of rain, sweeping low and fast across the sea. And caught in its path—tiny against the vast black—were five Spanish ships.

"They've seen it," Pharaoh's voice crackled across the conch shell relay. "They're trying to turn."

But it was too late.

Even from this distance, Raven could see the chaos unfold. Sails snapped as wind slammed into canvas. One of the galleons tilted, its mast groaning under the strain. Another ship began to drift sideways, rudder broken or seized, its decks a frenzy of scrambling sailors.

"They won't make it," Raven said flatly, lowering the glass.

"No," Jeffrey agreed, voice low.

Aboard *The Sea Witch*, the Spaniards under Pharaoh's command fell into a hush, crossing themselves. They recognized the flags of their homeland—Castile, León, the Cross of Burgundy—and some whispered names, perhaps of kin.

But none would raise a hand to help. The storm was coming too fast.

Lightning lanced across the sea like a blade slicing the sky, briefly illuminating the doomed ships.

One galleon's powder magazine ignited in the chaos, and a thunderous roar echoed across the water. A fireball erupted where the ship once floated, then was snuffed instantly as the rain smothered the flames and swallowed the wreck.

The others fared no better.

One by one, the ships were taken—broken by the wind, overturned by the waves, or simply dragged into the depths by forces unseen.

No cries reached *Destiny*. No sound but the wind and the rising rumble of thunder. Raven's hair whipped around her face as the first cold drops struck her skin.

Then the strangest thing of all happened: **the storm stopped moving**.

Just as it neared the place where Raven's fleet waited—calm but ready—it halted. The wall of black clouds stood at a fixed distance, wind howling at its edge but never crossing over. It was as though the sea itself had drawn a boundary.

The storm turned away.

It curled back eastward, back toward the open sea, leaving only churned water and broken timbers behind. The last mast of the Spanish galleon slipped beneath the waves like a vanishing hand.

Raven stood in silence.

Jeffrey whispered, "They were a sacrifice."

She didn't answer. She couldn't. Her thoughts were on the woman in the water—on the way the clouds had shaped her face in Raven's dreams.

Pharaoh's voice echoed once more from the conch shell, grim and hollow:

"Real ships. Real men. Gone without a chance."

Raven nodded slowly. "She's warning us. Or threatening. I can't tell which."

The water was still again. Too still.

And far below the keel of *Destiny*, something ancient stirred.

Night came again with no stars.

The sea was unnaturally calm again, as if the storm had scoured the world clean and left only silence behind. Raven stood alone on *Destiny's* forecastle, her hands resting on the rail, her eyes on the black water that lapped gently against the hull. The shattered remnants of the Spanish fleet had long since sunk beneath the waves. Not even a barrel floated now. It was as if they'd never existed at all.

Jeffrey had tried to speak to her after dinner, but she'd asked for time. He understood. He always did.

Still dressed in her rain coat, the collar turned up against the breeze, she looked out to sea and whispered, "Why them?"

She felt no triumph in their deaths. They had been enemies, yes—but sailors all. Men who loved the sea, who feared it, who died in service to a flag or gold or maybe just the promise of surviving one more voyage.

The storm had swallowed them whole like a beast... and then turned aside. Why?

She knew the answer. Felt it like a stone in her chest.

Because it wasn't *them* the sea wanted.

It was *her*.

She pressed her palm to her chest, right where her heart beat slow and heavy. That same pull, that same whisper in the dark part of her dreams—the voice of the woman in the water. Not screaming now, not commanding—but waiting.

Waiting for her to speak the name.

"Why do you want it?" Raven murmured into the night. "Why me?"

The wind didn't answer. But the ocean shimmered strangely under the moonless sky, and for just a moment-no more than a heartbeat—she saw the glint of gold beneath the water. A flash, like the edge of a crown. Then gone.

Raven shuddered and backed away from the rail.

She turned and strolled across the deck, her boots quiet on the damp planks. The crew gave her space—whether out of respect or unease, she didn't know. All of them had seen the storm stop short. All of them had seen the sea choose.

She paused by the mainmast, her hand brushing the salt-stained wood. Somewhere high above, the conch shell tied to the rigging swayed slightly in the breeze. It didn't sound, but Raven heard something all the same.

A name, almost spoken.

Not Raven. Not Richard.

Anaíra.

She closed her eyes and whispered, "Not yet."
And the sea, for now, was silent.

226

CHAPTER 24

The fleet had not spoken of the storm since the day it passed. But something darker had taken its place—an unease that crept into the bones of every ship, thick as mildew and twice as hard to shake.

Each night, the wind whispered over the decks in a tongue no one could quite understand. The sea was too calm. The lanterns burned low and strange. And every few nights, someone claimed to see her.

The Lady in the Water.

She never climbed aboard. Never spoke aloud. She simply floated—just beyond the edge of the ship's light—watching. Her pale face just beneath the surface, hair drifting like seaweed, her eyes fixed on those above as if waiting for one of them to say her name.

On *The Sea Witch*, the Spaniards had begun to break.

Pharaoh stood grim on the quarterdeck, fists clenched behind his back, watching as two men were lowered into the sea—one wrapped in canvas, the other still bare, his body twisted from a long fall from the rigging.

"He jumped," whispered a deckhand near the rail. "Said he heard her whispering in his ear. Said she called him by name...Marco."

Raven, arriving silently from her dory, caught the last words as she stepped aboard.

"He said she promised him peace," the man finished. "Said the only way to silence the voice was to go to her."

Pharaoh turned sharply. "Enough."

The man nodded quickly and fled below.

Raven stepped up beside her friend, scanning the weary, pale faces of the crew. "That's the third this week," she said softly.

Pharaoh gave a curt nod. "Only the Spaniards. The Africans—your people—they ignore her. They spit over the rails and chant prayers. But the Spaniards... they see a ghost in every wave."

Raven's jaw tensed. "She's not finished. Not until I speak the name."

Pharaoh looked sideways at her. "And will you?"

Raven said nothing.

From *The Royal Victory*, a conch shell blew—a single, hollow call. Alexander's signal. Another man lost. Another one drawn to the sea.

Later that night, Raven stood watch from *Destiny's* quarterdeck, eyes sweeping the black waves. Beneath the surface, the water shimmered with faint, unnatural light.

Jeffrey joined her, silent.

"She's closer now," Raven murmured.

He didn't ask how she knew. He just slipped his hand into hers.

Somewhere in the dark, a soft voice echoed over the water.

One of the Spaniards on *The Firebird* began to scream.

Night still clung to the fleet like a damp shroud when the single, ragged scream shattered the hush.

Raven didn't hesitate. She leapt onto *Destiny's* dory before it touched the water, boots splashing as she and Jeffrey scrambled aboard the waiting rowboat. Two oarsmen pulled hard, the only sound the hiss of water under the blades. Ahead, *The Firebird* rocked gently, her lanterns throwing nervous arcs of light across the black sea.

Aboard, men clustered near the forecastle. Attila—bare-headed, coat half-fastened—leaned over the rail, lantern in one hand, pistol in the other. He looked up as Raven's grappling hook caught the bulwark.

"Starboard bow!" he barked. "We've got a madman."

Raven vaulted the rail. The deck smelled of pitch and brine, but underneath she caught the same faint perfume of rotting lilies that now haunted every ship.

Jeremy Finch met her halfway, eyes wide. "It's Santiago, one of the new Spaniards. He was on lookout. Started ranting about a woman calling his name, then carved something into the deck with his belt knife. Tried to jump."

"Where is he now?"

"Pinned under the bowsprit grate. Still breathing—but barely."

Raven pushed past the circle of sailors. Santiago lay on his back, arms lashed to a cleat with rope. His eyes rolled, whites showing; his lips moved soundlessly. On the planking beside him, fresh gouges formed a half-finished **spiral-eye symbol**, the cuts slick with blood instead of tar.

Raven knelt, pressing one hand to his shoulder. His skin was icy.

"Santiago," she said quietly, switching to Spanish. "Look at me."

His eyes stilled. Focused. A whisper slid from his cracked lips:

"Dice... tu nombre. *It says...your name.*

Anaíra..."

Raven's pulse hammered. Behind her, crewmen muttered crosses and prayers.

Attila crouched. "He woke half the ship screaming. Said she was at the bow, calling him by name."

"Which bow?" Raven asked.

"He pointed straight down."

A cold draft slipped over the deck—against the wind.

Raven rose, stepping to the stern rail. Lantern in hand, she leaned out. Water gleamed like polished obsidian. For a heartbeat, it was empty—

—and then a face surfaced. Pale. Serene. Eyes open and luminous, looking only at her. Hair drifted like black kelp; lips moved, though no sound broke the water's skin.

Raven's breath frosted in the warm night air.

Jeffrey caught her elbow. "Do you see her?"

"Yes." Her voice shook. "And she's waiting."

The face sank without ripple.

Behind them, Santiago gave a final, shuddering sigh. The line holding him slackened, water beading along its fibers as if drawn from the air. He was gone. Vanished beneath the grate, leaving only the blood-cut symbol and a puddle of seawater.

A sailor retched. Jeremy backed away, hand over his mouth.

Attila exhaled through his teeth. "That makes five."

Raven touched the still-wet carving; the cuts stung her fingertips like ice. She stood, eyes sweeping the hushed crew.

"Listen well," she said, voice carrying. "What hunts us feeds on fear and names. Bolt every hatch. No man stands watch alone. You hear a voice, you tell me—before you answer it. Understood?"

A hesitant chorus of "Aye, Captain" drifted back.

She turned to Attila. "Signal the others. We sail at first light—southwest, away from these depths."

"And if the storm follows?" he asked.

Raven's gaze flicked to the dark water where the woman had been.

"Then we keep moving," she whispered, more to herself than to him. "Until the sea hears a different name... or I decide to give it mine."

Above them, the conch on *The Firebird's* mast swung in a breeze only Raven seemed to feel—its hollow mouth poised, as if ready to cry out the moment she did.

The fleet left just after first light.

As the pale sun crawled over the horizon, casting weak gold across the bruised sea, Raven stood at the helm of *Destiny*, watching as *The Sea Witch*, *The Royal Victory*, and *The Firebird* peeled away from the island one by one. The sails snapped with life again—for the first time in days, the wind stirred in their favor.

Still, the water barrels were low. Too low. They'd made landfall only long enough to bury the dead and take on a few casks of brackish rainwater. It wouldn't last. Now they pushed southwest, hunting a river mouth or an uncharted cay with fresh springs.

"Keep watch for birds or driftwood," Raven ordered her crew. "Anything that smells of land."

She glanced at the horizon. "And if the sea speaks... don't answer."

The crew nodded, wary and silent. No one so much as whistled as they pulled at lines and adjusted sails.

That night, the ships rocked gently under a sky choked with stars. The wind had calmed again—not dead, but quiet, as if the sea were catching its breath.

Jeremy Finch stood alone at the bow of *The Firebird*, wrapped in a wool coat and staring out over the starlit water. His watch was half over. The ship creaked gently, ropes swaying, lanterns swaying with them—nothing out of place.

Then came a sound.

Soft. Wet. Like fingertips brushing wood.

It came again. Just under the wind. Like someone whispering his name, drawn out long and slow:

"Jeremyyyyy…"

He froze. His pulse spiked. At first, he thought it was the creak of the rigging above him—a trick of the sea. But the voice came again, clearer.

"Jeremyyy… She trusts you."

He gripped the mast tighter, breath fogging. "Who's there?"

"You've always been her shadow… her eyes… her little brother."
"You could protect her, if she would only say it…"

"Say what?"

Silence. Then a splash below, too deliberate for a fish.

He looked down—and there she was. A pale face, just under the surface, turned upward toward him. Her lips didn't move, but the words slid into his skull like wind slipping through a crack in the hull:

"Tell her to speak her name… or she'll lose everything."

He shuddered. "No. I won't."

"You don't have to tell her. Just…ask."

The face vanished, swallowed by the dark.

Jeremy slumped back against the mast, shaking. His breath came in gasps, his heart hammering. Below, all seemed calm—but he knew what he'd heard. What he'd felt.

He closed his eyes.

And in the stillness of that lonely night, for the first time since he was a boy, Jeremy was afraid of the sea. Not for its storms, or its pirates, or even for its hunger—but for its *voice*.

And what it wanted from *Raven*.

The following day dawned hot and windless, a glassy calm settling over the sea. The sun hung low and sullen in a haze-streaked sky. But aboard *The Firebird*, something else disturbed the morning.

Jeremy Finch stood at the bow, hands clenched tightly on the rail, staring out across the mirror-still water. His jaw was tight, his eyes shadowed from a night with no sleep. He hadn't touched breakfast. He hadn't spoken more than two words since the shift change.

Attila watched from the quarterdeck, arms folded over his chest. The boy—no, not a boy anymore—had always been dependable, sharp, a bit quiet, but steady as bedrock. But now... something had cracked behind his eyes. He wasn't himself.

"Something's wrong with that one," the helmsman muttered.

Attila nodded and crossed to the rail, scanning the deck of *Destiny*, which sailed just ahead.

He raised the conch and gave a short, deliberate call. A reply echoed back moments later. *Destiny's* sails adjusted course to come alongside. A grappling line was thrown over, and the two ships came together.

Minutes later, Raven climbed over the rail of *The Firebird*, boots thudding on the deck, red coat flaring like wings.

"Where is he?" she asked.

Attila motioned silently toward the bow.

Raven approached slowly. Jeremy hadn't turned around. She noted how stiff his posture was, how pale his knuckles had gone where they gripped the railing.

"Jeremy."

He flinched at her voice. Then, slowly, he turned.

When she saw his eyes, her gut twisted. Black circles surrounded them. Haunted. Distant. Like someone who had stared too long into a storm and found something staring back.

"You haven't spoken to anyone," she said gently. "You barely looked at Attila."

"I didn't sleep," he said. "Didn't feel like talking."

"Why not?"

He hesitated. His gaze dropped.

"I saw her," he whispered.

Raven said nothing, just waited.

Jeremy looked out over the water. "After my watch. She called my name. She knew things. About us. About *you*."

A silence stretched between them.

"She wanted me to get you to speak your name," he said. "Your real name. Said you trusted me. Said I could protect you—if I helped her."

Raven inhaled slowly. "And did you answer her?"

"No," he said quickly. "But... I *heard* her in my mind. It was like she was inside me. And even now, I still hear her. Not words, exactly—just the *pressure* of her voice."

He finally turned to face her fully. "Raven...it's like she planted something in me. And it's growing."

Raven stepped closer and placed a hand on his shoulder. "You did the right thing telling me."

"I didn't want to," she said, voice tight. "I didn't want to bring you more of this... curse. But it's not going away. I appreciate your trying to protect me, Jeremy. But...that's not your job."

"She's getting bolder," Raven murmured, more to herself than to him. "And closer."

She looked to the sky, then back to him. "Jeremy, if she comes to you again, you *don't* speak with her. Not even in your mind. Not even a whisper. She's not a dream or a spirit. She's *ancient*—older than anything we understand. And she wants something from me that she has no right to take."

Jeremy nodded. His voice broke slightly. "What if I'm not strong enough next time?"

Raven looked him dead in the eyes. "Then *I* will be."

She turned to Attila, who stood a few paces away, listening in silence.

"Keep him close," she said. "Watch for signs. And if she comes back..." Raven's jaw tightened. "We change course. She doesn't get to choose where we go."

Jeremy watched as she stepped away, red coat catching the wind like a banner.

But in the pit of his stomach, something coiled.

Because the voice hadn't lied.

He *had* always been her shadow.

And now, something in the dark wanted to *use* that shadow to reach her.

CHAPTER 25

T he sea was black glass beneath a blood-red sky.

Raven stood barefoot on the surface of the water, her reflection rippling below her. The wind was hollow, without direction, and the horizon offered no promise of land. No ship. No stars. Only the endless, silent sea.

She heard a whisper curl around her ear like breath.

"You know the name. You always have."

She turned—and her mother stood behind her.

Margaret Ashworth looked just as Raven remembered: auburn hair falling loose over her shoulders, eyes like burnished amber, soft but fierce. She wore no shoes, no jewelry. Only a pale dress that clung to her as if soaked, though she was dry.

Raven winced at the sight of her. She was in pain...no. Was it fear? She had seldom felt such fear, if that's what it was. Her body tensed at the sight of her mother after so many years.

"Am I dead?" Raven asked.

Margaret smiled gently. "No. But you're closer than ever to the place where death and life intertwine."

"I don't understand," Raven said. "Why won't anyone tell me the truth?"

Margaret stepped forward and cupped her daughter's face. Her touch was warm, heartbreakingly real. Raven barely remembered her mother's touch, but recognized it now.

"Because it's not something that can be told. It must be *remembered*. And the remembering comes with a cost."

"Is it true?" Raven asked. "Was I born with another name?"

Her mother's smile faded. She whispered something—too soft to hear.

And then the sea boiled beneath them.

A flash of silver light split the horizon.

La Dama de Sangre rose from the waves, towering, spectral, masts torn and sails dripping with seaweed and red salt. Her black figurehead wept blood from its eyes. Behind her, a storm churned—a wall of water that hung suspended in midair, waiting.

And on the deck of that cursed ship, *he* stood.

Geoffrey Neely. Just as Raven had seen him before—eyes hollow, skin pale, long white beard, clothes tattered from centuries at sea. He raised his hand to her in greeting.

"You've always been the one, Raven," he said. "But it's not me you owe the answer to."

Suddenly, the water around her grew cold.

A woman's laughter echoed from the deep, melodic, and cruel.

The sea parted, revealing a great whirlpool of glowing green, and from its center rose *her*, the woman in the water. Her black hair streamed like kelp, her face eerily beautiful and inhuman. Her eyes glowed like molten emeralds. Her skin glowed like starlight.

"You *know* me," she purred.

"I do," Raven said, trembling. "You're the one who's been calling to me."

"Calling you *home*," the woman whispered. "Say your name. Say it, and all the blood in the sea will bow to you. The gold. The storms. The dead. All of it—yours."

"I'm not ready to believe you," Raven said, backing away. "I won't be your puppet."

A thousand voices screamed from the depths—men and women, sailors and slaves, those taken by sea and salt and silence—her old friend Captain Horatio Billings among them. She saw him rise from the depths as he called Richard's name.

The woman reached out a dripping hand. "You were born from the storm and the scream. Say your name, *Anaíra. Say it.*"

Raven turned—and saw herself standing on the deck of *Destiny*, wind howling, conch in hand, her voice rising like thunder.

She spoke the name.

The sea shattered.

Lightning burst from the sky. The dead screamed in ecstasy. Gold poured from the mouths of waves.

And Raven, the real Raven, staggered back in horror.

"No..."

She fell—

—into the arms of her mother once more.

Margaret held her tight as the storm closed in. "You can choose *when*," she said softly. "But you can't choose *if*. The sea will take what it is owed. Just don't let it take *you*."

Raven's eyes flew open.

She was in her cabin, drenched in sweat, the first light of dawn bleeding through the window. The conch shell at her bedside was vibrating.

And outside, a whisper rode the wind.

"*Anaíra...*"

The shutters of Raven's cabin slammed open with a crack of thunder.

Jeffrey burst in, his hair wild with wind, his coat dripping from the first sheets of rain. He stopped short when he saw her—Raven was on her knees beside the bed, breath ragged, hair plastered to her neck with sweat. Her nightshirt clung to her like a second skin.

"Raven—" he rushed to her. "You're burning up. What happened?"

She looked up at him, eyes wide and unfocused. "She was there again," she whispered. "The woman in the water. My mother. Geoffrey Neely. I saw it—I *heard* it."

Jeffrey knelt beside her. "Heard what?"

"My name. My *true* name."

She reached for him, trembling. "I said it, Jeffrey. In the dream. And the sea changed. Everything changed."

Jeffrey held her, but the tension in her body didn't ease. Outside, a deep rumble rolled across the heavens. The lantern swayed violently on its hook.

Jeffrey glanced toward the door. "There's a storm coming. The sea's turning fast. We need you on deck."

Raven stood slowly, still pale, still shaking. But the fire in her eyes had returned.

"Then we'll face it," she said.

Raven quickly dressed, donning her rain gear over her leather britches, linen shirt, and leather waistcoat. She moved quickly to the quarterdeck to stand with the other officers and the helmsman.

Waves crashed against *Destiny's* hull as the fleet pitched and rolled in the rising storm.

Rain lashed the sails in horizontal sheets. Lightning split the sky in jagged arcs, lighting up the roiling clouds in ghostly silver. The four ships were scattered across the water, barely visible through the mist and spray. Conch shell blasts pierced the thunder, calling out over the chaos—*hold course, reef the sails, watch the rigging.*

Walter Parpart gripped the wheel with Raven and Jeffrey beside him. Pharaoh's voice echoed from *The Sea Witch*, relayed by signal lanterns: "Wind's shifting fast! We're in the heart of it!"

Raven's gaze swept the horizon, trying to keep all four ships in her mind, to tether herself to the living while the dead whispered in the howl of the gale.

And there—at the crest of a towering wave—*she saw her.*

The woman in the water.

Floating effortlessly, arms outstretched, sea foam hair fanned around her, eyes glowing with unnatural green light.

She wasn't fighting the storm.

She *was* the storm.

The whispers pierced the roar of thunder:

"Say it again. Let the sea crown you."

Raven's fingers dug into the soaked wood of the helm.

"Don't listen to her!" Jeffrey shouted beside her. "Raven, stay with me!"

But the voices came from every direction now.

"Anaíra..."

"Anaíra..."

"Child of blood and brine..."

And suddenly, Raven's feet left the deck. Jeffrey reached for her, but she was quickly out of reach.

"Raven! Come back to me!"

The sea rose beneath *Destiny* like a living thing. Water lifted her skyward, encircling her in a spiral of glowing mist. The crew screamed. Jeffrey reached for her, but she was already gone, suspended above the deck like the eye of a hurricane.

In the eye of the storm, all was silent.

Rain and sea and sky circled her, but Raven stood in calm. Her mother's voice whispered on the edge of the wind.

"Say it, and become what you were born to be."

La Dama de Sangre loomed in the distance, sails aflame with ghost light, the dead gathered on her decks in silent expectation.

And beneath her feet—deep in the water—the woman waited, mouth open, hands rising.

Raven closed her eyes.

Tears slipped from beneath her lashes and vanished into the wind.

She thought of Jeffrey. Of her papa. Of Pharaoh, Jeremy, Attila, Alexander, the fleet she'd kept together with sweat and fury. She thought of Margaret. Of the moment she had first dressed like a boy to follow her father into a life at sea. Of the woman in the mirror of the water—waiting always.

And then she opened her mouth and screamed her name to the sea.

"ANAÍRA!"

The sky split.

A wave of force rippled from her chest like a cannon blast. The sea heaved backward, the clouds sucked upward into the heavens, the wind shrieked in triumph.

La Dama de Sangre vanished.

The storm broke like shattered glass.

And Raven collapsed to the deck of *Destiny*, unconscious, as the rain fell gently once more, warm and soft.

The sky was eerily clear, the stars blinking through the last strands of broken cloud. The sea, which only moments ago had risen like a wrathful god, now lay calm, flat as hammered silver.

And at the heart of the deck, Raven lay motionless.

A single lantern, somehow still burning, swung from the mizzenmast, casting long, flickering shadows. The crew of *Destiny* stood frozen in place, soaked, wide-eyed, as if unsure whether the storm had ended—or simply changed shape.

Jeffrey was the first to move.

He dropped to his knees beside her, dropping his ear to her nose and mouth.

"She's alive!" he called, breath catching. "She's still breathing!"

The tension broke like a snapped rope.

John shoved past two stunned gunners and knelt beside Jeffrey, eyes wide with panic. "She just—she flew, didn't she? I saw her *fly*..."

"No," whispered Caleb, one of the older Africans, "the sea *lifted* her... like it *knew* her."

Others whispered among themselves. "She said something." "A name." "It wasn't her name, not the one we know."

Pharaoh appeared, dripping and grim, having just boarded from the *Sea Witch*. His face twisted as he saw her, his fierce captain, sister of the sea, laid low. "What happened?" he demanded. "What happened up here?"

"She screamed," Jeffrey murmured. "Not in pain. Not fear. She—*named* herself. And the storm broke."

"She summoned it," said one of the Spaniards who had followed Pharaoh from *The Sea Witch*, stepping back in awe. "Or banished it."

"Witchcraft," muttered another. But no one took up the word. Not here. Not now.

Jeffrey carefully gathered Raven into his arms, lifting her like something sacred. Her face was pale, but peaceful. Her damp hair clung to his arm, and her lips moved faintly—as if still speaking to something only she could see.

"We need to get her below," he said. "Now."

As he moved toward her cabin, the crew parted in silence. No one dared speak. No one dared meet each other's eyes.

Above them, a wind picked up—not the howl of a storm, but something older. Deeper. Almost a sigh.

From the crow's nest, a sailor called down, voice trembling.

"There's something in the water."

Pharaoh climbed the rigging and cursed softly under his breath.

In the moonlight, the sea glistened.

The crew slowly turned toward the captain's cabin, where Raven—Anaíra now lay unconscious.

And not one of them doubted.

The sea had claimed her.

But it had *not* taken her.

Not yet.

CHAPTER 26

The first rays of dawn had barely kissed the sea when the conch shell sounded from *Destiny*. It was a low, trembling call—more cautious than commanding. The captains sent crews out onto the water to investigate the gold that floated along the surface of the sea.

"Be careful," Alexander instructed his men. "Gold shouldn't be floating on the surface like that. It might be something devilish."

Dozens of dories bobbed in the golden wake, oars dipping silently as the crews from all four ships moved to collect the scattered treasure trailing behind them. The coins shimmered like stars caught in the water, beckoning with a siren's gleam.

"Easy now," Pharaoh warned as his crew reached for the nearest doubloon. "Keep your eyes open. The sea's never this generous."

Attila warned his men, "Remember all of you. This treasure belongs to us all. If anyone is caught stealing, he will be severely punished according to the Articles each of you signed."

The men dipped nets and hands into the water. Some muttered prayers, others kissed medallions or whispered names of saints and ancestors. All of them felt it—that this was no ordinary harvest.

Jeffrey stood at *Destiny*'s stern, arms crossed, eyes locked on the horizon. Raven remained below, resting, her breath even but her presence stretching out over the fleet like a living tether. It was as if she saw the movements of every crewman. Everyone felt her presence. No one dared to take any of the treasure for himself.

Then, the ocean sighed. Everyone froze.

A tremor rolled beneath the boats—barely more than a ripple, but enough to stop every hand mid-reach.

And then... *the sea split.*

The waters churned all around them. The sea began to bubble like a boiling pot, yet the water's temperature remained unchanged.

From the depths, ships rose.

Masts pierced the surface first, their sails long-rotted or tangled in seaweed. Barnacled hulls groaned like the dead awakening. Some had ironclads bent by centuries of pressure; others were wooden, shattered along the beams but still climbing, creaking, gasping like leviathans returned from the deep.

One after another, they emerged—twenty, thirty, more than any man could count—spilling forth as if the sea itself were surrendering a hidden kingdom. Galleons, longships, merchant vessels, war frigates—all lost to time and storm—now reborn.

And on every deck... *treasure of every kind.*

Chests burst open, jewels spilling in rivulets of light. Idol heads glinted in the morning sun. Cannons engraved with forgotten seals jutted like broken teeth. Scrolls. Silks. Silver plate. Carved thrones. Beads. Bones.

Everyone who witnessed it, whether on a ship or in dories, stared with their mouths agape.

But then came the silence. *Deafening silence.* No sound of crashing waves against ship hulls. No call of the sea birds from the air. Not even the ships' riggings creaked as the ships rocked in the soundless waves.

And in that silence, the dead rose.

They came not as vengeful spirits, but as phantoms of memory—men and women from every era, every skin, every uniform. Sailors clinging to splintered timbers. Soldiers clutching ragged flags. Children. Priests. Courtesans. Seamen. They lifted from the decks and from the waves, their eyes not on the living, but skyward.

A Spaniard in a dory wept openly as a figure passed above him—a man with his same face, older, draped in conquistador armor corroded by salt. The ghost gave no sign of recognition, only floated upward, arms outstretched to something unseen.

Pharaoh recognized one of the spirits as his half-brother. Captured long ago and placed on a ship bound for the Carolinas.

One of Alexander's crew whispered. "This... this is Judgment."

"No," said Sean O'Toole, his voice strangely calm. "Dis is *release.*"

"These spirits have been held captive by the deep for centuries. Waiting. And now...Duh Red Raven has released 'em."

The dories drifted, forgotten. Oars slipped from fingers. Gold clinked softly in nets, but no one reached for more.

Above the rising fleet of the dead, the sky broke open into a haze of morning fire. The spirits faded into it one by one—some in peace, some wailing, some silent—but all ascending.

Back on *Destiny*, Raven stirred.

She gasped awake, eyes wide, whispering a name only the sea could understand.

Jeffrey turned at once, a chill racing down his spine.

From the quarterdeck of *The Firebird*, Jeremy shouted, his voice shaken.

"Attila! Something's happening to the *La Dama de Sangre!*"

Raven stepped barefoot onto the deck of *Destiny*, her skin damp with sweat, her dream still pulsing behind her eyes like lightning trapped behind clouds. Jeffrey followed close, his hand at her back, steadying but silent.

The entire crew stood motionless.

Above the sea, the sky burned with an unearthly shimmer. Dozens of spectral ships floated like strange relics of a dream—each a ruin, and each impossibly suspended by some divine breath. And there, on the horizon, framed by the drifting mist and the orange fire of dawn—

La Dama de Sangre.

She was rising, not with groans or splashes like the others, but in complete silence, the red-stained figurehead parting the sea like a blade.

Her sails were still intact, impossibly so, crimson and whispering as if windless breath moved through them. Her timbers glowed faintly with sea salt and shadow. A long gash along the hull bled no water—only a slow curl of black mist that turned the waves below her dark.

"She's not like the others," Jeffrey murmured.

"No," Raven said, her voice low. "She's never been."

John approached from the helm, eyes wide. "The spirits rose from every ship... *except* her."

Raven's jaw tightened. The woman in the water had always been tied to *La Dama de Sangre*—they were echoes of the same curse, reflections in opposite glass.

"She's watching," Raven whispered. "Waiting."

But for what, she still didn't know.

The awe of the moment passed quickly. Sailors' eyes drifted from the sky to the treasure-strewn ships, and the hunger returned.

Not greed exactly—not yet. But ambition. Possibility. Fear that this miracle might vanish with the tide.

Raven turned to her captains—Pharaoh, Alexander, and Attila—who had each gathered on *Destiny*.

"We're not hauling it all aboard," she said. "Too risky. Too much attention."

Pharaoh nodded. "And no merchant port would believe how we came by it."

"Then we take it in pieces," Raven said. "Sort and stow the choicest loads in waterproof barrels. We'll mark the ships they came from, record what we leave behind."

"And where do we take it?" Attila asked, already knowing the answer.

"The Robin's Nest," Raven said. "We move what we can to the uncharted island nearby—hide it inland, under our protection. That island is cursed in sailors' tales. No one dares go near it."

Alexander folded his arms. "They might now."

"Not if we plant signs of madness," Raven said. "Symbols. Stories. We make the land itself unholy. Let superstition do the guarding."

Sean O'Toole grinned. "And when the time comes, we ferry it home—quiet, light runs, month by month. One golden whisper at a time."

As the meeting ended, Raven turned once more toward *La Dama de Sangre*. The mist around her had thickened, and the sea beneath her glowed faintly red, as if the blood she was named for was not just painted wood, but real and stirring.

Then something changed.

The sails... moved.

No wind touched them, yet they fluttered once—twice—and then froze.

And on the quarterdeck of the ghost ship, something stood.

It was a woman.

Long hair clung to her skin like kelp. Her dress was tattered silk, soaked and shining. Her eyes were hollow, glowing faintly. And in her hands—

—*a name,* etched in dripping light.

Raven could not hear her, but she knew what she said. The lips moved slowly, deliberately.

"Anaíra."

Then the ship began to drift, slowly pulling back from the others, as if receding into another realm entirely.

Raven did not speak. But her hands were clenched at her sides, and the sea, though calm, shivered around her ankles.

Raven's boots creaked on the gangplank of *Destiny* as she crossed to the dory. The crew watched in silence. Not even a conch sounded. A stillness had fallen across the sea—watchful and unnatural.

The boarding party consisted of only four members: Raven, Pharaoh, Attila, and Jeremy. Each was armed, though the weapons felt almost ceremonial, like swords brought to a funeral.

The small boat cut through the waves toward *La Dama de Sangre*. She loomed ahead like a cathedral of rot and ruin. Her hull, though whole, wept streaks of black brine. The red sails hung like torn flesh from bone.

As they neared, they saw the ship didn't float so much as hover, barely breaking the water's surface, as if the sea itself feared to touch her.

Pharaoh muttered a prayer in Swahili under his breath.

"Steady," Raven said. "If this is what she wanted, we'll face it head-on."

The woman in the water was nowhere to be seen. Yet her presence pulsed like a heartbeat through the planks of the boat.

They reached the ladder, slick with algae, but firm. Raven climbed first. Each step was heavier than the last, as if the ship itself were resisting her. When she pulled herself over the rail, she stood alone.

The deck was empty.

No crew. No rot. No gulls. No sound.

Just the *smell*—wet parchment, salt, and something sweet beneath it... decayed roses, long dead.

Then the others came up, one by one.

The deck was clean, untouched by barnacles or the ravages of time. The ship groaned like it remembered a thousand storms.

"Where is everyone?" Jeremy whispered.

"They're watching," Attila said, eyes scanning the rigging. "From wherever the dead go when they sleep."

They moved toward the captain's cabin, Raven leading.

The doors stood closed, but not locked. As she reached for the handle, the wood beneath her palm *breathed*. Not a trick of the sea. Not a gust of wind.

It exhaled.

Raven opened the door.

The cabin inside was untouched by time. A large desk stood before a cracked window. A map was spread across it—hand-inked and illuminated in red. Her heart caught.

It was a map of the Caribbean.

But the islands were not as she knew them.

Some had new names. Others—long-lost ones, marked in ink. And scrawled across the sea in flowing, coral-red script was the word:

Anaíra.

Jeremy gasped. "That's your name, isn't it?"

Raven didn't reply.

She stepped forward. Her hand trembled as she reached for the map.

But then—

Footsteps.

From the aft hallway beyond the cabin came the slow, measured steps of something… approaching.

The party turned as one. Blades drawn. Breath held.

The door creaked open.

And there, standing in the shadows of the corridor, was a figure in red.

Not the woman in the water. No.

This was a man—tall, skeletal, eyes like smoldering coal. He wore a Spanish admiral's coat, tattered and stained with sea brine. His skin clung too tightly to his bones.

"You have come far, *Anaíra*," he rasped. "Too far to turn back."

Raven raised her cutlass. "Who are you?"

The man smiled, lips drawn too wide. "The one who named this ship. The one she defied."

He stepped into the light, and the red trim of his coat shimmered like fresh blood.

"La Dama was *my* ship," he said, "before she betrayed me. Before *you* were born."

He raised one bony hand.

The deck groaned.

Below them, in the hold, something stirred.

CHAPTER 27

The skeletal man in red took another step forward. The glow in his eyes flickered with memory, like a candle flickering in a long-forgotten tomb.

"I was Don Alvaro de Cortázar," he said, voice sharp with pride and bitterness. "Admiral of the Crimson Fleet. Spain's scourge upon these seas. Until *she* sank us."

"La Dama?" Raven asked.

"No," he rasped. "*Anaíra.*"

The name echoed off the ship like thunder.

Jeremy flinched.

Pharaoh muttered a curse.

The admiral pointed a long, rotted finger at Raven. "Your mother was meant to be mine. She had the gift... the tongue of tides, the name of storms. But she ran, fled into the bloodlines of lesser men. Hid you from the sea's call."

Raven's cutlass lowered just a fraction. "You knew Margaret."

"She was the lock," Alvaro said. "You are the key."

Then came the sound again—from the belly of the ship. *A moan.* Not mechanical. Not wood. **Human.**

Something alive—or nearly alive—waited below.

Raven turned back to Alvaro. He was gone.

Attila remarked, "That wasn't odd at all, now was it?"

Raven replied, "Nothing surprises me anymore."

They descended into the lower deck—Raven in the lead, Pharaoh just behind, the others wary.

What met them was not ruin, nor cargo.

It was **a shrine.**

The hold had become a cathedral of the dead.

Candles burned with green flames. Ropes of kelp draped the beams. Bones were lashed together to form an altar, and across it were etched symbols—the same symbols Raven had seen in her mother's journal.

In the center of the hold stood a sarcophagus—ornate and sealed in coral and pearl.

"What is this?" Jeremy whispered.

Pharaoh's voice was barely audible. "An offering... or a prison."

Raven stepped closer. Her hand hovered over the lid.

As her fingers touched the stone, the ghost admiral's voice rang out behind them.

"She waits inside. The one you've heard whispering. The one who longs for your voice."

"The woman in the water," Raven breathed.

"Her name is lost," Alvaro said. "But if you speak your own, she will rise. Whole again. And she will reward you."

"What is she to me?"

"She is the sea, child. She is the part of your mother you never knew... the part that died *so you could live.*"

Raven pulled back from the sarcophagus.

"I'm not ready," she said.

Alvaro's grin widened, revealing blackened teeth. "Then she'll keep calling. And the sea will never be quiet."

Above, the ship groaned again. The sea slapped at the hull.

Then—a violent *shudder.*

Destiny, anchored nearby, let out a warning **conch blast**. Something was stirring in the deep. Something old. Something awakened by their presence aboard *La Dama.*

"We need to go," Pharaoh said. "Now."

But Raven hesitated. Her hand still tingled from where it had touched the coffin.

"She's waiting for me," she whispered.

"Yes," Alvaro murmured. "And she will not wait forever."

Raven stood alone before the sarcophagus. Pharaoh had called her name once, then fallen silent, giving her space, though he stayed close. Jeremy hovered at the stairs, unsure, and Attila watched from the shadows, eyes dark with worry.

The coral lid glistened as though freshly wept upon. The pearlescent etchings seemed to breathe, pulsing softly with each crashing wave outside the hull. Her fingers brushed along the carvings. They were smooth and cold, like bones left too long in the sea.

And then... she heard it.

"Anaíra..."

Not spoken aloud, but **inside her.** A vibration in her ribs. A song carried in salt.

She stumbled back as a vision struck her: her mother, Margaret, younger, standing before this very stone, pregnant, afraid, defiant.

A younger version of Don Alvaro loomed in the vision, offering power... in exchange for her unborn child.

"She refused him," Raven whispered.

"Because she saw what he didn't," came the admiral's voice from the shadows. "That the child would carry not only the sea's blood—but the heart to resist it."

Raven turned slowly. "Is that what this is? A test?"

"No. It's a door. And you are the only key."

Suddenly, a crack split the silence.

Not from Raven.

From the sarcophagus.

A hairline fracture glowed with blue light. Faint at first, then stronger. The ship groaned—no, sighed—as if the breath of centuries was being exhaled.

Pharaoh stepped forward. "Raven..."

"Everyone out," Raven ordered.

"But—"

"Now!"

As they turned to flee, the deck tilted sharply, the timbers groaning. Ghost light bled from the walls. Water surged up through the floorboards as if the ship itself were drowning in reverse—*resurrecting*.

The crew scrambled up the stairs. A rope ladder snapped as Pharaoh caught Jeremy's arm and hauled him bodily through a collapsing hatch. A lantern exploded behind them in a shower of green flame.

Raven was last up, the admiral's voice echoing after her.

"Anaíra, the sea remembers... and it will claim what is owed!"

They burst onto the main deck of *La Dama de Sangre*, now rolling underfoot like a beast waking from slumber. The masts creaked but didn't break.

Instead, they twisted upward, as though reaching toward the heavens. The sails unfurled on their own, red as fresh wounds.

"Launch the dories!" Pharaoh roared.

From *Destiny*, *The Sea Witch*, *The Royal* Victory, and *The Firebird*, conch shells blew in frantic alarm.

All around *La Dama*, the sea was beginning to churn.

Below the waves, shapes moved. Not ships. Not sharks. Not anything made by man. Something older. Watching. Waiting.

Jeremy grabbed Raven's hand as they leapt into the dory and rowed hard for *Destiny*. "What did you see?" he asked.

Raven couldn't answer. She was shaking.

The sarcophagus... the vision... her mother's voice... the name.

And the undeniable truth that if she opened that coffin, the sea would never let her go.

They sat alone on the quarterdeck of the *Destiny*, the stars barely peeking through clouds still boiling from the storm.

John Ashworth passed his daughter a flask. She took it without a word, letting the heat of the rum ground her, though her hands still trembled.

"I saw her, Papa," she said quietly. "Mama. Inside that ship... in the vision. She was pregnant with me. And she refused some sort of bargain."

John's weathered face stiffened, gaze fixed on the dark horizon.

"She never told you?" Raven added.

"She tried," he said. "But I wouldn't listen."

Raven looked at him sharply.

"I thought she'd gone mad, talkin' about curses and legacies. Thought she was just... grief-stricken. You were a babe when it started. Wailin' at night whenever we passed open water. Your mama swore it was the sea calling to you."

"And was it?"

He looked her full in the eyes.

"I don't know. But whatever's out there," he nodded toward the rising mists, "it ain't just the sea anymore. It's *part of you.*"

She let that settle. Then:

"There's a sarcophagus aboard *La Dama*. Something's inside. Something ancient. It knows my name."

"Anaíra."

He said it gently. But even the sound of it made the air thicken.

"I think Mama feared I'd speak it one day," she whispered.

John placed a rough hand over hers. "She feared what the world would *do to you* once you did."

The cove was narrow, ringed with black rock and jungle too dense to see through. A waterfall veiled the narrow entrance that led to a cavern just large enough to harbor a few longboats at a time.

This island wasn't on any charts. Pharaoh had confirmed it with a dozen coastal maps. Isaac Finch swore his grandfather had spoken of it in hushed tones as "Isla de la Sombra"—the island of shadow.

Here, the crews of *Destiny*, *The Sea Witch*, *The Royal Victory*, and *The Firebird* worked in grueling shifts, offloading treasure by torchlight and fog.

Jeffrey remained on the island as he counted and sorted the treasure as it was offloaded—gold bars, coins, jewels. Chests still wet from the sea. Relics that not even the oldest sailors could name. One appeared to be a crown made of coral and obsidian; another was a sword etched with runes that glowed faintly in the dark.

Raven stayed on the island with Jeffrey to oversee that each ship made good progress as they brought the treasure to the cave.

Each of the derelict ships was unloaded one by one. Mysteriously, once the treasure had been removed from any ship, the vessel slowly sank back into the depths of the sea. Raven knew within herself each time a ship buried itself back into the deep. She was connected to each one of them.

John commanded *Destiny* in Raven's absence. *Destiny* and each of the other ships were loaded with cargo from the ghost ships and then sent to the island to be hidden.

There was so much treasure and so many ships that it took nearly two months to transport it all to the island cave.

They buried the most precious cargo within a sealed chamber deep inside the waterfall cave. Pharaoh rigged traps using spring-loaded spears and crumbling tunnels. Attila drew runic warnings he had learned from his grandmother years ago. And Alexander carved symbols onto the cave entrance—old Spanish and even older tongues.

Before the cave was sealed, Jeffrey made an account of how much treasure each man or woman would be allotted according to their ranking within the crew. Everyone would be rich beyond their most incredible imagination. However, there was no need to divvy up the shares immediately. It would be far too much for each crewman to carry with them on the ship. Each of them was, however, given quite a large allowance of their share before leaving the island.

It was Jeremy, quiet since his own encounter with the woman in the water, who suggested placing one of the lesser treasures atop the main hoard—a gold chalice that always felt cold to the touch.

"It'll confuse anyone who doesn't know the signs," he said softly. "Draw them to the decoy."

Raven nodded. "Good. But if anyone does find this place..."

"We make sure they don't leave," Pharaoh finished.

She didn't argue.

And as the last crate was stashed away and the cave sealed, Raven looked back toward the sea and whispered:

"You're not having it all. Not yet."

CHAPTER 28

On the fourth day out to sea, *Destiny* led the way with the other three ships following in formation. The orange color of the sky gave Raven and the other captains concern for the storms that most likely lay ahead.

The fleet was on its way back to the Robin's Nest to take a break from their adventures in the Caribbean. Their hulls were filled with treasure, some belonging to crew members and some to the fleet, which was used to purchase supplies for the fleet.

Raven awoke with an unusual churning in her belly. She had never been one to get seasick, no matter how badly the seas tossed her ship about.

Raven quickly left Jeffery behind in bed as she scrambled out of her cabin, climbing to the main deck. Wearing only her bed gown, she ran to the port rail.

She gripped the rail of *Destiny* as the morning sun rose in streaks of gold and copper. The sea was calm again, deceptively so. Beneath her steady stance, her stomach churned—not from fear, nor hunger. It was a deeper queasiness, constant and unrelenting, as if something were shifting inside her.

She hadn't eaten properly in days. Even the smell of salt pork turned her pale. And the dreams-the ones filled with water, with light, with *names*—they had only grown more vivid since they'd left the cursed cove.

Jeffrey was on her heels as she woke him while she ran from the bed.

"Are you alright?"

Raven coughed several times, trying to remove whatever had turned her stomach.

"I'm alright. I guess I ate something that didn't agree with me."

"Maybe you should let Mr. Greer have a look at you."

"*I'm Fine*!

Jeffrey raised his brows in surprise before replying, "Of course you are. That's why you're yelling at me for absolutely no reason at all."

Raven sighed, "I'm sorry, Jeffrey. I'm just feeling out of sorts. I'm sure there's nothing wrong with me that a little rest won't take care of."

"Well then...why don't we get you back to bed?"

"No, I'm hungry. I want some breakfast."

"Are you certain? After what I just saw, I'm not sure eating is such a good idea right now."

"Jeffrey, be a dear and ask Mr. Hardy to fix me some eggs and bacon. I'll be in the cabin getting dressed."

Jeffrey left her at the rail and walked across the deck wearing only his trousers. He was shirtless and barefoot as he entered the galley to find Mr. Hardy.

"Mr. Hardy, Raven would like some eggs and bacon for breakfast if you please."

"Aye, Mr. Hamilton. And how is our captain this morning?"

"She is cantankerous and hungry, as usual."

"Well then, I best get busy with her breakfast. Never you mind, sir. I'll have her all served up in a jiffy. Will you be joining the captain for breakfast?"

"Yes, thank you, Mr. Hardy."

"Right-o, Mr. Hamilton."

Jeffrey returned to Raven's cabin and found her dressing for the day's events. She had already donned her linen blouse and was tucking it into her leather britches. The buttons on her britches were giving her trouble. She managed the first three buttons, but for some reason, the fourth button would no longer reach its hole.

"Jeffrey, dear, would you please lend a hand?"

Jeffrey stepped closer and took her waistband into his hands, pulling the two ends together. Raven grunted as he squeezed her belly beneath the leather britches to button the final button. Jeffrey noticed Raven's middle was growing larger over the past few days, but he dared not mention it to her.

"Ah! Are you trying to kill me?"

"Sorry, my love. I hope I didn't hurt you."

"No, but I'm finding it difficult to breathe. Is it possible my britches got mixed up with someone else's? Someone smaller than I?"

"I don't think so. Your clothes are always washed alone. Never mixed with anyone else's."

Frustrated, Raven replied, "Well, they've shrunk then. Quickly. Unbutton the top button for me. I'll leave it open and cover it with my waistcoat."

A knock on the door.

Raven finished buttoning her waistcoat, with some difficulty near the bottom, and said, "Enter."

Kupika entered carrying a tray with Raven and Jeffrey's breakfast. She set it on the table just as Raven exclaimed, "Oh! What is that smell?"

Kupika replied, "Your eggs and bacon, Captain. Just as you requested."

Raven blew her cheeks out in disgust at the smell.

"Take it away, Kupika. Take it away."

Confused, Kupika looked at Jeffrey for help.

"It's alright, Kupika. It isn't your fault. The Captain is just having a bad morning."

Kupika asked, "Mr. Hamilton, would you like me to leave your breakfast?"

Before Jeffrey could answer, "No! Take it away!"

"But, Raven. I'm hungry."

"*Then eat it outside. It smells rancid.*"

Jeffrey took his plate from Kupika and followed her out of the cabin. As they exited onto the main deck, Kupika said, "I'm sorry, Mr. Hamilton. I did not mean to make her angry."

"It isn't your fault, Kupika. She's just having a bad day."

"Is there anything else I can get for you, Mr. Hamilton?"

"Now that you mention it, would you please ask Mr. Greer to join me as soon as he is available?"

"Aye, Mr. Hamilton."

Jeffrey knew.

He'd known before she had.

The old doctor came up the companionway with the slow, deliberate pace of someone who'd tended to sailors long enough to recognize storms before they came. His leather bag creaked at his side, his hat in his hand.

Raven saw him and frowned.

"Is someone ill?"

"Yes," Jeffrey said gently, stepping beside her. "You."

She straightened. "I'm not sick."

Greer inclined his head. "No, Raven. Not sick. But perhaps… changed."

She looked between them. "Jeffrey. What have you done?"

"I've done nothing but worry about you. You're pale. You haven't slept. You nearly fainted yesterday in the chart room. You're hungry, but you can't stand the smell of food."

Raven opened her mouth to protest—then closed it.

Because he was right.

She turned toward Greer, jaw tight. "What do you want me to do?"

"Let me check you. That's all."

She sat on the edge of her bed, the lantern swaying with the rhythm of the sea. Greer examined her in silence, measuring her pulse, her eyes, the pallor in her skin.

Then he pressed gently along her abdomen.

She winced.

He sat back slowly, a flicker of something unreadable in his gaze.

"Well?" she said sharply. "What curse have I caught now?"

He gave a slow smile, tinged with something almost reverent.

"No curse, Captain. Not this time. I believe you're with child."

The words hit her like a cannon blast. The air left her lungs.

"That's not…I…no."

Jeffrey stepped forward and knelt before her, taking her hand.

"I've suspected for weeks," he said quietly. "I didn't want to believe it, not while all this… ghost madness was unfolding. But you've changed. You feel it too, don't you?"

Raven stared at her hands.

The dreams. The voice in the water. The stirring inside her.
The way the sea seemed to watch her more than ever.

"This can't be real," she whispered. "Not now."

"Especially now," Greer said, packing his things. "Life doesn't ask if it's convenient, Raven. It just *is*."

Then she looked at Greer and said, "Mr. Greer, I would prefer this be between us. Don't tell anyone until I'm ready, please."

"I understand. Don't worry."

Later that night, Raven stood alone again, the wind brushing her hair across her face.

She laid a hand against her abdomen, heart pounding like sails in a storm.

She was not afraid of battle. Not of ghosts. Not even the name Anaíra.

But this?

This was something different.

Something pure. Something fragile. And perhaps something the woman in the water would want...

"The child of sea and blood," the voice from her dream had once said.

Now it meant something more.

Behind her, Jeffrey stood silent, letting her choose whether to acknowledge him.

Finally, she spoke.

"This changes everything."

"It doesn't have to," he replied.

She turned and looked him in the eyes. "It already has."

The candlelight flickered inside Raven's cabin, casting soft shadows across the maps and charts she no longer had the heart to study.

She sat at her desk, elbows on the worn oak surface, chin in her hands. The gentle motion of *Destiny* should've calmed her, like it always had. But tonight, even the familiar creak of timber felt foreign.

A child.

Her child.

The sea outside sighed and whispered against the hull like it already knew.

Jeffrey was asleep in the bunk behind her. He hadn't pushed her for more. Not after Greer's quiet declaration. He had taken her hand, kissed her brow, and said: "We'll face it together."

But that was the thing, wasn't it?

Could they face it together?

Could *she* face it at all?

She had fought off slavers and storms. She had taken on curses, ghosts, and monsters. She'd buried friends and killed enemies and carved her name into the bones of these waters.

But now?

Now she was afraid of her own blood.

She rose slowly, wrapped her cloak around her shoulders, and slipped quietly up to the quarterdeck. The stars were faint, shrouded in mist, the moon a pale coin behind gauze.

She stood at the rail, staring out into the black.

Would the crew accept her? Would they see her as weak?

She was their captain—their *Red Raven*. And the sea demanded strength. No mercy. No softness.

But now...there was life inside her.

By dawn, she found her father sharpening a blade near the stern rail. He looked up as she approached, and his weathered eyes searched her face.

"Couldn't sleep?" he asked.

"I've had a lot on my mind."

"Aye," he muttered, setting the whetstone down. "Ever since that blasted ghost ship."

She folded her arms. "There's something I need to tell you."

He studied her a moment, as if he already knew.

When she said the words, they came out in a whisper. "I'm with child."

John didn't react at first. He just stared at her—no shock, no outrage, just the slow tilt of the sea behind his eyes.

After a long silence, he said, "Is it his?"

She blinked. "Jeffrey's? Of course it is."

He nodded. "Then that's a small mercy."

"You're not angry?"

"I'm... terrified," he said simply. "Not of being a grandfather. But what does this mean? You're already hunted by curses, Raven. Now you carry something pure. And that makes you a target."

Raven looked down at the deck. "I don't know whether to hide it or tell the crew. I don't know how to lead like this. What happens if I can't... do what I used to?"

John stepped closer and placed a hand on her shoulder.

"You don't have to be what you were. You only have to be what you are."

"And what am I now?"

He smiled—sadly, proudly. "Still, my daughter. Still a captain. And now... a mother with fire in her blood and salt in her soul."

Raven stood before the mirror in her quarters. She touched her stomach again—flat for now, but no longer empty.

She would not announce it. Not yet.

Let them see her strength as it is. Let the sea come for her.

She would decide when the truth would be known.

But one thing was clear now, clearer than the maps on her desk or the stars above her ship:

The future had already begun shifting beneath her feet.

And whatever the woman in the water wanted—whatever curses waited on the horizon—they would face her not just as Anaíra.

But as a mother who would burn the sea to protect what was hers.

It had been four weeks since the words were spoken aloud in Greer's low, reverent voice.

"You're with child."

And since then, Raven had tried to command as she always had—sharp, steady, defiant. But the change inside her was undeniable.

Her body ached in ways it hadn't before. Smells turned her stomach. The roar of cannon drills gave her headaches. She could no longer keep down morning coffee or make it through long watches without bracing herself at the rail.

Worse still, the dreams were returning. Only now, the voice that called to her in sleep no longer whispered her name alone—it whispered something smaller, gentler.

Another name. One not yet spoken.

Something was different in the way the sea moved around her. As if it, too, knew she was no longer sailing alone.

She had tried to hide it, wrap herself in layers, avoid the knowing glances of Greer and Jeffrey. But it was time.

She could not lead in the shadow. Not anymore.

She called her captains to meet with her for a conference.

The captains gathered aboard *Destiny*, below deck in the chartroom, lit with lanterns and quiet tension.

Pharaoh lounged near the window, arms crossed. Alexander leaned forward with elbows on the table, sharp-eyed and silent. Attila stood stiff, hands behind his back, his posture a soldier's even at sea. John Ashworth waited off to the side, brow furrowed, arms folded.

Jeffrey and John were the only ones who already knew.

Raven entered last, steady on her feet despite the nausea still clinging from the morning.

They stood as she entered—instinct, respect, and maybe something more. She didn't ask them to sit.

"I've called you here," she said, voice quiet but firm, "because it's time you knew something that will change everything."

The silence that followed was absolute.

Raven stepped around the table and laid her hand gently on her belly.

"I am going to have a child."

Attila's jaw tightened, but he said nothing. Alexander raised his brows. Pharaoh stared, blinking once.

"I've tried to hide it. I told myself it wouldn't matter, that I could push through it as I always have. But this fleet doesn't move unless we trust one another. And if I lie to you... I don't deserve your trust."

Still silence.

Then John spoke softly. "She's not asking permission. She's telling you."

Alexander leaned back. "You're sure it's wise to continue at sea?"

"I'll decide when I stop," Raven said. "Until then, I will remain The Red Raven, and captain of *Destiny*. My child is not a weakness. It's a reason to fight harder than ever."

Attila finally spoke, slow and deliberate. "You'll have our loyalty. That's never been in question. But I won't lie—I worry for what this means. What will it bring?"

Raven met his eyes. "So do I."

Pharaoh chuckled quietly, breaking the tension. "If your child turns out anything like you, I'll sleep better knowing it's on *our* side."

That drew a faint laugh from Alexander.

Even Attila gave the barest nod.

John looked at his daughter with something close to awe. "Your mother would've been proud."

Later, as the captains returned to their ships, the wind finally picked up, gentle and clean, carrying the scent of distant land and new beginnings. Raven looked forward to reaching the Robin's Nest.

Jeffrey stood beside her at the stern.

"You spoke like a queen," he said.

"I feel like a storm," she replied.

He smiled. "Then may the sea make way for you."

Raven looked out over the water. Her hands rested on her stomach.

The sea no longer felt like an enemy, or even a mystery.

It felt like it was watching. Waiting.

Raven no longer feared what was to come.

Things were changing. Everything was changing. It no longer mattered. She was going to be a mother, and she would do it with everything in her strength.

CHAPTER 29

After weeks at sea, the first sight of the southern shores of the Gulf of Guinea stole the words from every throat aboard the fleet.

Even for those who had seen it before, The Robin's Nest always struck the eye and heart with quiet wonder.

From the sea, it was almost invisible, tucked behind low cliffs draped in jungle and mist. Only those who knew the signs could navigate the narrow passage between two outcroppings of volcanic stone. But once through, the inlet opened into a hidden cove lined with pale golden sand and canopies of green that spilled down from the high ridge above.

Water trickled from a waterfall nestled deep in the hills, emptying into a clear pond that shimmered in the dappled light.

This was her favorite place. Raven's home away from the sea.

The ships of her fleet—*Raven's Destiny*, *The Sea Witch*, *The Royal Victory*, and *The Firebird*—lowered sails and drifted quietly into the cove, one by one. Men and women let out sighs of relief, some crossing themselves, others laughing aloud. The very air here felt cleaner. **Safer.**

There was no sign of the woman in the water. No whispers in the wind. No blood in the tide.

Just peace.

Raven stepped off the dory and onto the sand barefoot, the warmth of the earth grounding her. Her fingers brushed against the green leaves as she climbed the path that led to the waterfall.

It hadn't changed. The little pond. The flowering trees. The stone outcrop where she and Jeffrey had exchanged vows.

It was here that she felt most like herself—not the pirate, not Anaíra—but Raven Ashworth, woman of the sea, and soon... a mother.

She knelt by the pond, hand resting over the gentle curve of her stomach. *Let this be our beginning.*

Later that day, Raven summoned carpenters from among her crews—men who had helped her shape secret docks, hidden vaults, and ship repairs in hostile waters. Now, she asked them for something new:

"I want a home here," she said. "Stone walls. High windows. A hearth. Room for Jeffrey. And for our child. I want it to face the falls so I never forget why I came here."

Pharaoh grinned and clapped her on the back. "We'll build it better than a fortress."

Jeffrey knelt and sketched a rough outline in the dirt beside her, asking questions about the rooms she wanted, how wide, how open. Raven's answers came with laughter and lightness she hadn't felt in months.

The crew set to work that very evening, while the rest of the fleet hauled crates of gold and relics deeper into the jungle caverns for safekeeping.

The ground at the base of the waterfall was rich and solid, shaded by fig trees and palms, with soft ferns crowding the base of the hill. Raven paced the space slowly, barefoot, one hand on her hip, the other trailing through her curls as she envisioned the house that would soon stand here.

"I want the front open," she told Jeffrey, "with wide shutters that swing like sails and catch the sea breeze from the north."

He nodded, sketching lines in the dirt with a stick. "Wraparound porch?"

"With carved rails," she said. "Each one different. I want Pharaoh's men to carve symbols into them—bits of their past. African, English, Spanish. Doesn't matter."

"Like a story," Jeffrey said, smiling.

Raven looked up at the falls. "Precisely."

The crews set to work at once. Nearly three hundred men and women volunteered to help—carpenters, shipwrights, even the young ones eager to carry stone and lash ropes. They had built siege weapons in the Caribbean. Some of them had built huts on the island where Raven had first become *The Red Raven*. But this? This was different.

They were building something *meant to last*.

Pharaoh and Mr. Greer oversaw the construction. They chose black volcanic rock from the far side of a nearby island and had it ferried back in the small boats. The base of the house was built into the slope, half-sunk for coolness and stability.

"I don't care if a hurricane rises off the blasted moon," Greer said, planting a beam. "This place won't shift an inch."

Attila supervised the reinforcement. He drew lines with chalk and char on the stones—symbols of protection learned during his service and from older texts, Raven didn't ask too many questions about. "They're just lines," he said. "But I've never seen a storm take down a roof where they've been drawn."

Alexander designed the chimney and hearth, shaped in an old English style with arched brickwork and sufficient space for cooking, warmth, and a mantle carved with the crest of *Destiny*—the Raven.

The house rose over weeks—first walls, then beams, then the high, sloped roof with carved eaves that looked like wings when seen from the trees above.

The master room faced the waterfall directly, with floor-to-ceiling shutters that opened fully. Raven had chosen it herself.

"I want to wake to the sound of the water. Every day," she told Jeffrey.

Beside it was a small room for the child—bare now, but painted in pale ochre and deep blue. It's single window faced the pond, and already, the crew had gifted Raven a carved cradle and a woven hammock.

A guest room was built at the opposite end of the house from Raven and Jeffrey's room.

At the center of the house was an expansive sitting room with built-in shelves and a long bench positioned beneath a window that overlooked the cove. A small kitchen stood to one side, with a tiled washroom just beyond it—stone-floored and fed by a channel cut from the stream.

Outside, a footpath led to the pond, flanked by torches, and a narrow wooden dock reached into the calm water. It was here that Raven sometimes stood at dusk, hands resting on her belly, dreaming not of storms, but of stories she might one day tell her child.

When the final beam was raised, the crews gathered to celebrate the project's completion. They roasted fish over an open fire, played drums and flutes, and told stories of ports from Madagascar to the Carolinas.

Pharaoh led a toast with rum laced with cinnamon and citrus.

"To the house that Raven built!" he roared.

"And to the child who'll rule from it someday," Alexander added with a wink.

Raven stood on the steps of her new home, the light of torches flickering across her skin, and for once, she allowed herself to smile without caution.

This house was not armor. It was not a fortress.

It was *hope.*

At night, Raven stood beneath the stars outside her tent, the beginnings of her house taking shape behind her.

She breathed in the wild scents of flowers, wood smoke, and earth.

The sea murmured far below. The air was warm and still.

The dreams hadn't come in nearly two weeks.

No voice. No visions. No La Dama.

It was as if the woman in the water had let go.

Or was waiting.

But for now, Raven let herself believe that peace was genuine.

She turned back toward the falls, where fireflies drifted like stars drawn close to the earth.

Home.

For the first time in her life, it felt like something she could hold on to.

The heat of the Gulf had softened as the season turned. Gentle rains came more often now, falling in warm, whispering curtains across *The Robin's Nest* and feeding the deep greens of the jungle that surrounded Raven's new home.

The stone house, once just a sketch in dirt and a muttered dream, now stood complete, solid, warm, alive with memories and labor. The sound of the waterfall was constant, a lullaby woven into every corner of the house.

Raven's steps were slower now. The weight of her belly curved her forward as though the sea had placed an anchor inside her. But she did not hide her swelling form. She walked the gardens barefoot, her tunic light, her hair braided against the heat. The crews had come to respect her even more, not for her sword, but for her strength in peace.

For her softness that did not shatter her steel.

Each morning, she and Jeffrey shared a ritual. A quiet breakfast under the porch eaves while the mist lifted from the pond. Some days, he read aloud from old journals or sea logs. Other days, they sat in silence, her hand resting on his, both of them listening to the child shift and stir within her.

Her father came often now, never overbearing, never apologetic. Just present.

"You were born for fire," he said to her once, "but even fire must know when to burn low. That child inside you...they're the flame you've yet to understand."

Sometimes, when Raven lay down for rest in the hottest hours of the day, she placed her hands over her belly and whispered stories—not of war, but of stars, birds, and far-off islands. She imagined the little one sailing alongside her, not in a fleet of warships, but in calm seas with music, laughter, and light.

Greer came every few days to check on her. "You're near the end of it," he said one afternoon, brushing his fingers lightly across her wrist. "A week or two, perhaps less."

She met his gaze. "And you're sure the child is healthy?"

He gave her a tired, warm smile. "Stronger than any I've seen. Almost like they *know* where they're going."

That night, thunder rolled somewhere far out at sea—not a storm yet, but the promise of one.

Raven stood at her window and looked out over *The Robin's Nest*. She watched the lanterns flicker on *Destiny's* deck, watched Jeffrey sharpen a blade out of habit, and watched the crews finish their tasks like clockwork.

She pressed a hand over her belly, and the child kicked in response—strong, sure, alive.

She closed her eyes and whispered, not a name, not yet, but something ancient and quiet:

"I'm ready."

Whether the sea heard her or not, she didn't know.

But it answered with silence, and for now, that was enough.

The pain began just after midnight.

It came not as a scream, but a ripple—a tightening in her back, low and persistent, like the rumble of a distant wave. Raven stirred in the dark, breath caught in her throat as her hand flew instinctively to her belly.

A second wave followed. Then a third, closer, stronger.

Jeffrey woke at once, as if tethered to her soul. "Raven?"

She didn't answer right away. She rose slowly from their bed, her hands braced on the carved post. Another contraction struck, sharp this time, radiating through her like lightning across open sea.

Her face was pale, her jaw set. "It's time."

Jeffrey was already moving. He called for Greer. A runner was dispatched for John and Pharaoh. The fire was stoked. Fresh water was heated. Linens were prepared. The cradle was moved close to the hearth.

Outside, thunder muttered over the ocean—but the rain held off.

Inside, *Destiny's* captain prepared to bring new life into the world.

Greer arrived with a practiced calm, his satchel swinging from his shoulder. Two women from the crew followed—Miriam, a seasoned sailor with midwife's training, and Ebele, one of the African sisters from *The Sea Witch*, who brought her own herbs and quiet strength.

"Raven," Greer said gently, kneeling at her side. "Are you ready to fight the final storm?"

Raven, already on hands and knees before the hearth, gave a breathless laugh. "I've fought worse."

And then the pain reached its crest.

Hours passed in sweat and silence broken only by the cadence of whispered prayers, murmured encouragement, and Raven's low, guttural moans as she worked through wave after wave of agony. The candlelight made her sweaty skin glow, her long braid was damp, and her eyes were glassy but fierce.

The midwives forced Jeffrey and John to wait outside the bedroom. Jeffrey paced in front of the hearth, while John watched and tried to remember if he had been as nervous when his daughter was born.

"I see the head," Miriam whispered. "She's almost there."

Raven clenched her jaw, shoulders trembling.

One final push—and the room seemed to hold its breath with her.

And then—*a cry.*

High. Raw. Beautiful.

The storm beyond the cliffs let loose a sudden gust, as if the wind itself had exhaled.

Ebele caught the baby in her strong arms and wrapped her quickly in a cloth. Greer whispered something in Latin. Miriam was weeping.

Raven was relieved. Then the pain came once more.

Ebele said, "Wait. There is another."

Raven was shocked by Ebele's statement.

"What?"

"Raven, you are having twins."

Raven was delighted, shocked, and terrified.

She screamed again.

Ebele caught the little one and wrapped him in a cloth. When both babies had been adequately cleaned, they were laid side-by-side in the cradle next to the hearth.

Raven collapsed back against her pillows, sobbing with both joy and exhaustion.

Outside, the first drops of rain began to fall—soft and steady, not a storm, but a baptism.

John Ashworth stood under the eaves, arms folded, as he looked out at the fleet moored safely in the cove. He heard the newborns' cry and let out a long breath, his eyes wet with unspoken emotions.

Jeffrey still nervously paced inside the great room.

Raven held both children close against her cheeks, their skin touching hers. The babies rooted, nuzzled, and began to nurse, their tiny hands wrapping instinctively around Raven's fingers.

Mr. Greer stepped out of the bedroom to deliver the news.

"Jeffrey. You have a son and a daughter."

Shocked, Jeffrey nearly fainted. Greer steadied the young man and led him into the bedroom to see his children for the first time.

Jeffrey knelt beside them, brushing a damp strand of hair from Raven's cheek.

"You did it," he whispered.

"No," Raven replied softly, "*we* did."

They stayed like that for a long time—mother, father, daughter, and son—wrapped in the hush that follows storms.

And in the low cradle of her voice, Raven said the name she had kept hidden even from herself.

"Anaíra," she whispered to her daughter. "You carry what I once feared. But now, it's your light."

Jeffrey asked, "What did you say?"

"She will be named Anaíra. Anaíra Elizabeth Hamilton."

Jeffrey asked, "And the boy?"

Raven thought for a moment, looking around the room for inspiration. She saw the man standing nearby, whom she had worked with for so many years. When she was Richard, he taught her how to be both a ship's carpenter and doctor. She loved him almost as much as her own papa.

"We'll name him, Andrew. Andrew Ashworth Hamilton."

Mr. Greer's eyes filled with tears. He stepped outside to find John to deliver the news that Raven was now a mother of two beautiful babies.

CHAPTER 30

The days that followed the birth were unlike any Raven had known. The world slowed. The sea softened. The birds of the jungle seemed to sing for her house alone.

Two babies. Not one, as Greer had expected.

First, the fierce and sharp-voiced *Anaira Elizabeth*—born fighting, fists already clenched, wailing like a storm against the injustice of being pulled from the sea of sleep.

Then, her brother—*Andrew Ashworth*—quieter, wide-eyed, born minutes later with a sigh and the barest furrow in his brow, as if weighing the world before letting out his own small, strong cry.

Raven wept when she held them both, one nestled on each side of her chest, her heart twice full. Captain Billings, who had been brought over from *Destiny*, sat on Raven's shoulder to get a closer look at the tiny humans.

John was the first to whisper, "Twins run in your mother's family."

Greer, exhausted but honored, looked touched beyond words when they told him of Andrew's name.

"These two," he said, "were always meant to be born together."

Jeffrey couldn't stop staring. He rarely left the porch those first nights, standing guard under the starlight, listening to the lullabies of frogs and falling water.

In the soft light of dawn, the babies were bathed in the waters of the pond—the same one where Raven had been wed. Pharaoh himself held Anaíra, and Ebele cradled Andrew as Jeffrey poured the cool water gently over their small heads.

"They've touched salt and spring," said Pharaoh, placing a protective charm on each of their woven cradle blankets. "Let the sea know they are its children—but not its to claim."

Every ship in the cove hung banners that week. Bright cloths and ribbons flew from every mast. Meals were shared under canopies. There were no drills, no missions, no whispered hauntings: just music, stories, and the scent of woodsmoke and jasmine on the wind.

For the first time in a long while, *no one dreamed of the woman in the water*.

No one thought of treasure or riches.

The celebration of thoughts was only on Raven and her new family.

By the second week, Raven was strong enough to walk again. Her hands still bore the faint swell of late pregnancy, but her eyes were sharp, her voice clear.

She summoned her captains to the house—Jeffrey, Pharaoh, Alexander, Attila—and brought with her a decision she had been shaping since the moment she saw Anaíra's eyes open. Others were summoned as well, not knowing or understanding why they were called. However, each was eager to see the newborns who had blessed their world.

Everyone stood before Raven as she sat on a large chair in the great room.

"I'm *not* stepping down," she said, "but I *am* stepping aside. The fleet must move even when I do not."

They listened. And she laid out her plans.

- **Jeremy Finch**, only just past seventeen, would captain *Destiny*.

He had earned the helm. Brave, loyal, tested in fire. Raven gave him her compass personally.

- **Simba**, the tall, fierce sailor from Zanzibar, once a fighter in the holds and now a tactician, would serve as Jeremy's first mate. "She'll keep the boy honest," Raven said with a smile.

- **Mdago**, the quiet navigator with an uncanny feel for wind and current, was promoted to second mate aboard *Destiny*. He had never asked for recognition, which made him all the more worthy of it.

- **Bila Meno**, with his booming laugh and razor mind, would take his place beside Attila as first mate on *The Firebird*. "You'll challenge each other," Raven told them both. "Which means you'll be stronger."

Raven added, "Isaac will move back to *Destiny* to serve under his son as helmsman. Walter Parpart will take Isaac's place on *The Firebird*."

"Here is your mission: You will continue to sail together until all the treasure is transferred here to the Robin's nest. I've selected twenty men and women to remain behind to help with duties here. Part of that duty will be to protect our boundaries from those who would invade us."

She looked at her papa, "John Ashworth, you will remain here to lead those who remain behind. However, your number one priority is...to be a grandpapa to my children."

Raven smiled.

John broke down into tears and gave up trying to hide them as they spilled down his cheeks.

Raven continued, "Captains, you will operate as a council. None of you will have dominion over the others. You will work together. Make decisions together. When you can't come to a consensus on any decision, you'll put it to a vote among the crew. It is the way of the seas. After the treasure has been transferred here, we will assess the reconstruction of our fleet and determine our next steps. I will meet with the captains when that time comes. We will make that decision together.

Later that night, Raven sat beside her babies in the warm nursery lit by oil lamps and ocean breezes. Anaíra slept with her tiny brow furrowed. Andrew curled against her, breath soft and even.

Raven looked out the shuttered window toward the dark sea.

A conch shell sounded faintly from one of the ships.

Peace still held.

But in the wind, she thought she heard something old shifting.

Not a threat.

Not yet.

But a watcher.

Waiting.

And Raven whispered to her sleeping children, "You are of the sea and me. May you rise with the tides, and may no name ever own you.

Others have gone first so that you may go farther."

Author Bio

Michael L. Clark is an award-winning historical fiction author. He and his wife of more than 40 years live in the Pensacola, Florida area after Clark retired from the U. S. Postal Service in 2022. His stories captivate readers with a wide range of subject matter, whether it be time-travel in the frontier of Tennessee, riding with the Pony Express in 1860, or sailing with pirates in the early 18th century. Clark's stories will leave you begging for more. Be sure to see all of his works on his website

www.author-michaellclark.com

Other Titles By
Michael L. Clark

The Shimmering Trilogy

The Shimmering
The Diary of Gus Childers
The Prophet

Young America Series

Ambush at Horse Creek

The Red Raven Pirate Series

The Red Raven
Raven's Destiny
Raven's Lost Island
Raven's Lady of Blood

9 781965 756133